Mark of a Crescent Moon

Clara Fay

PRAISE FOR *MARK OF A CRESCENT MOON*

"Through the experiences of Fleur La Salle, author Clara Fay leads readers on an exploration of concepts related to spirituality, intuition, portals, and dreams and visions. Ms. Fay breathes life into these mysteries by staging them against a background of Scotland's Hebrides islands and Scottish history. This book is rich and beautiful in details without slowing or stalling the unraveling of the story. Definitely worth the read!"

—Sandra Valencia, award-winning author of The Chikondra Trilogy and the Legends of Turand series

"*Mark of a Crescent Moon* is a fantastical and intriguing novel. Clara Fay knows how to paint a beautiful picture with words, and the lyrical narrative and beautifully portrayed setting transported me into a fairytale-like world. Fleur is an intriguing character, warm and passionate—her passion was what drew me into her story. I saw her haunting dreams to be an opportunity for her to get back something she lost and maybe even gain something new. Magical and suspenseful, Clara Fay's *Mark of a Crescent Moon* took me on an unforgettable adventure of romance, magic, and so much more! Excellent work!"

—Jessica Barbosa for Reader's Favorite ®

"*Mark of a Crescent Moon* is a gorgeous debut from author Clara Fay. A blend of fantasy and historical fiction, Fay's tight command of prose and character development elevates this book from your standard genre fiction fare. This is a story of secrets, a story rich with Scottish history and lore, and, perhaps most important, a story of dreams and visions—the power of spiritual development to transcend time and place."

—David Arthur, Goodreads reviewer

Mark of a Crescent Moon

A forgotten legacy.
A portal to the past.
And one chance for a better future.

Clara Fay

WILD GEESE
Bookworks

Wild Geese Bookworks
Paperback ISBN: 9798987216903
EPUB / Electronic Book ISBN: 9798987216910
Library of Congress Control Number: 2022950273

Wild Geese Bookworks, Hamilton Bermuda.

WILD GEESE
Bookworks

To my parents, and theirs, and theirs.
To my children, and theirs, and theirs.
To ancestors behind, and descendants ahead.
To every moment that led to this moment.
And to all connecting us with who we are now.

CONTENTS

When we know about our ancestors,
when we sense them as living and as supporting us,
then we feel connected to the genetic life-stream,
and we draw strength and nourishment from this.

—Philip Carr-Gomm
Druid Mysteries: Ancient Wisdom for the 21st Century

CHAPTER ONE

ANTIGONISH, NOVA SCOTIA, CANADA, 1987

The last tendrils of sun crept across the bay, melting into the early twilight, a period of ambiguity, a pause to inhale mystery and wonder.

Fleur stepped onto the wraparound porch sipping her chamomile tea, knowing she would not feel the usual joy from the vista this evening. Preoccupied with other musings, her mind kept her artist's eye from noticing the splendor of the sunset.

She loved to sit on her porch gazing at the beauty surrounding her cottage. With a slight squint of both eyes, she could isolate all the details that only an artist can see – the angles of the shadows, the multiple hues of color, the depth of light. No matter the season, the views from Blue Bird Cottage delighted her, the sole occupant.

In spring, a yellow wildflower-carpeted meadow curved from the hilltop where the cottage rested to the ledge that dropped off to the bay, filling the air with an abundance of sunshine. In winter, a brilliant white sheath of virgin snow swept across the icy inlet to the small Nova Scotian town of Antigonish. On this early spring evening, as the setting sun's soft glow winked out, fog glided over the inlet, reaching out to Blue Bird Cottage with a dream-infused vapor. The mist and the shadows suited Fleur's mood.

The day marked one year since Fleur moved back to her hometown after her divorce. She wasn't sad about the breakdown of her marriage. It had taken a long time to reach that stage. Fleur had come to realize parting from Arthur Boden had been a blessing. His subtle, passive-aggressive behavior, especially towards her passion for painting, had eroded her confidence. Also, he had assured her that he had wanted children, when in fact he did not. She very much wanted a child; it was a connection to family and a clear identity which she craved. Fleur concluded in hindsight that Arthur had been jealous of her artistic talent. That would explain why he destroyed the last canvas Fleur had been working on, blaming the pungent smell of oils for his rage. His actions had broken her heart.

This evening, sitting in dusk's half-light, Fleur was distracted thinking about the dreams she started having a few weeks ago. They began when she rediscovered meditation to calm her mind. Though the dreams hadn't been frightening, they had been realistic, as vivid as if the woman in the dreams was in the room with her, breathing the same air, living the same life. Each time the woman came to Fleur in her dreams was a visceral encounter, a parallel universe of increasing mystery.

The close proximity with the woman's energy made Fleur tingle with a familiar feeling, like the sensation of her grandmother's vitality as an intuitive healer. Fleur's keen awareness of the woman's life force made the dreams seem more real. Though she was a bit disconcerted by the intensity of the dreams, at the same time she was intrigued to discover the story they revealed.

The dreams started the same way, with the woman sitting on the dirt floor of a primitive hut near a fire, swaying and muttering words like a chant. The woman would then open her eyes and beckon to show Fleur a scene from a tribal village that appeared to be some kind of North Sea clan. Each time she had the dream, Fleur wondered, *What does the woman want from me?*

The next morning, Fleur startled awake to the sound of the very words: "What do you want from me?"

It took Fleur a minute to realize *she* had shouted those words.

She trembled, the words a familiar mantra as she struggled to pull away from the gripping dream. Fleur exhaled to release the spike of fear. She searched for soothing words to relax her rigid body into the expanse of her white linen sheets. *All is well. I am Fleur La Salle, raised by loving grandparents Eileen and Joe Lewis in Antigonish, not a tribal village from the remote past.*

Her surroundings came into focus as the dream receded and the woman faded. The dream woman's face was etched in Fleur's mind, with features that were very much like her own. It was a solemn face with clean angles framed by a heavy curtain of honey blonde hair that grazed the shoulder blades, and steady, clear grey eyes that held another's gaze a fraction longer than comfortable and saw deeper than the surface.

There were differences Fleur noticed as well. The woman held herself with confidence, an inner knowing of her power and influence. It shone through her manner, even when she appeared to be pleading with Fleur. This confidence was an aspect of the woman's attitude to life that Fleur herself longed to have.

Wisps of the dream evaporated, and Fleur became aware of the soft early morning light filtering through her window, the one facing the bay. She sat up in her bed and stared out at the peaceful inlet, trying to soothe her heightened emotions. The angst in the woman's eyes made Fleur feel helpless; she wanted to help but did not know how. She wasn't sure if the woman wanted her to go somewhere, or to do something.

Ten years ago, before she had met Arthur, she would have leapt at such an intriguing dilemma. She had been confident about her intuition, and she would have used it to find a solution to what the dream woman was asking of her. But now, Fleur was too unsure of herself. She had forgotten who she was.

With a mental shake, Fleur flung off her duvet, pulled by the desire to be outdoors. She needed to feel the earth beneath her feet and find her balance through nature's beauty.

As she rounded the corner into the living room, Fleur was startled by her grandmother coming through the front door, unexpectedly. Fleur knew something wasn't right. Perhaps she heard Fleur shouting in her sleep. Fleur's grandmother was a formidable woman, a trait well suited to her career as a nurse. Seeing the set of her jaw, Fleur knew she was on a mission. Fleur hugged her Grana hard with a forced smile, inhaling her rose blossom signature scent, a fragrance that conjured feelings of safety and love.

Fleur was slightly shorter than her Grana, who still stood tall and erect, benefiting from her solid Scottish frame. Even at 86 years of age, her stance was perfect, a factor of years of conscious attention to the importance of good posture. Only a slight limp hinted at the childhood disease that never slowed Eileen Lewis down.

"Grana, what brings you around so early?" Fleur asked before she realized her grandmother wasn't buying her nonchalant act. Her Grana's raised eyebrows and pursed lips told Fleur everything without her Grana uttering a single word.

"You heard me, then?" Fleur murmured, aware her Grana couldn't be fooled. "Yes, it was the same dream. The woman showed me her village life, then motioned for me to come nearer. Her intense pleading look stays with me. It's like she desperately needs help."

Her Grana put her hands on her ample waist, smiled at Fleur, and asked, "Well then, dearie, now that you've fessed up, can you tell me what the woman wants from you?"

That was the difficult part. Fleur always woke up too soon. "I just don't know, and the building tension is worrying me," she said as she busied herself making coffee. "I don't think there's any danger. It seems like the woman wants me to do something or to go somewhere. Her energy was stronger today, like she was in the room with me."

Fleur looked up when she heard her Grana's rapid inhale. "What is it? Your concern is obvious."

Shaking her head, her Grana spoke in a measured tone. "I've been thinking about the meaning of the dream. I'll tell you when I'm more certain. For now, don't concern yourself."

Fleur respected her honesty. Grana wouldn't brush aside anything that might be significant; if she said that she would deal with it, she would. She might take matters into her own hands, using the old ways.

"That's alright," said Fleur. "When you're ready, I'd like to hear your interpretation. I've been puzzling over it myself. Sometimes I think the dream is about me seeking answers for myself or looking for help, as if *I'm* the woman in the dream. Come to think of it, she does look like me. She has the same hair I do, and a long face with grey eyes just like mine."

Her Grana raised an eyebrow and teased, "Well, that's an interesting thought. You could've saved some money and gone on more adventures with Matty instead of going to that fancy therapist."

Fleur grinned. She had often wondered if those months of therapy after her marriage fell apart had helped. True, her self-esteem had improved significantly, but she still experienced a lingering sense of dissatisfaction, not knowing the purpose of her life. Her Grana's observation was spot on; Matty's company was better than psychotherapy. Her friend had been supportive of Fleur during her separation, divorce, and later when she moved from Montreal back home to Antigonish. Matty had pulled Fleur along on exceptional travel adventures and immersions into different cultures.

Matty Dorval, or Mathilde as her Acadian mother called her, pronouncing the last syllable as a staccato, was Fleur's best friend, and she couldn't remember a time before Matty. From the moment she met Matty standing her ground against the school bully in kindergarten, with her wild raven curls, creamy white complexion, brilliant green eyes blazing, enormous dimples, and joyful irreverence of life, Fleur knew they would be inseparable.

Fleur's childhood was spent as though she were another Dorval child, falling into the fray of six siblings and a lively Acadian household. She loved the ruckus and good-hearted shouting of the Dorval household, such a contrast to the sedate life with her elderly grandparents.

"Oh, Grana, thank you for the reminder that Matty is coming for the weekend."

Her Grana lifted a well-used pie plate from the bag she was holding. "Here's a hearty meat pie for your supper. I even put a wee bit of hug-wort in it."

Fleur chuckled at her imaginary remedy for childhood hurts. "You're the best, Grana," she said. "Hug-wort is truly magical. You should've bottled it and shared it with the neighborhood kids. Thank you for your help."

Her Grana leaned in to give Fleur a hug. "That's what grandmothers are for," she said, putting her handbag over her arm. "I'm off then. Mary-Beth and I are going to the parlor to get all dandied-up for the seniors' tea this afternoon."

"Good for you, Grana. Give Auntie Mary-Beth my love. Will you be home tomorrow if I pop by before work?"

Her Grana patted her shoulder, "Be glad to see you. I'll have a pot of tea ready."

Eileen left her granddaughter's cottage that morning with a growing unease after Fleur told her the woman's energy seemed to be increasing. She had determined that she would keep a close watch to make sure Fleur was safe.

Something else had bothered Eileen. Fleur's description of the land in the dream had seemed familiar. Not anything Eileen had experienced herself, more like recollections from ancestors, echoes from the past, oral traditions passed down through the generations.

Eileen wasn't her usual buoyant self when she and Mary-Beth met at the beauty parlor. While Eileen was never ungainly despite her large, buxom size, that morning she had been clumsy. Poor Sally Ann Parsons, the beautician, had ended up covered in hair perm affixing solution as a result of Eileen's distraction.

"Do you have time for a cuppa?" Eileen asked Mary-Beth as they left the beauty parlor. "I've something to get off my chest, if you don't mind."

Her friend patted Eileen's hand and replied, "I was wondering when you'd spit it out. You haven't been yourself all morning. Let me put my groceries inside, and I'll be right over."

As Eileen went through her front door, she almost stepped on a letter dropped through the mail slot. Her heart sank when she turned the envelope over and saw the return address. Eileen knew the letter would come one day, but she always imagined it would be after she departed from this world.

Eileen saw that the envelope was addressed to Fleur and thought the timing couldn't be worse. Fleur seemed so much happier lately, the best she had been since her husband left. Eileen trusted that the timing was right, just as her own grandmother had assured her long ago. Right timing or not, there it was, resting on the floor the entire morning while Eileen and Mary-Beth had enjoyed being pampered at the beauty parlor.

Eileen heard the creak of the porch steps behind her as Mary-Beth approached. *I must look a sight*, she thought staring at the envelope in her shaking hands.

Sure enough, she heard Mary-Beth ask, "What's the matter, Eileen?"

Eileen shook her head as she walked to the kitchen, motioning for her friend to sit down. "The letter has come, and it's for Fleur."

"Why, Eileen, the envelope isn't even opened," said her friend. "How can you know it's bad news?"

Eileen cleared her throat. "Well, my own grandmother, Fiona Kintrell, told me this tale when I was nine. You remember my grandmother growing up, she was a fearsome determined woman. And she had the fey in her."

Mary-Beth nodded in agreement. "Oh yes, she was a strong-minded woman, your grandmother," she said, "much like you. I'm certain it was her determination that had you walking when no one believed you ever would.

We called you 'the Girl in the Window.' You sat with that iron contraption on your leg, happy to be watching us play outside."

Eileen recalled the endless exercises to strengthen her left leg, deformed from birth. Along with the series of stretching and flexing, her grandmother made her drink horrible-tasting medicines, concocted from herbs she grew herself and also collected from the woods.

Eileen put on the kettle and told Mary-Beth the background behind the letter. "The tale is an ancient one, about generations of women raised by their grandmothers, one after the other. One of the pair, either grandmother or the granddaughter, would be a healer, and the other an artist or a creative one. Sometimes a combination of both artist and healer."

Eileen could almost see her dear grandmother telling her the tale of an ancestry of proud and courageous women from a barren land. Women who faced hardships to survive and take care of their own. Lost in this memory, Eileen shivered though the day was warm.

"There was a curse placed upon one of our ancestors that has created this endless cycle, a line of women raised each by their grandmothers, not by their own mother. Never knowing a mother's love. Not knowing true love. It is said that the curse would be lifted when the last descendant in the line does the work," Eileen concluded with a puzzled look. "Though I don't know what the work is, I have my suspicions."

Eileen heard the exasperation in her dear friend's voice. Mary-Beth scoffed, "An ancient curse? Eileen, your grandmother used that to get you to behave as a child. Curse indeed! This is 1987, not the Middle Ages. Anyway, what does that have to do with the letter?" Mary-Beth pointed to the offensive envelope shaking in her friend's hand.

Not taking her friend's admonishment the wrong way, Eileen nodded her head and got up from the kitchen table to attend to the tea making. "Yes, I know how it sounds. I thought about it many times over the years, and I don't think there is a hex kind of curse," she said. "I think it's more like a pattern of behavior or learning passed down from one generation to the next. The ultimate self-sacrifice. But I don't know, I never found out."

Eileen raised an eyebrow as Mary-Beth shifted in her seat with impatience. "And the letter?" asked Mary-Beth. "How do you know it has anything to do with that?"

Turning the envelope over in her hand, Eileen pointed to her friend. "Look at the stamp. It's from the Isle of Mull. I was born on the northeastern shore of the Isle of Mull," she said.

"What do you mean? Mull is one of the Scottish islands of the Inner Hebrides," said Mary-Beth with an inhaled breath. Eileen knew she would be surprised, for her friend thought she had been born in Canada.

"Yes, confusing, isn't it. You didn't know that my grandmother immigrated from Scotland after the land clearances, and brought me to Canada with her. I was only three months old."

Mary-Beth asked the next logical question, eyes wide with shock. "How can you possibly know this letter is related to your grandmother's story about a curse?"

Eileen tried to explain as best she could. "I don't have the strong intuitive powers my grandmother had, " she said. "But I do have some intuition, and it tells me this letter is indeed connected with my grandmother's story."

The story Eileen's grandmother told her ended with a call to action. She remembered the words, though she didn't dare share them with Mary-Beth. "Answer the call from home, and return whence you come. Do the work for your line, for descendants ahead, and ancestors behind."

Mary-Beth cocked her head to one side and smoothed down her skirt. Ever practical, she asked, "What are you going to do about this letter? I assume you never told Fleur the true story about your birth?"

Eileen knew this would be a problem. She had meant to tell Fleur, but never found the right time. Her granddaughter would have more questions than she had answers.

"We'll have to see when we get to that bridge, now won't we," Eileen replied, patting her friend on the knee. Eileen tilted her head to the side and wondered if this situation would help Fleur realize her intuitive powers.

Fleur pulled her thick hair into a ponytail and threw on some joggers for a fast-paced walk to start to her day. She craved connection with nature, to be in tune with the rhythm of the earth. There had been a time when she could perceive the subtle vibrations of the earth under her bare feet and feel plant energy when she touched trees and foliage. Though that sensitivity had dimmed in recent years, she still appreciated nature's healing energy.

Fleur settled into a brisk walk on the country road which led to Pomquet Beach a mile away. She focused her mind into a stream of appreciation to soften the whirling thoughts of worry about the dream woman. Her Grana had taught her that thoughts impact reality, so Fleur would list the positive aspects of any situation to adjust any dissatisfied notions.

At the top of Fleur's list of appreciation was her Grana, who was strong, determined, yet loving and compassionate. Eileen Lewis had been dedicated to nurturing her granddaughter, and ensuring that she appreciated the everyday magic of life.

Fleur recalled a dark period during her preteen years when she felt adrift, and often wondered where she came from. Though her grandparents cared for her with the same love and attention as parents would have, she thought it unfair she didn't have parents, or even an extended family. At times Fleur had even been embarrassed by her old grandparents, and felt angry that her parents died in a car accident. She remembered those times with shame, especially after her grandfather died when she was twelve. It had taken time, but Fleur learned to appreciate her grandparents' role in her life.

As she continued with her practice of gratitude, Fleur thought of her new home. The cozy cottage at the end of a quiet country lane within walking distance to her favorite place, Pomquet Beach, brought her peace. It was the first home that she lived in alone, and she was enjoying the freedom. As Fleur considered her cottage, her brows scrunched together recalling the many times during her marriage that she had wished for the freedom to paint as much as she wanted to, the very freedom she had now. She wondered again what was stopping her from painting.

It didn't take Fleur long to reach the beach, a place of happy childhood memories. In this place of ocean, sand, and swaying dune grass, Fleur had let her imagination run rampant as a young girl. Looking out on that lonely expanse of sea, her innermost fantasy of being an artist had risen as high as the ocean waves. Fleur chewed her lip as she considered the pain it caused her that she lacked the courage to capture her favorite place in oils.

Fleur emerged through the thicket of reeds from the rough wooden boardwalk and glimpsed the clean stretch of sandy beach. The beach was separated from the ocean by a line of pebbles that danced with every rolling wave. The early morning fog mirrored Fleur's lack of clarity. The ocean, still as an illusion, was the perfect backdrop for her restless thoughts. Fleur returned to the significance of last night's dream, and wondered if *she* was the woman.

A detail she hadn't remembered until this minute teased its way into her consciousness. The woman worked with her hands. Maybe she was an artist. Fleur noted the irony, for she herself was an artist, or rather had been one. She still longed for the ease of total absorption in the creative process, of being in the moment and letting everything else fall away.

Even as the familiar desire gripped her, discomfort welled up and she started to shake, her breath rasped, and her heart pounded. The momentum of the negative energy immediately sent her to a place of fear, so she attempted to distract herself.

At the shoreline, Fleur toed a beach pebble as though the action would help her cross a threshold and relieve her fear. Maybe she would find ease by discovering what her purpose in life was, learning to stand strong in her own identity, or finding a connection akin to her longing for family. If only she could leave the irrational fear behind and remember that she was an artist at her core. She was unsure if this resistance to doing what she loved most was because of her experience with Arthur, or if she had forgotten her identity. Fleur shook her hair out of its ponytail and ran as fast as she could down the length of the beach, exhilarated by the sensation of blood pounding in her heart.

When her friend left, Eileen busied herself in the kitchen, baking a tart and keeping her hands occupied to calm her mind. She considered the dreams Fleur started having recently, like they were foreshadowing the arrival of the letter, and wondered if there was a connection. It seemed too much of a coincidence for a letter to arrive from the place of her birth now.

Eileen had no doubt it was time to tell Fleur the details of her family history. She would put the feelings of guilt about waiting so long behind her. She had been aware of Fleur's longing for family while growing up. It had been hard of Fleur to lose both of her parents at such a young age.

Though Eileen and her Joe had given Fleur all the love and support they could, Eileen knew that Fleur keenly felt the absence of extended family. Many years ago, Eileen had an intuition that she might have a sister or half-sister in Scotland. She was ashamed that she never investigated that possibility. Life had been busy raising Fleur on her own after Joe died, and she never had time to find out the truth.

She wondered if it was too late to do so now. Eileen suspected the answer would come on its own, so she resolved not to mention the possibility of family being in Scotland to Fleur.

Eileen was unsure if she should show Fleur the letter first to find out what it contained or tell Fleur the story about her birth to give a background into why the letter might have arrived from the Isle of Mull.

With a snap of the kitchen towel, Eileen decided she'd wait until after Fleur enjoyed her weekend with Matty to give her the letter. Then together, they would work out what it all meant, if there was indeed a connection.

Chapter Two

Fleur's anxiety had lifted by the time she arrived at the Dragonfly Café for her shift that morning. The walk to the beach, followed by a short meditation practice, had curbed her inner turmoil for the moment. She loved the drive to work, sitting behind the oversized steering wheel of the green vintage Singer Vogue sedan that had been her Papa Joe's pride. That old car made her feel like a carefree teenager, instead of a thirty-one-year-old divorcee. Fleur grinned at the tires grinding on the gravel in the parking lot.

She caught sight of Rosalind at the bakery counter window. Rosalind O'Donnell, a plump sixty-something hometown girl who never married, was a kind soul. She took care of her staff like a mother hen. Rosalind liked to watch out for Fleur and give her lectures about the dangers of reckless driving. Fleur appreciated that her boss kept an eye on her. When she started to have those dreams, Rosalind had noticed her fatigue and asked her immediately what was disturbing her sleep.

Fleur had regretted telling her boss about the dreams for now Rosalind scanned her daily for telltale signs of a sleepless night. It was going to be tricky today to hide it, but she didn't want to worry Rosalind. The first time Fleur had mentioned the dreams, Rosalind had shared a painful story about a recurring dream she had after her fiancé had died, a realistic dream about a baby in distress. Fleur knew that her boss had shared the story as an example that she should nurture herself after a traumatic experience and give herself time to heal.

Fleur had taken the waitressing job for three days a week. It was supposed to be temporary to allow her time to figure out what she was going to do with her life. A year later, she still enjoyed the thrum of characters that came into the Dragonfly as well as her colleagues and their idiosyncrasies. It was like having a large family, or at least what Fleur imagined it would be like to have lots of siblings.

The Dragonfly Café, located on the outskirts of town, was decorated in light wood paneling and gingham reminiscent of a 1950s diner. Known for its simple, healthy home cooking and decadent baked goods, it was popular especially with university students. They came for economical food and Rosalind's friendliness. Fleur had spent quite a bit of time at the Dragonfly during her university days to chat with friends about art and to enjoy the home cooking. She had fond memories of Rosalind encouraging her and her friends in their aspirations.

With St. Francis Xavier University campus forming the centerpiece of the town, Antigonish was inhabited by many artists, both students at the university and mature artists. Numerous professional artists settled in the area to capture the surrounding natural environment. Miles of windswept beaches and steely ocean, framed by a craggy land, translated well through a range of artistic mediums. The small university town offered a greater sense of community and belonging than the larger metropolis of Halifax, which was only a couple of hours away by car.

Fleur smiled as she passed Rosalind and shrugged her shoulders to hide her flushed cheeks at being caught in a moment of abandoned joy. She was determined to avoid Rosalind's inspection today, knowing that her boss would ferret out her latest dream.

She stepped into the kitchen to start her shift, jerking back to avoid getting knocked over by her co-worker. "Hey, Norma, anything interesting happen this morning?"

"Did you have a good beauty sleep?" said Norma, dripping sarcasm. Norma could be a force to reckon with on the best of days.

Fleur was surprised at her colleague's rebuke but didn't answer. She was not an argumentative person and learned long ago that it was best to leave Norma alone when she was in one of her moods. Her colleague had no time for small talk and little patience for the eccentric people who came into the diner.

With one hand on her hip, Norma sneered in disgust, "That uppity Massey Grand was in for her weekly bacon orgy. Her poor husband ain't allowed any kind of fat, yet she wolfs down a plate full of bacon all by herself."

Fleur nodded. George Grand was a gentle man who winked at her when his wife harangued him about his food order. Fleur liked Mr. Grand and admired the tenderness he showed his wife of 45 years. It was endearing that he could be so mild hearted towards a wife who said quite hurtful things to him. Fleur sympathized with Mr. Grand, knowing how it felt to be criticized by a spouse in public.

She allowed Norma to rant some more while she put on her apron. "If I were him," said Norma, waving a butter knife in the air. "I would cut off that silly little fox she wears around her neck no matter the season and feed it to her. The pretentious cow!"

Fleur smiled as she moved through the swinging doors towards the dining area, glad that everyone at the Dragonfly was in character this morning. She resisted the urge to flinch as she walked toward her section. Sitting near the window was Len, the gangly manager from the hardware store who had been pestering her for a date since she arrived back in town. Fleur avoided him whenever possible, put off by his persistence. Too late to turn around, she put her shoulders back and moved toward his table, wishing under her breath for someone to save her from Len's advances. While she was too kind to rebuke him, she found it painful to speak with him.

Before Fleur got to the table, Norma swooped out of the kitchen and breezed past her, nearly knocking her over. She told Fleur that she would take the window section today and instructed her to seat the group of four who had just come in. With a whispered "you owe me," Norma arrived at the window table and said in a gruff voice, "Whaddayou want today, Len."

Fleur didn't register how quickly her wish was answered; instead she was relieved from the stress of fending off Len's advances. The lunch crowd kept her busy until her shift ended, and it wasn't until then that Fleur recalled how she had avoided an interaction with Len by merely wishing it.

Fleur cut her shift short after accepting her boss's suggestion that she leave to get ready for Matty's arrival. She stopped at Sobeys grocery store to pick-up food and the all-important wine, which must be red, dark, and robust to satisfy her friend Matty.

Midway down the dairy aisle, Fleur caught sight of Sally Ann Parsons from The Set beauty parlor. Too late to avoid the town gossip, Fleur tried to appear engrossed in her shopping list, hoping that the older woman would get the hint she was too busy to chat.

She flinched when Sally Ann called out to her. "Fleur! I saw your grandmother this morning. Whatever is the matter with her?" Sometimes Fleur believed that Sally Ann's sole purpose in life was to inform people about problems they didn't know they had.

Stepping back, Fleur responded, "What do you mean? I saw Grana earlier and she was fine."

Fleur wasn't impressed with Sally Ann's faked look of sympathy. "Why, your grandmother was in an absolute dither," said Sally Ann, exaggerating a pause. "She couldn't focus on anything. She was all over the place, and she made me spill a whole bottle of perm fixative. Do you suppose your grandmother is going senile?"

Fleur set her jaw, "There's nothing wrong with my Grana. She's as strong-minded as an ox. Likely, she just had something on her mind."

"Well, if you say so," said Sally Ann, shrugging her shoulders. "I know it's a painful subject when our old folk start to lose their senses. I remember my own granny going around the bend; there was no telling my mother that she had to be put in a home."

Fleur scrunched her eyebrows and shoved her grocery cart forward. "Don't worry, no one is going around the bend in the Lewis household, unless it's to get milk on the next aisle." Fleur thought Sally Ann should knock something over to know how her meddling felt. A half second later, Fleur heard a crash of tins from the direction where she'd left Sally Ann.

Fleur looked over her shoulder, and pushed her cart to the cash register at the front of the store, eager to be as far away as possible from the aisle where she spoke to Sally Ann moments before. Surely, she had nothing to do with the tins crashing down.

Fleur barely set foot on the step when the front door of the cottage flew open, and Matty bounced onto the porch. "I found your key—you should hide it better. Wonderful to see you, Boo, I hope there's meat in that grocery bag. I swear there is no way I'm ever going near one of those new-age starve-you retreat centers again," greeted Matty in a single breath.

Fleur should have anticipated Matty's dramatic appearance. As usual, her friend made a wildly energetic entrance accompanied by an avalanche of words, delivered in her sweet Acadian pronunciation.

"Hey Matty. Great to see you too," she said, giving her friend a big hug. "Let's go inside. Just give me a minute to change out of this uniform, then you can tell me all about it." It was good to hear the nickname her friend had given her in grade school, even though she'd long outgrown her tendency to be easily startled.

Fleur came out of the bedroom after changing into her usual comfy jeans and button-down gingham shirt, a shade of green that made her grey eyes stand out and sparkle. She loosened her hair from the low side ponytail she usually wore to work, and it hung around her shoulders like a veil. Fleur unpacked the groceries while Matty told her about the latest exploits involving her work as a travel agent.

"Pass the bottle, and I'll tell you about my awful week," she said, waving around the corkscrew. "Vegan-ism and to top it all, imagine no wine. Should have been my first clue."

Fleur took the offered wine and looked at Matty, eye-to-eye, to clink glasses. "Eye contact," they said at the same time, a habit they decided as teenagers would ensure they had good sex in the future.

"Cheers! It's good to see you," Fleur said. "Start from the beginning, you lost me. Vegan – you? That doesn't make sense. Hang on while I put Grana's pie in the oven."

Matty sighed, "Oh thank heavens, your grandmother's meat pie. I am saved, all will be well."

Fleur smiled at her friend's theatrics and went about preparing their dinner. She loved her cozy kitchen area. It was separated from the living room by a counter where three bar stools allowed her guests to chat with her while she prepared their meal. She basked in the orange sunset glow that streamed through the double window over the sink with a view of the back lawn and fishpond. Beyond the kitchen, Fleur enjoyed the openness of her living and dining area, sectioned by couch, chairs, and a fold-up wooden table. Floor-to-ceiling windows on two sides of the cottage showcased the sweeping lawn that carried the eye to the bay. A black pot belly stove on the colorful flagstone floor added contrast to the wooden floors of the rest of the cottage and enhanced the coziness.

Fleur watched in amusement as Matty dropped onto the large red double-seat armchair in the living room, popped one leg over the ample arm and chattered about her latest exploits. "I can taste that delicious pie already," she said. "I've been dreaming about meat pies. Now let me tell you about my horrid week."

Matty launched into her tale. "It all started when this save-the-planet guy published a book about a new way of eating," she said. "I heard about a retreat center in Ontario that had based their philosophy on this book. You know, clean living for a healthy environment. They only serve vegan food, just like it says in the book. Of course, I had to experience the retreat center before I could recommend it to my clients.

"You've heard about this vegan trend?" asked Matty. "It's stricter than vegetarianism. You can't eat anything to do with animals. No eggs or cheese. I thought no meat was bad enough."

Matty paused for breath and turned her attention to the song playing in the background. "Great tune – love The Bangles, isn't this their new hit single?" she said as she jumped off the armchair and walked around the living area like an Egyptian, in sync with the song playing on the radio.

Fleur smiled at her friend's tendency to be easily distracted. "Go ahead, keep talking," she said, sipping her wine and taking a seat across from Matty on the couch.

Matty plopped back on the chair and took a large sip of wine. "Anyway, it sounded like the kind of trendy place my clients would like to visit," she said. "It was a cool spot – beautiful grounds around a lake and lots of wooded lands for hiking and horseback riding. I did meet a lot of interesting people. You know me, I love to hear people's stories. Anyway, in the evenings there were guest speakers who talked about different New Age stuff. The week I was there, a shamanic healer talked about connecting with your inner spirit animal."

Fleur suppressed a giggle thinking what Matty's spirit animal might be and spluttered the first question that popped into her head. "Let me guess, was yours a man-eating tiger, or tigress?"

"Very funny," said Matty before adding her own twist to the joke. "You have no idea how hard it can be to train your inner animal. It takes lots of practice." Matty put her hands in front of her, scratching the air with pretend claws and growling.

She continued her story. "I admit, the place was great. The problem was I signed up to stay for five days, but by day two I was going nuts with all that clean eating. I enjoyed the New Age stuff, but the vegan eating business was too hippie for me."

Fleur smiled at the irony of Matty's statement, taking in her long, multi-colored paisley skirt, the white ruffled peasant blouse, and the lopsided bandanna holding her riotous black hair in place. Her friend's wardrobe was miles from the more conservative clothes she wore, mostly jeans and button-down shirts with the occasional shift dress thrown in. They made quite the pair, standing side by side, almost total opposites in looks, style, and character.

"It must have been a good break for your digestive system. Did you enjoy it?" asked Fleur, well aware of her friend's atrocious eating habits.

Matty smirked and glanced around her shoulder before answering. "No problem for me," she said, using her stage whisper voice which was a sure sign of mischief afoot. "I snuck in a huge deli box of cold cuts, a large bag of all-dressed chips, and several bottles of Pinot Gris. I figured the fridge in the room must be for essentials."

Fleur gasped. "Of all places to sneak wine and meat, a vegan, holistic retreat center! Did it feel as good as the time you climbed into the living room window of the boys' dormitory during Lent, with strings of chocolate kisses tied around your neck and wearing only a bra and knickers?"

Matty tossed back her head and howled, curls shaking from the exertion. "You know that nothing short of scoring with Wayne Gretzky could make me feel that good."

With the mention of Canada's hockey legend Gretzky, the conversation turned to Matty's college conquests. The friends laughed as they reminisced about her year-round buffet of collegiate sports stars. In the fall, Matty dated the football all-star players, in the winter it was the hockey stars, and in the spring the all-star basketball players.

"You'd take a break from athletes during summer to concentrate on your intellectual side – dating science majors, pre-med or pre-law students," said Fleur. "But don't forget rule number one, never date an acting student. Maybe a writer or an artist now and then, but never someone savvy about acting! They might see through your bullshit!"

Matty spluttered, holding her hand up while she caught her breath from the laughter. "Yes, and I mostly stuck to that rule," she said. "Almost veered off course with Hubley though. He was so yummy back then, funny, and what a wacky point of view. We had great laughs together. Good thing it worked out like it did, we're best buddies now, and he's a super fab boss."

Fleur asked the question that always surfaced when the friends got together, "What's going on in your love life?" she asked. "What about the oilfield guy, what's his name?"

Matty placed her wine on the side table so as not to spill it. "Oh my, that one was a real driller," she said. "Approached sex like he was taking core samples. But boy, could he lay down a pipe!"

Fleur was used to the outrageous way Matty described her conquests. "Sounds like fun, I think. Is he still around?" she asked, knowing full well that oilfield guy must have moved on if Matty referred to him in such a nonchalant manner.

"Nah, I had to cut him loose because his blowouts were kind of gross."

Fleur held up her hands. "Whoa, you're getting too technical for me," she said with a grin, delighted that her friend still enjoyed playing the weary, woman-of-the-world character. Fleur knew her friend's bravado hid a lack of confidence in her allure and sexuality. She had witnessed it many times; when Matty was interested in a long-term relationship, she was stone silent and never divulged details.

Matty glanced at Fleur through wild curls, showing her deep dimples as she attempted to hide a smile through her response, "All right, you got me. oilfield guy took off at full gallop when I asked him where he lived."

"What do you mean?" asked Fleur. "Why wouldn't he want you to know where he lived?"

Matty frowned. "Yeah, I thought it was odd too. Crazy that it didn't occur to me that after three months of dating this guy, I still didn't know where he lived. The coward broke up with me on the phone. Told me it wasn't my fault, and he said that he was so confused."

As they talked, the friends set the table with the Portmeirion Botanic Garden dinner plates Fleur had brought back home from Montreal. At least something nice came from her marriage, Fleur thought as she held the plates.

"How about you?" asked Matty. "Have you dated again since the disaster with that architect from Ireland? A few months ago, wasn't it?"

Fleur shook her head, still puzzled by her encounter with Dr. B. Thomas Hayden. "I'm still licking my wounds about that one," she said. She had been intrigued to meet Dr. Hayden, because his articles showed a deep passion for his work, but things changed after she met him.

Fleur gazed out the window with a wistful look. "I remember that feeling at the bottom of my belly. When I looked into his eyes, my stomach turned to jelly. I've never seen such intensely blue eyes, almost navy. Then when I heard him speak with that silky Irish lilt that is so sexy, I nearly passed out. Almost worth the humiliation of him running out on me, just for that feeling of mushy longing again. It's been a long time."

Matty leaned closer and asked, "What happened? How did he not fall in love with you immediately? Look at you, a tall cool sip with a personality to match. Smoky grey eyes, perfect curtain of hair, which I could kill for. Heck, I'd fall in love with you myself!"

Fleur nodded, "I know, it's all about the hair envy."

"You don't know what it's like to wrestle a comb through this mop," said Matty, shaking her head and causing her curls to bounce. "Go on then, continue what you were saying. I need more details about that hunky Irish architect."

Fleur served up the meat pie with some tossed salad and sat down at the table. "I stayed in the back row when the lecture ended, like a groupie hoping to catch his eye," she said. "It sure seems pathetic now, but I have to admit that it was as though the world would never be the same if I didn't meet him."

Fleur paused to summon the strong intuition she felt when she saw him. It was as though their meeting was somehow meant to be, that she was supposed to be with him. "Some students stopped him to ask questions after the lecture. I was acting cool, pretending to read his article. Next thing I knew, I looked up from the magazine, and there he was standing beside me and asking me to have a drink with him."

"Now that's the magnetism I'm talking about. The man's got taste after all," exclaimed Matty. "So, what happened next? Did he sweep you off your feet?"

"We went to the Thirsty Duck and sat at the back where it was quieter," said Fleur, smiling at the memory. She could feel the warmth of contentment sitting across from Thomas Hayden, enjoying conversation and a drink together. "It was magical, like we'd known each other forever rather than just having met that night. We had so much fun. At least I thought we did."

Matty got up to open another bottle of wine. "So, what happened?" she asked, pouring a generous portion into her friend's glass.

Fleur shook her head and paused as she took a sip from her glass. "He stood up, looking all rattled, and said he had to go. My mouth must have been gaping in disbelief. I had no idea what happened. We were laughing and enjoying ourselves. In fact, he had asked me for my phone number earlier in the evening, which I took as a sign he was enjoying my company. I never heard from him after that."

"That's weird. What were you talking about when he left?"

Fleur chewed her mouthful, turning the memory of her meeting with Thomas Hayden in her mind. "I've replayed it in my head, looking for a clue. The only thing that happened before he left was I leaned back in my chair and lifted my hair off my neck, you know how stuffy the Thirsty Duck can be. I caught him staring at my neck like he'd seen a ghost. You don't suppose he was grossed out by my birthmark?"

"No way," Matty replied with a roll of her eyes. "That little thing is hardly noticeable."

"But don't you think it is a bit strange, a brilliant blue crescent-shaped mark?" asked Fleur with a degree of persistence. "It looks like I put it there. But it's not a tattoo, just a weird birthmark behind my ear."

"Nah," said Matty, shaking her head so hard her curls bounced. "It was hair envy. You know how men privately wish they could have long straight hair."

Fleur laughed. "You're right, I'm being silly. Maybe something popped into his mind. The way I look at it, like my Grana says, everything's a gift. There must be a reason."

Fleur had a strong notion that she would see Thomas Hayden again. There was no doubt in her mind they had connected at a deeper level. She didn't know how or where, as Dublin was a long way from Antigonish, but Fleur sensed they would indeed meet once more. Even now, many months later, she could still feel the timbre of his voice reverberating in her chest, the intensity of those eyes staring into her being and sending a shiver down her legs. Yes, she was going to see him again, she thought. She lifted her wine glass in a silent salute to the man who had affected her in such a short period of time.

CHAPTER THREE

The next morning, Fleur tiptoed into the kitchen to grab a coffee and bagel before heading to the Heliotrope for her half-day shift. She and Matty had enjoyed large quantities of dark burgundy wine last night, and Fleur feared waking her friend, as she would be none too chipper.

"Is that something with caffeine in it I smell?" asked a wild-haired Matty from the bedroom door. "I could use a cup of that expresso, immediately if not sooner."

Fleur covered a chuckle with a cough and asked, "You mean espresso? Are we feeling a bit hungover this morning?"

"I don't know a thing about this *we* business, but I sure as heck am a little less than 100%," said Matty. "Why are you up so early? Oh right, heading to the gallery for a few hours, I forgot, you told me. But I didn't forget you telling me about those dreams. I can't believe you kept that from me. It sounds very exciting. A bit spooky maybe but exciting at the same time. I wonder what the woman wants from you?"

Fleur winced. In a moment of weakness, she had told Matty about the dreams when they ended up in the backyard hot tub. Relaxed by wine and warm, bubbly water, Fleur confided about her recurring dreams of a tribal woman seemingly asking for help.

The dream was more intense last night, likely fueled by too much wine. Fleur was mesmerized by the dream, eager to see where it would take her. The story was developing like a mini-series plot. In fact, last night's dream was like listening to a story, oddly comforting and familiar, like a rerun of a movie.

Fleur didn't want to talk about it yet. She was glad that Matty understood the subject was closed for discussion. "Don't you go worrying about a single thing, Boo," said Matty. "I won't breathe a word about the subject again if you don't want to talk about it."

Of course, that just made Fleur more apprehensive. Matty never left a subject alone if she thought there was a chance to help fix a problem. Nevertheless, she had to take Matty's words at face value if she wanted to arrive at work on time.

"Thanks for understanding," she said. "I appreciate your sensitivity. I'd like to keep this low key." Fleur put on her raincoat with her back to Matty, but could feel her friend smiling, a sure sign she was plotting something.

"I'm going now, enjoy your day," Fleur said on her way out the door.

Fleur parked at the edge of town alongside the garden commons a few blocks from the art gallery so she could savor the early morning atmosphere as Main Street came to life. Lined with trees and flower planters, the street smelled of lavender and greenery. The comforting aroma of freshly baked bread wafted from the bakery.

When Fleur walked through Main Street people knew her. The shop-keepers at the haberdashery, the butchers, and the florists all waved as she passed. She pressed her nose against the windowpane of the candy shop to see what treasures were there. Mr. Troms brought out a piece of rock candy, her favorite treat when she was a kid. She should feel a sense of belonging, but she didn't. Fleur worried, if she couldn't feel like she belonged where people knew her so well, then where could she feel at home?

Fleur unlocked the gallery door, anticipating the pleasure of discovering the new treasures that had arrived since her last shift at the gallery. She looked forward to being alone with the many expressions of creative talent presented at the gallery in oils, watercolors, pencil drawings, and sculptures.

Fleur considered the art gallery a safe place to embrace her passion for art. She felt pleased when she could find the perfect piece for a client, one that pulled them emotionally. While it saddened her to feel so paralyzed at the thought of painting, working at the gallery gave her a connection with her passion through conversations with clients about the various art works, as well as discussions with local artists about their craft.

The morning was an easy one, with only a few customers coming in to browse. She unpacked, catalogued, and placed in inventory fifteen new pieces of art that arrived from the Halifax exposition the gallery's owner recently attended.

As Fleur was putting away the final piece, her attention went to the front window where she glimpsed the top of Professor Donaldson's green tweed

MARK OF A CRESCENT MOON

flat-cap. Dread plummeted her stomach. He had been her mentor at university, and now made it his mission to coax her to paint again. He reframed his nagging as concern, though every encounter with the professor only added to her worry. Since her return home, Fleur had tried to figure out why she had such an irrational fear of painting. She had wondered if her ex-husband's negativity had accounted for it. Attending therapy sessions had helped her understand the emotional damage he had caused her, but quite a lot of time had passed. Fleur thought she should be over that angst by now.

Not wanting to talk with the Professor Donaldson this morning, Fleur whispered under her breath for him to go away. To her surprise, the professor placed a hand on the door handle, paused, and then withdrew it. Turning back down the five steps to the gallery, he headed off towards Main Street. Fleur sighed her relief of avoiding another lecture. Her next thought was a niggling one as she wondered what caused the professor to turn around and leave.

She froze a few minutes later when the bell signaled someone entering the gallery. It was only Tammy, the art gallery's owner. "Was that Professor Donaldson I saw heading down the street?" asked Tammy, placing a tray of doughnuts and a coffee for Fleur on the desk. "What am I thinking, of course it was. It's the last Saturday of the month."

"You're right," said Fleur, helping herself to a doughnut, "But for some reason he stopped short of coming in. He must have remembered something he had to do. He turned around and went away without a backward glance." Taking a bite of the treat, she added, "You remembered that strawberry is my favorite, that's so sweet of you."

"You're quite welcome. You say the professor just turned around? That's odd, but great, you've been saved. Maybe he won't bother you again until next month. He is persistent though, isn't he?" Tammy paused to gesture at the art Fleur had unboxed. "What do you think of the new artwork that came in last night?"

Fleur touched the landscape she liked the best. She considered the large-scale oil by Dalton Daly captured the tranquility of Pomquet Beach precisely. "This one is quite evocative," she said. "I haven't heard of the artist. Is she new here? The way she paints Pomquet is like someone seeing the magic of it for the first time." Fleur drew her hand away from its gentle caress when the pain of not being able to paint her favorite place in the world washed over her.

"I thought you might like that piece best, knowing your love of Pom-quet," said Tammy. "Were there many customers this morning?"

"A few people came in to have a look around," said Fleur, glad Tammy had not noticed her momentary sadness. "Coincidently, they were all looking for Mi'kmaq art. The Johnson sisters came in for their usual Saturday browse around, and Dante popped in again. She looked familiar to me last week when she came in, but I couldn't place where I'd seen her before."

"Dante is lovely," said Tammy. "Her niece is an artist, specializing in Mi'kmaq work. Dante has always been a good supporter of her people's artistic talent."

Fleur handed Tammy the appointment list. "A few clients are coming in this afternoon. Will you be able to handle them yourself, or would you like me to stay?"

"No need, I'll be fine. Enjoy your afternoon. It's your lucky day; the professor didn't bother you."

Fleur grinned but chewed her lip, the knot in her stomach appearing again at the mention of the professor. The incident this morning with him turning away from the door when she wished him to leave was the third example of her thoughts becoming reality. First with Norma saving her when she didn't want to deal with Len at the Dragonfly, then with Sally Ann knocking over tins when she wished her to know the mess she made by being a gossip.

Fleur considered that she could no longer think of these as coincidences, yet she didn't know what to make of them. She decided she would not think about that now but promised herself to be vigilant in taking notice in the future.

That evening, Fleur could feel Matty's pent-up excitement as they waited for their university buddy, Terrence Donavan, to join them at the Thirsty Duck. Matty had insisted they arrive early to get a good table as Saturday nights were busy. One of the oldest pubs around, the Thirsty Duck was warm and comfortable and included upscale décor such as stained glass panels separating the booths and tiffany lamps swinging above the tables.

Wiggling into a booth, Matty immediately launched into an account of her day. "Boo, you wouldn't believe the amazing time I had. Imagine, I enjoyed the interrogations by Maman. I even found that Papa's mutterings when he teased Maman were funny. The two of them banter back-and-forth all the time, and it's hilarious if you pay attention."

Fleur fixed a smile on her face as though she were listening closely to Matty's story. Mostly, she was taking in the sights and sounds of the pub and a rare evening out. "Then there was the luminating visit with Dante," added Matty, almost as an aside. "Maman took me to see the old lady the minute I told her about your dreams. Dante had some very interesting things to say."

Fleur snapped her head back to stare at her friend. "Whoa there, wait a minute. What are you talking about, Matty?" she asked. "You told Dante? Why were you telling people about my dreams? And for goodness sakes, the word is illuminating not luminating."

Fleur didn't often correct Matty's improper use of the English language, but she was upset. Her privacy was never to be compromised, that was *her* rule number one.

"Don't get your knickers all twisted up," said Matty waving her hands in the air. "I just mentioned it. Dante is like family; she comes over often for Sunday dinners. You've met her lots of times. The old Mi'kmaq lady, she's some kind of Indian spiritual healer. Don't you remember playing Maids in the Night under the moonlight when we were twelve? When we snuck up on her doing some kind of ritual."

Fleur relaxed. "Yes, I remember Dante. Odd name for a Native Indian," she said. "I've seen Dante recently. She came into the gallery last week, and again today, to look at some Mi'kmaq art. Very kind lady. But that's beside the point – you shouldn't be talking about me, especially about those strange dreams. That's my private business."

Matty jumped up, and wrapped her arms around her friend. Fleur's annoyance softened seeing the confusion on her friend's face. Matty looked conflicted; on the one hand she just wanted to help, but on the other hand she was apologetic about making Fleur feel uncomfortable by her actions. "I'm so sorry. I promise not to blather mouth again. But you should talk to Dante. She said you need to be true to yourself and to your Inner Being, that you have lost your way, and that you need to go back where you came from to find your way, or something like that."

Fleur leaned towards Matty, endeared by the awareness that Matty wasn't sure if what she said made any sense. "Ah, don't look at me like that," she sighed. "I know you always have my best interests at heart. I didn't mean to be abrupt with you, but you know I'm kind of weird about my privacy. Why don't we go see Dante tomorrow after lunch with your folks? I'll talk with her myself."

Matty beamed. "Sounds cool. Now where is Terrence Donavan? I can't wait to see him, I've missed our conversations, you know? The stuff you can only talk about with a gay guy."

"I can't believe you said that!" admonished Fleur. "But I know what you mean. Ever since Terrence admitted that he's gay, he's been more relaxed, despite being a big shot lawyer."

"Who's a big shot lawyer?" asked a voice behind them.

"Donavan," Matty cried out, giving him a tight squeeze. "Wowzer, check you out. You're looking as gorgeous as always. I've missed you."

Despite years of not seeing each other, Matty and Terrence fell into their usual comfortable banter. "You aren't going to launch into that soliloquy you called *The Trials and Tribu-relations of the Gay Donavan – the High School Years,* are you?" Terrence responded to Matty's cry of delight.

Matty threw back a retort with a saucy flip of her hair. "Ha, I always knew you and I lusted after the same guys in high school. I can't believe you pretended to like Shirley Parsnip. You couldn't fool me with your jock jokes. Those long locks of straight hair gave you away."

Fleur choked while taking a sip of her wine. "No, not hair envy again. Just accept it, you're never going to have straight hair," she said, sending them to laughter.

She was pleased to see Terrence enjoying Matty's good-natured teasing, though she noticed him flinch when Matty started to interrogate him about the state of his current love life. Fleur knew the details about Terrence's journey to accept himself as a gay man. Since university, she and Terrence had a great relationship and had shared their innermost feelings about life and their future. Even lately, since Fleur had returned home, they often got together, and she shared more with Terrence about her marriage breakdown than with anyone else.

Terrence answered Matty's question, tentative at first, then with enthusiasm. "There is someone," he said. "A mate of mine, Mark McEwen. I met him the summer I interned in Edinburgh. Mark is a partner in a law firm now, and he helped me out with a client who needed work done in Scotland. Things have been developing. I just need to find a reason to get to Scotland so I can see him again, to see if there is anything happening between us."

"Sounds like you have enough of a reason, if you ask me," exclaimed Matty.

"We'll see," said Terrence smiling at Matty. "Hey Fleur, are you feeling alright?"

Fleur stared at the candle on their table, twirling the wine glass stem in her hand. It took her a second to register Terrence's question.

"Oh, sorry," said Fleur, twinged by guilt at disconnecting from the conversation. "I was just thinking about Scotland. Is it like a cold and barren land? Does it feel almost tribal? I've never been there, but I imagine it must feel quite remote."

"Some of the islands of the Hebrides can feel that way," replied Terrence. "The Isle of Mull, Islay, and Jura do feel as though you've stepped back in time. You could describe the atmosphere as barren and almost tribal, I suppose. At least, that was my experience when I visited those islands. I haven't been to the other islands. The mainland is quite different, very lush, with green hills and lots of forests. Why do you ask?"

Matty answered for Fleur, clicking her fingers. "I bet it's those dreams about a woman calling her. We're going to see a spiritual healer tomorrow to find the meaning. Like maybe this woman wants Fleur to go somewhere, or to rescue someone."

Terrence raised an eyebrow, and Matty continued, addressing Fleur. "Wait a minute there. Do you think your dream woman is from Scotland? Wouldn't that be something!"

Fleur threw open the windows in her kitchen to let in the fresh morning air. She had a rare lie-in this Sunday morning, and she looked forward to spending the afternoon with Matty and her family. Moments later, Matty slinked bleary-eyed into the kitchen in search of coffee. Her riotous hair sloped to the left, and her half open dressing gown dragged on the ground.

Fleur hummed to herself as she pulled down two mugs upon seeing her friend in disarray. "Good morning, Sunshine!" she said, smiling at the irony that her upbeat friend had such a hard time in the mornings. "What a great evening, so much fun. Now tell me, what time is your mother expecting us? We don't want to be late for the Dorval brunch feast."

Matty winced and put a hand to her head. "We can back out, I'm not sure two days in a row with my family is good for my health."

Fleur frowned. She loved to be around the Dorval family. They gave her feelings of comfort, family, and connection. "But you promised we'd go. Didn't you have a great time yesterday?" reminded Fleur. "Besides, I think you're right, I should talk to Dante about those dreams. I had an interesting one last night." Fleur considered it a good tactic to persuade Matty that going to see her family was her idea.

Matty bobbed her head, awake in an instant. "You had a dream last night? A good one? What was it about? I can't wait for us to solve the mystery," she said.

Fleur smiled to see her tactic working and sat back on the stool to tell Matty about the dream. "The woman appeared to be more hopeful, like she knew help was on the way and she could relax," she said. "She spoke to me, said these words, 'To know whence you come, it will help you know where you're going,' or something like that."

"That sounds like what Dante said to me. That must be it," said Matty, clapping her hands. "The dreams must be about your identity crisis, and not knowing what you want to do with your life."

Matty continued to explain her theory, ignoring Fleur's confused expression. "First you were excited to be an artist. Then you married Arthur and wanted to have a family, but he surprised you by not wanting children, and then he showed just how mean he is by not wanting you to even be an artist. Then he divorced you after all the compromising you did. It's no wonder you are struggling to know who you are."

Fleur decided not to take offense at how her friend summarized the last ten years of her life. When hearing the summary from Matty's perspective, it was no wonder she had forgotten who she was. Perhaps Matty was right after all. "Maybe Dante can help me understand. We should get going. I'm looking forward to seeing your folks."

Fleur grinned as she sat surrounded by Matty's boisterous family. A flood of fond memories came to her as she sat at the massive oak table, the centerpiece of life at the Dorval homestead.

She loved the cacophony of multiple languages and rambunctious shouting as Matty's family communicated with each other. She enjoyed being fussed over by Mrs. Dorval, who noted her quietness. "Ma petite Fleur, what are you thinking about? You're sitting there like a withering pat of butter," she said in her heavy Acadian accent. "Are you not over that no-good Boden man you married? I knew the minute he came whiffing around you, he would be nothing but trouble."

After answering Mrs. Dorval's questions about her personal life, Fleur gazed around the table at Matty's family, relishing the ruckus. The table's wooden boards groaned with the typical Acadian Sunday fare of roasts, meat pies, garden vegetables, and three potato dishes.

While Fleur was lost in nostalgia, Matty was in defensive mode, fending off her mother's attempts to discover why her eldest daughter was still not married.

Matty interrupted yet another question, "Hey, Maman, did you know that Fleur's dreams are now turning prophetical?" Mrs. Dorval asked Matty to explain.

Fleur glared at Matty to discourage her, but Matty continued unabashed. "Oh yes, Maman," Matty focused on her mother and ignored Fleur. "The woman in Fleur's dreams tells her she needs to find out where she came from before she can find out where she's going. Not everyone has visions giving them direction about their lives, or telling them stories about people from another time and place. Maman, you always said Fleur was special, and has unusual gifts. This just proves it now, doesn't it."

Fleur gave Matty her best *Stop Talking About Me* look. Before she could protest, she heard someone whispering beside her. "Answer the call from home, and return whence you come." The proximity of the soft voice made Fleur jolt and drop her fork.

Fleur turned to see who had murmured in her ear. It took a great deal of willpower to hang on to her composure. Dante sat at the corner of the table.

At least Fleur thought it was Dante. The woman sitting beside her looked like Dante but was the same age as when Fleur had seen her many years ago with Matty. She hadn't aged a day. Before Fleur could form a question, Dante continued, "Do the work for your line, for descendants ahead and ancestors behind." Fleur thought they were strange words, particularly with the ageless Mi'kmaq woman speaking with what sounded like a Scottish accent.

Fleur sat transfixed, and turned to take a sip of water. When she turned back to ask Dante what she meant, she was no longer there.

"You look like you've seen a ghost," Matty said, having noticed something wasn't right with Fleur.

"I think I did," said Fleur, draining the water in her glass in one gulp. She had trouble getting enough moisture in her mouth to swallow. Noticing the lack of saliva made her try harder to swallow, which in turn made her heart pound with the building anxiety. Fleur took a few calming breaths to center herself before anyone could notice her internal turmoil.

"I was hoping to talk with Dante. Has anyone seen her?" she asked. Every hair on her arms stood on end in anticipation of the answer that she knew would only frighten her more.

Matty's mother smiled and said, "Dante could not be with us. She had to help her niece."

Fleur's instinct told her the truth. She grabbed her napkin to cover the red blotch she could feel rising on her neck, making the blue crescent-shaped birthmark stand out. This was a telltale sign of internal upheaval, which few people could spot. Matty was one of those people. Like smoke rising from a crater signaling volcanic action, Fleur's red blotch meant an emotional eruption was about to happen.

Fleur was relieved when her friend noticed her neck and concluded it was time to evacuate. "Maman, we have to go," said Matty. "Thank you, everything was great, and I'll call you tomorrow." Matty ran around the table kissing everyone on both cheeks, then whisked Fleur from her chair and rushed her out.

A good distance down the country road, Matty pulled the car onto the shoulder of the road. "Ok, out with it," she said without preamble. Fleur was happy her friend was so direct; it helped her calm down.

Staring straight ahead of her, Fleur explained what had happened. "I saw Dante, right there, sitting next to me. No one else saw her. She was so real. I didn't know that I was the only one seeing her until I looked back and she had disappeared. She whispered very strange words to me. I know it's hard to believe, but it's true."

"What did she say to you?" asked Matty, as though it was normal for a Native Indian healer to appear and disappear like a vision.

Following Matty's lead, Fleur answered as though the event was ordinary, though her voice warbled. "She said something similar to what the woman in my dream said last night. She said something like, 'knowing where you come from or going back to where you come.' Dante spoke with a Scottish accent, as if everything else wasn't weird enough."

"Those are similar words to what Dante said to me yesterday! I wish I was there."

Fleur laughed. "Matty, you were there. You just didn't see what I saw."

"What do you suppose it means?" pondered Matty, tapping the steering wheel. "Do you think that Dante came to you in a vision to heal you? Do you feel different? Maybe lighter? Do you think that you could make that happen again?"

Fleur shook her head and admitted, "No, I feel scared. Am I losing my mind? I'm not even sure if I saw her. Why would she appear and say those words? They didn't make sense."

"I need to talk to Grana," said Fleur, her body starting to tremble. "There's been a lot of stuff happening lately, not just the dream. When I think of something, it happens. Am I going crazy? Maybe I should just stop meditating? It all started when I began meditating again. That's when the dreams started, and all the coincidences. All of those things just happening when I wish them."

Matty patted Fleur's knee. "Hey, don't you remember how good you used to be at making things happen by wishing them? Remember the Kiss concert? We were complaining that we couldn't afford the tickets, and you wished we could go. About an hour later, the radio station called to say you won two tickets to the concert."

Fleur grinned at the memory. "I didn't even know there was a competition. But we took it in stride and enjoyed the concert. This just feels different somehow. The events lately all feel connected to each other. I'm not sure how that can be. I don't feel in control of things."

She couldn't shake the dread that something outside of her control was taking over her life. At least Matty was unfazed by it all, which made Fleur feel a little normal, more so than she might if she were alone. Fleur assured herself that once she had a chance to speak with her Grana, everything would be all right.

Her uneasiness grew when she remembered her last conversation with her Grana, who had expressed concern about the dreams. Her Grana said she would share her concerns with Fleur when she had a chance to think it through. Fleur wondered if there was a connection between the dream, the incidents, and Dante's vision. She couldn't shake the feeling that her Grana had answers.

CHAPTER FOUR

Eileen was sitting on her porch when her granddaughter's car pulled into the driveway. She had been expecting Fleur, knowing she would be coming to ask questions. She was almost positive that Fleur's recurring dreams were connected to the truth of her birthplace, the family curse, and the letter addressed to Fleur. There were too many coincidences; it had to be the culmination of the foretelling by her grandmother. The story about the ancestors had made Eileen anxious as a child, and she had wanted to safeguard Fleur from that same anxiety. *What's done is done, and better 'twere done and over with,* Eileen thought as she recognized that she could no longer keep Fleur in the dark; she had to know the truth.

Eileen stood to greet her granddaughter at the top of the stairs. "Hello, dearie. Come, let's go inside. We'll take this tray to the kitchen and I'll put on another pot." Knowing that Fleur was too polite to confront her, Eileen decided she would ease into the discussion after assessing her granddaughter's emotional state.

"How was your visit with Matty, dearie?" asked Eileen. "Did you polish off the meat pie? I know how much Matty loves comfort food." Eileen watched Fleur, and saw her granddaughter tapping her index finger on her knee before she covered up the nervous habit by clasping her hands together.

"Matty is good, I just dropped her off at the cottage to pack and run some errands," said Fleur. "We had brunch with her family. Thank you for the meat pie, we enjoyed it."

"Glad you liked the pie," said Eileen. "What's the news from her family?" Eileen noticed Fleur shift in her seat as though she were preparing to be on the defensive. "I've come straight from visiting the Dorvals to see you," she said. "Something happened there. I think it was a hallucination, and I'm confused and frightened. So many strange things have happened recently."

Eileen scanned her granddaughter, thinking she appeared composed enough despite her words to the contrary. She noted that Fleur's emotions were in check as she relayed seeing Dante at the dining table. Fleur recounted the event as though it were ordinary, speaking to someone who wasn't there.

Eileen couldn't help but feel proud at how unruffled her granddaughter was in the face of such a strange situation.

Fleur proceeded to tell her grandmother about the small incidents happening to her. Eileen listened, nodding her head as Fleur told her how, over the past few days, she would think about something, and it would happen. Fleur mentioned the bothersome Professor Donaldson turning away from the gallery just as his hand was on the doorknob; about Norma rescuing her from Len Dawson's advances at the café; and also about Sally Ann Parsons knocking over groceries to create a mess in the store, just like her gossip created chaos. She told Eileen that the dreams were changing, the woman seemed to want her to do something to help, the woman was pleading with her. She explained that Dante whispered familiar words to her, but in a Scottish accent.

"Grana, you don't seem at all disturbed. Can you tell me what's going on?" asked Fleur.

Eileen was not in the least surprised by these examples of Fleur's power. Her granddaughter came by these intuitive powers as her birthright. It was a matter of time for her granddaughter to understand and use them. This was the start of Fleur knowing who she really was. She waited for Fleur to finish, then asked an important question.

Fleur heard her grandmother's soft sigh, a sign that she was preparing to discuss something difficult. "Do you remember the words that Dante whispered to you, dearie?" asked her Grana.

Before she could gather her thoughts, Fleur felt her body turn numb, and she experienced a sensation like something outside of herself was controlling her breath. Fleur heard herself uttering the words Dante had spoken, "Answer the call from home, and return whence you come. Do the work for your line, for descendants ahead and ancestors behind."

When she stopped speaking, the dead weight of extreme tiredness hit her. She slumped in her chair. She noticed her Grana had refreshed the teapot. A piping hot cup of tea was the antidote for physical or emotional turmoil, according to her Grana.

Her Grana stared into her eyes and said, "There's something I need to tell you."

Fleur's blood pressure pounded in her ears. She remembered her Grana telling her that she would share her thoughts about the dreams when the time was right. Fleur wondered if that time had come.

Pouring tea for the two of them, her Grana started to tell her a long story. "Don't worry, it's not that bad," she said, glancing at Fleur. "It's about my birth. I was born on the Isle of Mull, not here in Nova Scotia as you believe. You've heard of the islands of the Scottish Inner Hebrides off the west coast of mainland Scotland?"

Fleur set her teacup down so it wouldn't drop. "Yes, I've heard of the Hebrides, though you've never spoken about them before," she said in a flat voice. "I had no idea that you were born on the Isle of Mull. Why didn't you ever tell me?" A myriad of thoughts tumbled in her mind, painful memories of longing to have an extended family. Years of feeling like she didn't know who she was or where she came from. It was a lot to take in, that the story she was told wasn't quite true.

"I know, this must be a great shock for you. It was for me too when I found out the truth of it, when I was nine years old," said her Grana. "I don't know much about my birth, as my own grandmother was closed-mouthed about such matters. But I promise to tell you everything that I was told."

Fleur held her breath as Grana continued, starting with the land clearances of Scotland in the 1700s. "As you know, your great-great-grandmother, Fiona Fleur Kintrell, after whom you had been named, had been an artist and a writer born in Scotland," she said. "Her work depicted the devastation of the land clearances. Though she had been born in 1856, at the very end of those times, my grandmother had lived with the aftermath, the decimation and destitution of the population, especially on Mull where she had been born. Her family was fortunate not to have been swept off their land, but they had very little to sustain themselves and were at the mercy of the Laird of Dowart Castle, who owned the land they lived and toiled on. Many died of poverty."

Fleur covered her cup with her hand when her Grana tried to refill it, restless for her to continue her story. "In 1901, Fiona's daughter Moira gave birth to a child, suspected to have been fathered by the Laird, or one of his sons. The baby girl was maimed from birth, not expected to survive. But she did, and when she was three months old, Fiona immigrated to Nova Scotia to save her daughter the humiliation and to keep the baby away from the Laird. Before she left the Isle of Mull, she made sure her daughter was married to her fiancé. Suffice to say, I was that baby."

Those words made Fleur gasp from the weight of emotional pain pressing her heart. Her poor grandmother, an illegitimate child, not knowing who her father was and not knowing her mother's love.

Her Grana gently touched her arm resting on the table. "Don't fret. It all worked out," she said. "My grandmother and I arrived in Nova Scotia, and with the support of the academic community, she continued her work of documenting the history of the Scottish land clearances. She recorded the live histories of Scottish immigrants who arrived in the Pictou County area, people who became like family to me. I not only survived in the new world, but thanks to my vigilant grandmother, who was a remarkable healer, I thrived."

Fleur threw her arms around her grandmother. "Oh Grana, I can't believe we had similar experiences."

"Don't feel sorry for me," said her Grana. "I had a marvelous upbringing. But there is more to tell you, the reason why I never clarified the circumstances of my birth.

"There's an ancient tale in our family about generations of women raised by their grandmothers, all because of a curse. My grandmother said the curse would be lifted when the last descendent in the line does the work. I don't know what the 'work' is, I never found out. I don't believe that I was the one to be called."

Fleur shook her head. Long ago she learned to rein in her emotions as she never wanted to upset her dear Grana. But this talk of a family curse was too much to take. Her mind was whirling with disbelief. She could not sit still, and she went to the porch for air. Her world had just tumbled upside-down. Fleur paced, glad her Grana didn't follow her. She needed time alone.

Some time passed before Grana joined her on the porch. Fleur wasn't sure how long. Time seemed irrelevant. She turned to find Grana extending a glass of whisky. She smiled at the gesture. It was just what her Papa Joe would have done, offer his favorite whisky glass with a finger of the golden liquid.

"How are you coping, dearie?" asked her Grana after Fleur had taken a warming sip. "A lot to take in? I learned over the years the best thing to do was to put this to the back of my mind and carry on with life. It doesn't help to put your mind into an endless loop of seeking reasons."

Feeling the whisky relaxing her, Fleur gave her Grana a half smile to let her know she was indeed all right. Grana handed her an envelope and said, "This came for you a few days ago. I was waiting until after you'd enjoyed Matty's visit to give it to you, but I know now it was a mistake to wait."

Fleur took the envelope and examined the return address and noted it was from the Isle of Mull. The name of the sender, Pheill McDonnell & Sons, offered no clue as to the contents of the letter. With the new information about her grandmother's birthplace, Fleur concluded that this letter must be connected somehow to what she just learned. She asked, "Do you think this letter has answers?"

"Well, I don't know what the letter is about, but there is one way to find out," said her Grana, motioning to Fleur to open the letter.

Fleur sliced the top of the envelope with a shaking hand and drew out the typed page. Her Grana craned her neck to view the letter and waited until Fleur read and reread it. Fleur looked up and shared with Grana the contents of the letter.

"There's a lot of legal jargon I'm not sure I understand. Pheill McDonnell & Sons are solicitors representing John and B. Thomas Hayden, the new owners of Castle Dowart Estate. Apparently, the new owners are contesting my inheritance of the Factor's House," Fleur said in a flat tone. "The letter says that I have two months to appear at court on the Isle of Mull to appeal this motion, and another month to remove Ms. Glenna K. Currie from the Factor's House premises." With that, the two slumped on the porch lanai in total silence.

Fleur was the first to speak. "Well that's a lot to take in," she said, pausing to blow out a breath she didn't know she was holding. "An inheritance, in Scotland. I never imagined such a thing possible."

After pausing to let the information sink in, Fleur appealed to her Grana, "Do you recognize any of these names? I know you told me that your grandmother never talked about the circumstances of your birth, but do you recall hearing the name Glenna Currie?"

"No, dearie, that name doesn't ring a bell," answered her Grana. "It sounds as though she needs help. Poor soul, about to be tossed out from her home. It looks on the surface that you are the one who can help her. None of those names are familiar to you, I suppose?"

"Actually, I recently met a Dr. B. Thomas Hayden," murmured Fleur. "He was giving a lecture on historical architecture at the university. We had coffee together afterwards. I liked him, but something odd happened and he disappeared. I wonder if this could be the same person. If it is, I wonder if he knew about this inheritance when he met me?"

"I wouldn't go worrying and wondering about things you don't know to be true," said Grana, ever practical. "It will only bring chaos. I suggest you approach this mystery with an open heart as the gift it's meant to be. I've always said all things that come to us are gifts, though at first they might not appear to be. What will you do?"

"I promise not to fret," stressed Fleur. "I agree, this is a gift. You're right, it's an opportunity to help someone if nothing else. The first thing I will need to do is seek legal advice to understand what the letter means. For instance, how can an inheritance be contested if there is no inheritance in the first place? This letter certainly brings a lot of questions, not answers as we had hoped."

An hour after she drove home from Grana's house, Fleur was curled up on the sofa with a glass of wine trying to relax when Matty came in from her errands. Fleur figured she must look a sight when Matty stopped mid-chatter to ask what was wrong.

"I've had some news from Grana," said Fleur. "Not terrible news, just a lot to digest."

Matty sat down on the sofa next to Fleur, uncharacteristically quiet. Fleur realized she had never seen her friend at a loss for words.

"Relax. It isn't illness or death or anything disastrous like that," said Fleur, giving her friend a nudge.

"Thanking heavens," breathed Matty. "You gave me a fright, looking all sober like that."

Fleur chuckled and didn't bother to correct Matty on her wrong choice of words. Sober instead of somber, which made sense given how they overindulged during the weekend.

As Fleur recapped what her Grana had told her, the story started to sound normal, even the part about an ancient family curse. She became less apprehensive, as the shock wore off. Matty's enthusiasm and interest in details helped.

When she finished telling Matty about the letter, she heard the exclamation she'd been expecting from her friend. "You inherited a castle in Scotland? That is fantastic news," she said. "When do we go? We need to plan and pack. Is it cold in Scotland this time of year? Oh, I can't wait to see those men in skirts; do you remember 'thigh guy' at the Highland Games? There isn't much time if that legal stuff means you've got one month to sort things out. Do you know who the woman living in the Factor's House is – Glenna Currie? What a great name. I bet she's a lot of fun. Wait a minute. Do you think that she could be a long-lost relative? Wouldn't that be amazing!"

"Whoa there, Matty. Slow down. You're moving way too fast for me."

"But you're so right. I should be excited. Not everyone inherits property in Scotland. But I don't understand the legal jargon, and you know how I need to analyze everything. Do you think Terrence would come over tonight to have a look at the letter?"

Fleur paused for a moment as Matty's last comment filtered through the barrage of words. "I hadn't thought about the possibility of finding a family. I asked Grana, but the name Glenna Currie wasn't familiar to her. Then again, she never went back to Scotland."

Matty didn't hesitate. "Of course Donavan will help. Call him. Let's get him to pick up Indian take-out on his way over, and make mine spicy! All this excitement made me hungry."

While the two friends waited for Terrence to arrive, Fleur pulled out her encyclopedia to research the Isle of Mull. She was daunted by the logistics of getting there, involving airplanes, trains, cars, and ferries. Matty assured her that she would handle all of the details when the time came to make travel plans.

When Terrence came through the door with food in hand, Matty grabbed the Indian take-out, insisting they eat before he looked at the letter. While they devoured their meal, Fleur updated Terrence on the story her Grana told her, leaving out the part about the family curse. After dinner, she gave Terrence the letter from Pheill McDonnell & Sons, and waited for him to read it a couple of times.

The letter sounded ominous to Fleur when she first read it. She didn't know anything about an inheritance, so it was strange to receive a notice contesting one. Fleur worried most about Glenna Currie's removal from the Factor's House. The letter didn't say who she was or why she had been living in the Factor's House, but Fleur assumed she would be removed if the Haydens won the court case.

Terrence put down the letter. Fleur raised an eyebrow in Matty's direction to warn her friend to remain quiet while he spoke. "As you've probably guessed, there's a lot of information missing," said Terrence, stating the obvious in a bland tone. "This letter sounds like a rebuttal following a letter that would have informed you about being named a beneficiary of this estate, which I gather you never received. It's difficult to assess your rights without more details."

Fleur thought that would be the answer, but allowed Terrence to continue his explanation. "There are a lot of questions still to be answered," he said. "For example, what is your relationship to the person leaving you this inheritance? Who are they and why did they name you a beneficiary? It would suggest that you are a family member or have a connection with a family member that you are not aware of. These are key points in proving your legal rights. The only thing we know is the solicitors who sent you this letter are representing John and B. Thomas Hayden, who must have inherited the main Castle Dowart Estate and are contesting your claim to the Factor's House."

Terrence turned to Fleur and asked, "By the way, do you know what a Factor's House is?" At the shake of her head, he explained, "I remember from visiting the countryside. A factor is a superintendent or property manager who manages estates. My guess is that the Factor's House at Castle Dowart must have been inhabited by a factor for many generations in the same family. Based on what you told me of your grandmother's story, there could be a connection with her side. The tricky part will be proving what that connection is to uphold your right to inherit the home."

"So that I understand, in order to win any kind of legal case, if it comes to that, I'm going to have to prove that I have a connection with the person who named me as their inheritor? How does that work when I don't know who named me?"

Before he could respond, Fleur jumped in with another question. "What is the next step, Terrence? I'm concerned for Glenna Currie. I don't know why, but I have a feeling that she needs me to keep her safe in her home."

"I agree, you need to move now, given the time frame and a possible court case," said Terrence. "I'll contact my friend Mark McEwen, the lawyer in Edinburgh."

Matty looked at Fleur with an exaggerated lift of her eyebrow. With a smirk, Terrence added, "Yes, Mark is the friend I was telling you about last night."

Matty couldn't help grinning. "Well then, you have a reason to see him now," she said. "You must go to Scotland with us to oversee the legal stuff."

"Slow down," said Terrence. "I have a big court case here, I can't leave everything, much as I'd love to. But I'll call Mark and have him take care of this from Edinburgh. We need to understand the grounds upon which the inheritance is contested, and establish what tactics Fleur would need to follow in a case. That means we need to discover what happened to the original inheritance notification. We need to know where it came from, and why you were named to inherit the Factor's House. Glenna Currie might be the one person who can answer those questions. I assume Matty will organize the travel details?"

By the time Terrence left Blue Bird Cottage that night, Matty and Fleur had a plan of action. Upon her return to Halifax, Matty would make the travel plans for the two of them. Terrence would contact Mark and get the legal investigation started, so by the time the two friends arrived in Scotland, the path forward would be clearer.

That night, twisting in her bed trying to sleep, Fleur tingled in anticipation and in fear of the unknown journey she must make. She wondered if Scotland, the land of her grandmother's birth, would help her find a connection to family.

Fleur was excited about the prospect of experiencing new landscapes and terrain. She had a special connection to the earth, a relationship with the energy in nature that had kept her steady through tough periods in her youth.

She might not have known extended family growing up, but she'd had a clear bond with the universe. Fleur closed her eyes and savored the eagerness of feeling the earth her ancestors had tilled beneath her feet, and inhaling the atmosphere that they had breathed.

As Fleur fell asleep, she soothed herself with words that echoed the words Dante spoke: "I'm going home. Home to do the work – for myself, for my ancestors and for my descendants." She felt a strong yearning to truly believe those words, and it took all of her willpower to resist the urge to allow feelings of unworthiness overwhelm her, which would leave her feeling unfit for the task.

She dreamed of the tribal woman standing calm and elated on a hilltop looking down upon lands stretching out to the sea. The woman smiled a knowing smile: confident, certain of things about to transpire. Fleur had the sense the woman was put at ease by something she experienced at the hilltop, perhaps a burden that was on her mind had been relieved. Could it be the woman knew that Fleur was coming to her land? Or was there something else? Whatever the situation, Fleur sensed that the woman's energy was lighter since last she encountered the woman in her dreams.

CHAPTER FIVE

AN ISLAND OF THE HEBRIDES, AD 560

T'Eilin paused beside an ash tree at the edge of the hilltop, emerging from the stupor of a deep trance. The dawn's artistry was lost on her as she surfaced from contemplation of spirit.

She had traveled to the hilltop a few hours journey from her village at the Spring equinox looking for answers. She had experienced a growing unease about strangers coming to her land who would bring change.

An ancient circle of stones, hidden behind a meager patch of trees, stood sentinel over the land of her ancestors since the beginning of time. T'Eilin had come to commune with the stone circle, attuned to its energetic field; a vortex which connects all time and all people. The knowing was in her blood, passed down the matriarchal line from healer to healer, intuitive to intuitive, linked through her lineage to the power of healing and foretelling.

T'Eilin drew her linen tunic closer to her body against the fresh breeze as she pondered what she learned. Strangers were indeed coming. It was her duty as the tribe's intuitive to assess the meaning for her people. Would the strangers bring a better life for her people, or would they bring demise, T'Eilin wondered.

The last attack on T'Eilin's people was a vivid childhood memory. Her great-grandmother had foretold the event, receiving her wisdom by communing at the stone circle to warn the warriors with the details of the attack.

T'Eilin's grey eyes cleared as she gazed at the distant headland, and discerned the glimmer of fire from the broch atop the bluff. Manned for early warning, a broch fire could be seen for miles. One fire indicated a return of village warriors, while two meant strangers were approaching.

T'Eilin saw that there was one fire on the broch, telling her that the group who set off in late winter returned. If she left right away, T'Eilin could be back in time to report to the tribal elders.

Glancing over her shoulder, T'Eilin offered gratitude to the divine intelligence within the circle of stones. She spoke words out loud to clear any heavy energy. "Everything is working out for my people. All is well with my tribe."

Arriving just before the start of the meeting, T'Eilin walked through the group of elders gathered inside the healing hut, greeted each by name, and kneeled in front of her grandmother, the Healing Mother Naghaire.

As the Irie's leader and healer, Naghaire sat elevated upon a stone bench facing the eastern opening. "Child, you are returned," she said, turning her blind eyes towards T'Eilin, and touching her shoulder. "We will hear the news from the North first, and then you will tell us the wisdom from the stones."

T'Eilin settled in her place next to her grandmother, then stifled a tremor when she noticed Tonnick in the back corner of the hut. The dark and brooding Tonnick looked uncomfortable in the presence of the elders. His eyes darted around the room, not focusing on any one person. When his gaze settled upon T'Eilin, she cringed but kept her own eyes steady. She would not allow him the satisfaction of seeing her react to the venomous look he cast upon her.

"Orgah and Tonnick have returned from the mainland with news," said Naghaire. "Orgah, tell us of the voyage in search of betrothing women."

"There is much to tell," began Orgah, pleased with the opportunity to showcase his skills as a leader. "We left for the mainland at the beginning of the last moon cycle and made landfall in good timing. There were no encounters at sea. Trouble began when we made landfall west of the peninsula."

Naghaire waved her hand for him to continue his report when Orgah paused. "In short, we were ambushed. Norse attacked, but we took care of them. Agreed, Tonnick?" Orgah asked his brother.

Tonnick spluttered when he realized he was being addressed. "That is correct," he grumbled before glaring once more at T'Eilin.

"Right," thundered Orgah, scowling at Tonnick. "After we dealt with the Norse, we headed inland where we knew we would be welcomed. We returned with ten women of childbearing age, and soon a party from their villages will come for reciprocity. We need to prepare our best women for the honor," said Orgah, looking at T'Eilin, who was in charge of that task.

Naghaire motioned to signal Orgah that he should wrap the story up succinctly, then said, "That is good news, and T'Eilin will be vigilant in preparing them. Now, tell us of the other important information you were eager to relay; we are eager to hear it."

Orgah cleared his throat before he continued. "We heard about a man they call the Monk from Eyrie, traveling with a group of men to conquer King Bridei using magic. It is said this Monk heals people by raising his hand and calling the name of a revered elder he calls Christ. It is also said he makes solid rocks float on water, and wooden boats move across the seas without wind."

T'Eilin was not bothered by what Orgah said, for she had heard similar stories. However, the elders reacted with concern, punctuated by Tonnick's belligerent glee as he added to the tale. "This great Monk is said to dislike women, saying they are evil creatures that only want to keep men subservient," he said, staring wide-eyed at T'Eilin.

"Sounds like a man unable to appreciate the better qualities of honey," said T'Eilin under her breath so only her grandmother heard.

"We heard such stories in the past," said Naghaire, swallowing the urge to chuckle at T'Eilin's muttered words. "We need to determine if these stories affect our people's safety."

Orgah jumped to give his opinion. "Many tribes succumbed to this Christ overlord," he said. "We must plan defense from an invasion from these western isle folks."

"T'Eilin, it is time for you to speak of your discovery at the standing stones," said Naghaire.

T'Eilin nodded her head. "Healing Mother, this is indeed the perfect time to share the wisdom at the stones. I believe it is quite relevant to the story that Orgah told us."

"For some time, I have had a sense of strangers coming, and of things changing for our tribe. This intuition was confirmed at the stones."

Orgah interrupted. "See, there is truth to the tale. Let us prepare for battle."

Naghaire waved her hand to signal the elders to stop their muttering. Some of the elders were in favor of immediate action, but most wanted to understand the pertinent information before deciding action.

T'Eilin looked at her grandmother for a sign to continue, and then spoke as though uninterrupted. "Strangers from the western lands are coming, and they will bring change beneficial for the long-term prosperity of our tribe."

One of the elders, an experienced farmer, requested permission to speak. In his usual measured and deliberate manner, he said, "It's possible that change can be a good thing. Many seasons ago we experienced unusual weather that ruined our crops. But we adapted, and benefitted. We started to sow different kinds of oats that could withstand the climate changes and were better for our trade."

Naghaire nodded in agreement with the farmer's words, and then asked T'Eilin more questions about her communion at stones. "Do you know what form the change will take?"

"I only know the strangers will not come to take our lands, but to change our spirit," she said, explaining further as she sensed tension building. "That is, they come to teach us another way of living, and new ways of doing things."

The leader of the warriors, Alcorat, had been quiet throughout the discussion and now motioned for permission to speak. He turned to Orgah and said, "I thank you for your report and concern for the safety of our tribe. You are right, we must prepare. To be unprepared is foolish, but to take action before assessing all the information is irresponsible. Therefore, I suggest we prepare but take no action until we know more about the strangers."

T'Eilin added clarity to the situation with her words. "That is wise. Our tradition tells us that our western neighbors have been friends for many generations, since they helped us dispel invaders from the plains. This tradition matches the wisdom from the stones. We must gather knowledge to understand why they come, to assess how to react, and whether to expect more strangers to arrive at our shores."

Orgah acknowledged the directive from his warrior leader, and nodded his agreement with the words of the tribe's intuitive. He had no reason to oppose T'Eilin. He had come to know her power through instruction from her on his spirit journey. A small blue crescent moon tattoo behind his right ear marked his level of mastery.

As after every meeting of the elders, T'Eilin led the Healing Mother outside to speak to the tribe's people gathered awaiting word about decisions made. Naghaire spoke in a strong, clear voice that belied her fragile appearance. Silence, punctuated by the occasional crackling of wood on the fire, followed her declaration about the impending arrival of strangers from the western lands. Moments passed before a general burble erupted, telling of the tribe's confusion.

"With due respect, Healing Mother, how is this possible?" asked the head herdsman. "You are telling us not to prepare for an attack by men who are coming to our land? It goes against what we have always done to keep our tribe safe."

T'Eilin took her cue from her grandmother before she addressed the tribe. "Thank you for voicing your concern. Things are at work we don't understand. I have just now returned from consultation at the standing stones at the same time that Orgah returned with news of strangers from the western isles. It is confirmed that these strangers are coming to our land, but in peace, not for conquest. They will bring new ideas. We will be vigilant and prepared, but we need to understand what the strangers say and do. I do not fear them."

While the tribe's people trusted their intuitive, they also wished to hear from Alcorat. "Our warriors will be briefed on the preparations needed in these unusual circumstances," he said. "Our forces will be ready for anything that arises."

T'Eilin stood with her head bowed as the Healing Mother concluded with the words of closure and universal wisdom saying, "As above, so below. As within, so without." The tribe's people continued with their festivities as she took her grandmother's arm to guide her back to the healing hut where they lived.

When T'Eilin turned to lead her grandmother back inside, the back of her neck tingled. She looked around to find the source of the unease. She did not see Tonnick, but knew it was his negative energy cast her way. At the same time, she felt her grandmother's hand resting on her arm tighten its grip. She decided it was time to discuss this awareness of Tonnick's ill will with her grandmother.

When they were alone, T'Eilin guided her grandmother unto the comfortable resting place at the back of the hut and prepared herself to speak of the situation with Tonnick.

"Grandmother, if you are not too exhausted by this day's events, may I speak with you about something of a personal nature?"

Her grandmother patted T'Eilin's hand, "You are concerned about Tonnick. He still has tremendous negative energy toward you, ever since you spurned his advances long ago. I felt it this evening; his negativity is growing."

"That is what worries me," said T'Eilin, staring into the fire. "For many years I have tried to cleanse that heavy energy. I don't understand why I have not been successful. I am ashamed of my failure."

"Dearest granddaughter," said Naghaire, her voice gentle with love. "You know that sometimes what is personal is the hardest to heal. Trying to understand the why of things only traps your mind, but nothing shifts in your vibration. I can help you with the healing ceremony right now if you wish. It is always best to cleanse heavy energy as soon as possible before something unwanted comes of it."

T'Eilin agreed, and gathered the items needed. A bundle of sage to burn in the fire in combination with oak moss to purify the air. The ceremonial drum to keep the rhythm as T'Eilin grounded herself to lower her resistance towards the healing work.

She handed the drum to her grandmother, who tapped a sedate rhythm while T'Eilin settled herself cross-legged in the center of the room in front of the fire. T'Eilin shuttered her lids over her eyes, and focused on grounding her energy as the smoke emitted by the sage and oak moss curled around her head.

T'Eilin slowed her heart in harmony with the drum beat, and adjusted her breath in sync with every other down-stroke. She deepened her breath and focused on dropping it into her heart space to open her heart to the light of spirit. Before long, light of love energy pulsed within her heart. It was a warm light that grew and grew until it eclipsed her being. She felt encased in a cushion of love. Breathing with precision, T'Eilin chanted the name Tonnick, breathing inward on the first syllable and outward on the second, creating a sound like a light summer breeze rustling through the trees. It did not take long for T'Eilin to sense a positive shift in energy, an indication that the healing ceremony was doing its work.

The ceremony was nearly complete when a crashing sound alerted T'Eilin to an intrusion. She raised the lids from her unfocused eyes, continued to focus on her breathing, and waited to see what would happen next.

A hulking figure stood in front of her, encased by swirling smoke. "Witch, what spell have you cast on me?" roared Tonnick. "I should kill you now and be done with all of my trouble. You are nothing but an aggravation to me."

"I see you Tonnick, and I know you do not mean me harm," said T'Eilin as unemotional as the hard dirt beneath her crossed legs.

Tonnick lunged towards T'Eilin. He froze when he heard Naghaire speak.

"Tonnick, leave this room," said Naghaire from the corner where she sat unnoticed. "Watch your words and never threaten my granddaughter again, or you will feel my wrath. Do I make myself clear?"

Tonnick left the hut with one last withering glance at T'Eilin.

It took a few minutes for T'Eilin to rouse herself after Tonnick left the hut. "Do you think I should be worried?" T'Eilin asked, her voice sluggish from the exertion of coming out from her trance so abruptly.

T'Eilin glanced at her grandmother when she did not answer and kneeled at her side. Her grandmother's head moved from side to side as though she were denying something, and her entire body trembled.

"What is it grandmother? Are you feeling unwell?" said T'Eilin in alarm as she cradled her grandmother's hands in hers and looked into her unseeing eyes.

T'Eilin leaned closer to hear the words her grandmother spoke in a fragile voice. "I am remembering a foretelling many years ago," said Naghaire. "In a vision it was told that our ancestry would be cursed by a dark energy, only to be saved when a descendent returned to do the work. I am afraid this is the beginning of that curse."

CHAPTER SIX

EDINBURGH, SCOTLAND, 1987

Fleur sat on the edge of her seat in the cab to Edinburgh, observing how the pastoral land, dotted with sheep, reached to the edge of the bustling city. In the city, historic monuments and medieval structures stood next to classic architecture. The quaint streets and lively pedestrian zones intrigued her, but Fleur was focused on her consultation with Mark McEwen the next morning.

The last few weeks had passed in a blur. The logistics of the unexpected journey had overwhelmed Fleur, and she appreciated how her friends had stepped in to help. Matty took care of the travel details and Terrence coordinated the legal pre-work for her meeting with Mark while she sorted her work commitments, finances, and passport.

Fleur had also tried to contact Glenna Currie by telephone about her and Matty's arrival at the Factor's House. The last thing Fleur wanted was to arrive at the door without a proper introduction and an explanation.

When she managed to get in touch, Glenna was pleasant, and told Fleur that she had been expecting her call. Glenna said she was aware of the inheritance case. This relieved some of Fleur's anxiety, but also raised many questions. However, at that time it was important to assure Glenna not to worry about the Factor's House. They would have ample time to discuss matters when Fleur arrived. Just before hanging up, Glenna had said something rather strange, "I look forward to seeing you remember who you are."

In the cab, Fleur appeared to have her emotions in check. However, on the inside she was conflicted. She was excited to meet Glenna Currie and find out if she knew something about her grandmother's family, while at the same time fearful of the disappointment if Glenna didn't know anything about Grana's family. She also wondered if one of the Hayden brothers disputing her inheritance was the same Thomas Hayden she met at the university.

Fleur looked across the backseat of the cab to find Matty staring at her. Matty gave her a pat on the knee. "Don't worry, Boo," she said. "We'll get to the bottom of all of those questions flitting around in your head. Remember, this is a great adventure."

Fleur smiled at her friend. Matty always looked for the positive aspects of any situation, even when deprived of caffeine. She considered her friend to be quick-witted, able to think fast on her feet. A perfect example was Matty trying to deflect attention away from herself and onto Fleur when they had visited Matty's parents. At that moment, Fleur thought of the words Dante whispered to her, and she wondered how she could have forgotten them.

"What's the matter, Fleur?" asked Matty. "Are you feeling car sick?"

Fleur shook her head, "No, not at all. It's the words that Dante spoke to me. I can't believe I forgot about them! 'Answer the call from home, and return whence you come. Do the work for your line, for descendants ahead and ancestors behind.' Can't you see? The words are true. I'm going to the land 'whence I come,' and that land is Scotland."

"You're right," exclaimed Matty. "Not just that, but it's like you are answering a call, don't forget that part." Her friend appeared excited now, despite her lack of caffeine. "I forgot too. This makes it even more of an adventure. Not only are you a queen of a castle, but maybe we'll solve the mystery of the woman in your dreams." Matty grew serious. "Which reminds me, you haven't mentioned anything about those dreams, are you still having them?"

Matty's excitement was contagious; even her questions about the dreams didn't concern Fleur. "I do dream about the woman most nights," she said. "She still beckons to me, and there is a sense that she is waiting for something, but she doesn't seem to be as agitated as she was before. It's as though she knows that help is on the way. I guess that help would be me." Fleur was more excited to discover what Dante's words meant, and if there was a connection with the woman in her dreams and with the inheritance.

Fleur and Matty stayed awake to counter their jet lag that afternoon. They went their separate ways as Fleur wasn't interested in seeing the funky, vintage boutiques found in the Grass Market district. She was happy for the time to wander the cobblestone streets alone. It cheered her to hear the Scottish accents and unique words and phrases her Grana often used. She spent the afternoon at the Scottish National Gallery, lost in the emotion captured by the old masters and the fabulous Scottish masterpieces on display.

The gallery included a room on the works of the nineteenth-century Scottish masters, dedicated to the history of the Highlands Clearances, which was of special interest to Fleur. The pieces depicted loss and upheaval, and emigration on an unprecedented scale. From the gallery notes, Fleur understood a number of Scottish artists had combined themes of displacement, homelessness, and noble suffering in their work.

Standing in front of a masterpiece of the genre painting named *The Last of the Clan*, Fleur placed a hand on her heart at the tragic emotion captured through the powerful immediacy of a quayside emigrant scene depicted by the master Thomas Faed. The words attached with the painting brought a tear to her eyes; "our once powerful clan was now represented by a feeble old man and his granddaughter, who, together with some outlying kith-and-kin, myself among the number, owned not a single blade of grass in the glen that was once all our own."

As Fleur studied the works, she noticed there were no women artists on display. She knew it was common that women were not involved in the arts then. However, her intuition told her there was artwork painted by a woman here in this very gallery. She wished that she could study a work of art created by a female artist from that period.

A moment later, her wish came true. Fleur noticed a painting at the back corner of the room. From the distance, Fleur sensed a woman's touch by the texture of the brushstrokes, the color palette, and the scene depicting a strong emotional connection between a mother and her children. She imagined a woman must have painted it. The painting captured the desperation of the mother being forced to leave her homeland while protecting her babes. Close up, Fleur looked with curiosity at the nameplate to see if she could tell if the artist was a woman. The artist's name was labeled F. Kintrell, giving no clue to the gender.

Fleur's breath caught in her throat as the memory of the name Kintrell surfaced. The name was her Grana's own grandmother's surname. Fleur wondered if F. Kintrell was her great-great-grandmother. The timeframe could make it possible, as her great-great-grandmother emigrated to Canada with her Grana more than eighty years ago.

Excited about what she might discover, Fleur asked the curator for information about the artist F. Kintrell. Fifteen minutes later, the curator handed

Fleur a dossier, telling her that much of the artist's work was lost, only a few paintings remained. The one in the Scottish National Gallery, and one in Glasgow Museum of Art, were the only works on public display. The documents revealed that F. Kintrell was indeed Fiona Kintrell, born on the Isle of Mull where her father had been the factor of Castle Dowart Estate.

Fleur paused to note this information. It certainly aligned with Grana's story. The artist's dossier discussed the theme of the young artist's work, as well as theme of the piece hanging in the Glasgow Museum. Fiona had taken on the plight of the Scottish women through her work, depicting the suffering wrought by the Highland Clearances. In addition to several large oils, such as the one installed in the Scottish National Gallery, Fiona had created line drawing depictions of the times that she had mailed to London in protest.

From the documents in the dossier, Fleur pieced together that Fiona had been the protégé of the Laird of Castle Dowart. The Laird had seen her talent and had paid for painting lessons for her. This explained how she had been educated at a time when women were not considered worthy of it. There must be an interesting story of how that came about.

Fleur walked back to the hotel later, her head reeling with what she had just learned. Through the fog of disbelief, she realized being an artist was in her DNA. She felt guilt about not using her "God-given talent," as the professor would say. On the positive side, Fleur hoped she might find the family connection she craved through her passion for art.

The next morning, Fleur arrived before her appointment time at the offices of Cummings & McEwen. She was anxious to hear what Mark McEwen had uncovered since speaking with Terrence.

"Hello, lassie," Mark greeted her. "It's so good to meet Terrence's best mate. Come on in, and let's chew on this inheritance situation of yours."

Fleur smiled, sensing an instant bond with Mark. He exuded an easy-going personality, and she knew he and Terrence suited each other.

Fleur sat on the red leather couch in Mark's office, leaning in to listen to his update. She learned Mark found the solicitor located on Mull who acted on behalf of the Castle Dowart Estate. Ian MacNeill had been the Laird's family solicitor for many years.

"Unfortunately, the solicitor had been a lone practitioner," said Mark. "His offices burned down several months ago. At first, I assumed he must have sent the notice of the inheritance to you, but learning about the fire I concluded the letter was never posted."

"That explains why I never received the original notice. Did you find any information regarding my connection with the Laird?" Fleur asked. "I assume it might explain why the Laird named me the benefactor of the Factor's House."

Mark shook his head. "For now we have to assume any proof was burned in the fire," he said. "The poor solicitor – the fire affected his health, and he is not able to communicate anything of use."

"How sad, I'm sorry to hear that," said Fleur. "How will I be able to claim an inheritance where there are no details about it? It seems that I learned about the inheritance by chance."

"Yes, that proves to be tricky," said Mark. "In a way it was a good thing the Hayden brothers are disputing your claim. Otherwise, it might have been a very long time before you would have heard about the inheritance, if at all. The good news is that under Scottish Succession Law, no claim can be made against someone who has been named heir of heritable property, being land and buildings. This comes from the culture of farming and landholdings. So, we're confident in that regard. At this point, since we haven't yet found the original inheritance document, we need to connect you to the Castle Dowart Estate for an airtight case. Do you have any thoughts about that?"

Fleur told Mark her grandmother's story about the possibility that Eileen was the illegitimate daughter of the Laird. "There is something else," added Fleur. "I was in the Scottish National Gallery yesterday and saw a painting by an artist named Fiona Kintrell. I believe Fiona is my great-great-grandmother, judging by the stories my grandmother told me. It turns out Fiona Kintrell was a protégé of the Laird of Castle Dowart."

"That's the ticket," Mark said. "We can trace the connection to the Laird from that angle. Could be that he had a fondness for Fiona and wanted to ensure that her descendants were taken care of financially."

"I thought of that," said Fleur. "It sounds plausible, except the timeline doesn't fit. The Laird during the time of my great-great-grandmother couldn't be the same Laird who provided me with this inheritance. The age doesn't match up."

"I see what you mean," said Mark. "The answers may need to wait until you speak with someone on the island who knows. Perhaps Glenna Currie? I'll put you in contact with a local lawyer to confirm information about Scottish Succession Laws being valid in the Hebrides. Colomie & Sons will be able to help you research the census records, which might give you a clue as to your connection with the Laird."

Mark provided Fleur the contacts to help with the legwork on the island. Time was running out, and Mark and Terrence needed to sort out a plan for the court appearance at the end of the month, two weeks hence.

"I'll continue to work from here," said Mark. "And keep Terrence updated on progress. I expect he'll arrive soon. His court case is going well."

Before she left, Fleur reiterated that she wanted to safeguard Glenna's rights.

"I understand your concern," said Mark. "Whether or not she is family, you don't want anyone to be put out of their home. Don't worry, perhaps she has a 'life tenancy,' as do most people living in Factor's Houses. That being the case, the Hayden brothers could not force her to leave. However, if she doesn't have a life tenancy, the Hayden brothers have a legal right, as the new owners, to ask her to leave. That is, if you lose the case."

Fleur was intent on winning the case, though she didn't know what she would do with a house in Scotland. From her point of view, this was more about learning where she came from. Perhaps she would find out what the tribal woman in her dreams wanted. Maybe all of this was connected to the ancestor's curse her grandmother had told her about. If there was such a thing as a curse, Fleur wanted it resolved.

After the meeting with Mark, Fleur and Matty left Edinburgh to catch the ferry to Mull. Fleur delighted in the sweet freedom of speeding along lush country roads in the rental car, past the picturesque villages that dotted Loch Lomond. They arrived at the Oban terminal just in time to check in and board the early afternoon ferry. The weather was fair and the seas calm, making the trip pleasant. Seals cavorted alongside the boat and the smaller islands they passed, but Fleur didn't notice, for she was lost in thought about what she had learned: a great-great-grandmother who was an artist, a family member bringing to the world's attention to the plight of the victims of the Highland Clearances, a ferryboat heading to an island off Scotland, and a Factor's House that she inherited.

Matty, who was standing beside her at the rail of the boat, interrupted Fleur's musings, "Do you think that you'll see that gorgeous Irish architect you dated?" she asked. "I know it's a long shot, but I have a feeling it's the same guy. It sounds like you connected."

"You're right, we did connect," said Fleur. "But it sure would be a slim chance this is the same Thomas Hayden." The memory of the rejection still hurt.

Matty tried to jostle Fleur out of her pessimism. "Girl, so what if he ran. It was your first date since your divorce. You should've posted the news in that gossip paper – is it still called the Antigonish Casket?"

Fleur leaned over the rail to get a better view of a cormorant in the water and laughed. "Yes, well if the so-called date had lasted more than a second I might have done that."

Fleur's mood changed again as the boat neared the shores of Mull. She became aware of the land looming closer, the details vivid to her senses. The land itself was pulling her forward like destiny's embrace. Fleur wondered why she had such a strong intuition the closer she came to the island like she was coming home. She had never been to the Isle of Mull.

A nameless anxiety caused her to clutch the rail and inhale a deep steadying breath. In that moment, Fleur saw the woman in her dreams. The blonde tribal woman was real, standing before her, motioning to her. Despite the tension that sent her stomach into a tumult, Fleur started to move forward, compelled to follow the woman. Her friend Matty yanked her away from the rail, bringing her out from the vision by gripping her arm. The woman faded away from view, receding like a dream.

The vision completely faded, and Fleur could see the ferry docking and the passengers on the deck preparing to go below to disembark. She tried to speak but couldn't utter a sound. Once the woman faded from sight, Fleur wasn't afraid anymore, though the experience left her drained of energy. She could feel that the pallor of her face must match the sense of upheaval she had felt inside. She allowed Matty to take charge and bustle her below deck into their rental car.

She wasn't quite sure what had happened, but it was like nothing else she had experienced before. Dreams were one thing, but seeing visions in broad daylight was another matter. Just like when she saw Dante in Matty's family home, Fleur didn't know what to make of the experience. She knew she needed to get to the bottom of the curse, or whatever was going on with this tribal woman who kept appearing to her. If this incident at the rail of the ferry was any indication, her safety depended on it.

CHAPTER SEVEN

ISLE OF MULL, SCOTLAND, 1987

Unnerved by the experience on the ferry, Fleur let Matty drive the rental car off the ferry while she processed what happened. Matty stopped at the first coffee shop they passed and got them two cups of strong black coffee. Fleur took a sip before Matty broke the silence.

"Girl, you scared me back there. What did you see? I expect you at least saw a ghost," said Matty. Fleur knew Matty was trying to make light of the situation. In a more serious tone, Matty said, "I know you'll need to think it through first. My guess is that you saw the blonde woman from your dreams. Just nod your head."

Fleur shook her head in frustration, wanting to talk about it, but not ready to do so. She would need to at some point for she owed Matty that much.

"Don't worry, we'll get to the bottom of this," Matty said. "Darn if I'm letting some dream woman interfere with your fun inheriting a castle and finding family."

Fleur appreciated Matty's teasing tone; it was just what she needed in order to feel normal. She sat lower in her seat and relaxed, distracting herself with the scenery.

The late afternoon sun was casting its golden glow on the land as the friends made their way to the Castle Dowart Estate. Following a single-track road heading west, they passed a number of tiny villages, some forested areas, and a craggy shoreline along placid sea lochs. Sheep and highland cattle were grazing everywhere. Matty had to stop the car several times for animals standing in the middle of the road.

Beyond the first sea loch, the pastoral terrain changed as the road carved inland through a valley between two looming mountains with rounded tops worn down with age. The landscape became majestic and barren, the type of topography that emptied the mind of all thought.

Matty pulled the car to stop at a layby positioned at the edge of the first sea loch beyond the mountains. "Wasn't that incredible?" breathed Matty. "It was like we were on the backside of the moon. I didn't expect such huge, stark mountains on this island."

"You're so right," said Fleur, breaking her reflective silence at last. "I've had goosebumps since we left the coast. This land makes me feel so small, like my problems are insignificant in the scheme of things."

Fleur placed a hand on Matty's arm in appreciation, "Thank you for how you handled that weird thing on the boat. I did see a vision of the woman from my dreams. I wasn't scared after the incident, but I just couldn't speak. Don't worry, I'm alright now, I don't feel weak or anything."

Matty laughed out loud. "You, weak?" she said. "Never. You're the most courageous person I know. Sure, you get really scared sometimes, but that never stops you from doing things you are afraid to do. No worries, I'm here, and we'll figure this out together."

Using the roadmap from the ferry terminal, they followed a stretch of coastal road until they saw a castle in the distance, sitting on top of a stunning bluff. The main track road swung away from the coast before they could see the castle again, heading inland. About a mile down the road from where they first spotted the castle, they could see it again, but behind them. Matty turned the car around to backtrack.

Looking at the sides of the road carefully, Fleur spotted a lane in a great thicket of woods, hidden from sight as approached from the other direction. The pathway emerged from the woods and ran through rolling fields, dotted by clumps of dark green evergreen woods. Patches of hedgerows divided the landscape into neat parcels. They passed a number of croft houses, and further along they came across an old red sandstone house partially covered with blooming wisteria. They knew it must be the Factor's House. It was almost as large as a manor house, and every bit as grand. The outer walls were the color of sanded coral, contrasting with the darkened grey stone walls of the croft houses. The offshoot lane beside the structure sloped upwards to include gardens. The house stood at the bottom of steep hills, which Matty and Fleur assumed would provide sweeping views of the Castle and the sea beyond the cliffs.

Matty parked the car and sat still. "Boo," she whispered, her tone almost reverent, "this place looks so right for you. Look, it even has a blue front door, just like Blue Bird Cottage. Maybe this is what you've been looking for all your life."

The front door of the house swung open to reveal a statuesque woman waving and smiling. She called out in a strong voice with a warm Scottish lilt, "There you are, oh how lovely. I couldn't wait to see you."

The woman enveloped Fleur in her embrace. "Ah, so good that you are here," she said. "I never expected to be so lucky. And this must be your friend. Welcome to you both." Matty was likewise given a tight welcome hug.

Fleur swallowed hard and blinked twice. She peered wide-eyed in disbelief over the woman's shoulder at her friend to see if Matty was having the same reaction that she was. The woman standing in front of her could be Grana's twin.

Large-boned solid frame, posture like a new pencil despite her age, and lively blue eyes shining with secret knowledge of wonderful things to be discovered, so like her grandmother. Even her hug penetrated the heart in the same way.

"Wow, I sure hope that you're Glenna Currie," said Matty, untangling herself from the squeeze. "Because I'm loving you already!"

The woman pulled back and laughed. "I get carried away. Please, call me Auntie G. It has a nice ring to it, don't you think?" she said. "Come in and let's have tea while I answer any questions. Then I suggest the pair of you get settled in your rooms for the evening, you must be exhausted from your travels. A good night's sleep will sort you out."

Fleur and Matty retrieved the luggage from the trunk of the car and followed Glenna into the house. She directed the friends to leave their cases on the landing at the bottom of the staircase and shepherded them into a spacious, comfortable kitchen at the end of the hall. The friends sat around the large well-used oak table while Glenna busied herself putting together the tea, all the while telling stories about ferry trips she had taken to the mainland over the years. Fleur was soothed by the pleasant chatter, and eased into a sense of homey comfort as her body relaxed into the cushions.

Glenna joined them, placing a tray loaded with a variety of sandwiches and scones in the middle of the table. She then spoke about weightier matters. "From the way you've been scanning me since you arrived, I suspect that my appearance surprised you, and that I must look like your grandmother," she said. "Which leads me to believe that you have no idea who I am or what our relationship might be, is that right?"

Fleur nodded her head, eyes wide in anticipation. "You do look very much like Grana," she said. "It's uncanny. Not just your looks, but your mannerisms too. The way you snap the tea into the pot, how you hold your head as you inspect the sandwiches on the tray. And you even have the same twinkle in your eyes as Grana. But how do you know about me and about my Grana? She doesn't know anything about you."

Glenna leaned forward, more attentive and alert. "Are you telling me that your grandmother is alive?" she asked. "I had no idea. That is phenomenal news!"

Fleur's confused frown prompted Glenna to explain. "Where to start the story? I think the best place to start is to tell you how I had known about you inheriting the Factor's House," she said, getting up to pour the steeped tea into three dainty teacups.

"About five, maybe six, months ago, I received a letter from dear old Ian MacNeill, our long-time family solicitor from town," said Glenna. "He had informed me that the Laird's last will and testament included a Fleur La Salle from Canada being named to inherit the Factor's House. He wouldn't share any more details, which struck me as odd at the time, especially as this house has been my home for seventy-seven years. My family took care of this estate for many generations."

Fleur was taking in all the details. Glenna continued, "I wasn't worried though, I know that what's for me will come to me. But I did wonder who Fleur La Salle was, and why she was from Canada. I'm familiar with the Laird's family story, and have never heard of this name before. Be that as it may, that's the reason I wasn't surprised when you telephoned me to tell me that you were coming. It must have been Ian who contacted you?"

Fleur appreciated hearing Glenna's side. "I did wonder why you weren't surprised," she said. "But it wasn't Mr. MacNeill who told me about the inheritance. I found out when the solicitors representing the Hayden brothers had advised me that they were contesting my right as beneficiary. I've since learned that Mr. MacNeill's offices burned down, and that is the reason I never received a letter from him."

Glenna leaned forward and exhaled as understanding hit her. "That explains why you are surprised I look like your grandmother. You don't know who I am."

Fleur held her breath in anticipation. Glenna didn't keep her waiting long. "Some time after I had learned about the Laird bequeathing the Factor's House, I found a letter that my grandmother on my father's side wrote before she died years ago, tucked in a novel when I was cleaning the library. My grandmother's sister-in-law Elizabeth, married to her husband's brother, raised me here at the Factor's House after my mother died giving birth to me. The letter explained that my mother had given birth to another child before she was married, a wee girl taken to Canada under odd circumstances." Glenna paused to refresh the tea pot.

"The letter wasn't very informative: it was dated after my grandmother's mind had begun to deteriorate. I asked Ian if there was a connection between Fleur La Salle inheriting the Factor's House and this letter about an unknown half-sister. He admitted to me that I did indeed have a half-sister who was taken to Canada, a story he had sworn to keep secret all these years. He was going to find out if she was still alive, but once he had suffered the loss from the fire in his office, as you know, he just wasn't the same person and never completed the task. But the pieces all fell together when you called. And now you tell me that my half-sister is alive. I'm very happy indeed."

Fleur inhaled the rose cologne smell of her grandaunt, the same as the cologne her grandmother favored, and grinned in utter contentment. The magic of it all was not lost on Fleur, and she felt happier than she had in a long time.

Fleur found Auntie G. in the kitchen when she wandered downstairs just before 6:00 a.m., glad to spend a few moments alone with her. She was correct in guessing that Auntie G. arose with the roosters, preparing for the day. Just like her Grana. A pot of soup bubbled on the hob, and a hearty breakfast of Scottish porridge oats and scones was already on the table to be enjoyed with a slathering of butter churned fresh, and homemade strawberry jam. It was apparent that Auntie G. was determined to feed her guests well.

"Good morning, dearie," said Auntie G. "Did you sleep well? Or did dreams haunt you?"

Fleur startled at the question. "The bed was very comfortable," she said with little enthusiasm. Perhaps she was reading more into the question than her grandaunt had intended. Fleur wondered if Auntie G. had the fey in her like her Grana.

The dreams returned last night. She wanted to share them with her grandaunt but wondered if it might be too soon. After the emotional turmoil of the previous day, Fleur was not surprised how vivid the dreams had been, so vivid that the smoke from the fire in the hut seemed to have lingered on her clothes. The dream had shown a gathering of tribal elders, presided over by an older woman whom the tribal woman showed clear deference towards. There was an air of anxiety at the gathering. The people spoke of fears of foreigners coming to take their land. Fleur wondered if that could be why the woman was asking her for help.

Fleur went with her initial instinct to share her dreams with her grandaunt. "Sorry to be a bit vague," said Fleur. "I've been having dreams lately, the same dream about a woman beckoning me. I think it has to do with this place, here on the Isle of Mull. The woman wants me to do something or go somewhere. I haven't been able to figure out what she wants of me."

Fleur shook her head to clarify her thoughts, still doubtful about how to tell her grandaunt. Auntie G. patted her on the shoulder. "Don't fret dear, there is time enough for us to discuss these matters," she said, as though she heard Fleur's doubts.

Auntie G. launched into a soliloquy about every person on the estate as she poured coffee, which made Fleur feel more comfortable. She talked about their personalities, likes and dislikes, who they were related to, which clan they belonged to, and what became of their children who moved away from Mull. Then she talked about the nearest village and described the quirky characteristics of the folks and shopkeepers.

Auntie G.'s chatter had the intended effect. Her rich voice with its lilting tones lulled Fleur into feeling safe and at ease with her newfound grandaunt. The stories added to her understanding of the world of her ancestry. It wasn't long before Fleur told her own stories about Antigonish, the people who came into the Dragonfly Café, and the Heliotrope Gallery. By the time Matty came downstairs, Fleur and Auntie G. were laughing and enjoying each other.

Rubbing her eyes, Matty said, "What's the racket about? Sounds like my Maman's home. I thought it was a dream about being on a peaceful remote island in Scotland!"

Auntie G. gave Matty a wonderful smile. "I believe you need this," she said as she handed her a large mug of black coffee. "Have you ever considered taming your busy mind first thing in the morning, maybe with meditation? It would be much better for you than your caffeine addiction."

Finishing up her own cup of coffee, Fleur raised an eyebrow at how perceptive that comment was. Before Matty could say anything, she jumped in with an explanation of all the laughter her friend had heard as she came downstairs. "Auntie G. was telling me the stories about the people on the estate and in the village," she said. "It appears there are characters here, just like Sally Ann and Norma in Antigonish."

"That's right dearie, folks are folks, no matter where in the world they live or what language they speak," said Auntie G.

Matty took a gulp of her second cup of coffee before she spoke. "I can't wait to talk to the Islanders and discover those stories myself," said Matty. "What great news last night. Did you telephone your grandmother already to let her know she has a sister?"

At the sink doing the washing up, Fleur turned to answer Matty, "I'll need to wait a few hours. The time difference makes it three in the morning in Antigonish. I'll telephone Grana this evening, if that's alright with you Auntie G.?"

The friends discussed plans for the day. Matty wanted to explore the island. "If you don't mind, I'd like to go off by myself, find out about how the locals live," she said. "Need to gather notes for my clients, they love all the details. Hubley would be upset if I didn't come back with a great travel itinerary for our clients for the Isle of Mull. Our clients would go for that, especially if we can offer to trace their Scottish ancestry. Now there's a great idea. I have work to do."

Fleur was glad to spend some time alone. She wanted to explore the estate and get a sense of the land. Later, she would call her grandmother to tell her the news of her meeting Glenna Currie, her grandaunt and her Grana's half-sister.

"Auntie G., I'm heading out for a walk-about," she said. "Is there anywhere I should or shouldn't go? Or anything specific to avoid doing?"

Glenna shook her head and smiled. "No dearie, all the lands as far as the eye can see belong to the estate. As owner of the Factor's House, you have the right to walk anywhere you please."

"I don't think I'm the owner quite yet," mused Fleur. "I'm not at all sure of the process, but assume there will need to be some official handing over of the property papers. With the case against me, I'm not sure it will be that straight forward."

Her grandaunt patted Fleur's arm. "No need to worry about that now, dearie," she said. "Go and enjoy some air. Breathe in the land, I know that's your dearest desire at the moment. If you intend to walk near the castle, the staff won't bother you. They know who you are, you're one of us."

Fleur had no intention of walking anywhere near the castle. It was the land that interested her. She wished to tune in to her ancestry, to get a feeling of what it was like to live and work this land.

She put on a light sweater to shield against the morning air, walked down to the end of the path alongside the house, and headed back towards the main road, the opposite direction from where the castle stood on the bluff overlooking the sea. Fleur was inspired to walk towards the hills beyond the flat pastoral land, pulled by a strong energy her intuition told her was guiding her in that particular direction.

The air was tangy with the freshness of sea salt and heather. Fleur inhaled deep into her chest as she walked past large open fields planted with grain crops, through pastures and meadows bordered by thickets of trees, and up towards the hilltop. She had a vague memory of having walked this land before. It was a pleasant feeling, the sense of familiarity, not at all disconcerting.

Fleur floated on the magic around her, the raw beauty of nature. Stopping now and then to take in the sweeping view across the estate and towards the sea, the feeling of familiarity intensified. Fleur crested the top of the hill well before noon. Admiring the vastness of the sky, land, and sea from this vantage point, Fleur could barely discern the castle in the distance.

A strong premonition took hold of her as she reached the top of the ridge. There was something she needed to see in this place. Fleur gasped when she turned around to inspect the area, startled to see the woman from her dreams at the edge of a thicket of trees gesturing for her to follow. She was powerless to resist. Just like the incident on the ferry, Fleur was compelled to follow the woman.

She inched towards the thicket, and peered through the trees, holding down the anxiety that was building inside her. The sunlight pierced the shadows and flooded a clearing in the center of the trees with a glowing light that exaggerated the impact of a most unexpected sight. In the middle of the clearing stood a large circle of lichen-mottled stones. Like soldiers standing at attention, the stones varied in height and width. They were slightly conical, and for the most part uniform in shape. Fleur counted 30 stones in the circle. Her skin tingled, and she concluded that this must be a sacred place.

Fleur moved around the stones, enjoying the peacefulness and at the same time looking for the dream woman. Though she could not find her, Fleur sensed the woman's energy. In that moment of recognition, Fleur heard a pulsation emanating from the stones, it vibrated straight into her chest. The sensation did not frighten her; it was familiar and unlocked a strange and wonderful longing from deep inside her. She walked to the middle of the circle and without thought of what she was doing sat cross-legged on the ground, and began to sway with a methodical and dancelike movement. Her actions were driven by instinct. She let go of her reserve and allowed bliss to take hold of her. Fleur was aware of dropping into a deep meditation.

With no conscious thought on her part, Fleur was swept into the midst of people who appeared to recognize and respect her and whom she recognized as the tribe's people from her dreams. The experience was visceral: she smelled the tilled earth as she walked past farmers tending the fields; she heard the vibration of clanking swords from the warriors training in their skills; and she felt the pulsing heartbeat of every child she stopped to place a loving hand upon. All the while, a sense of responsibility for the wellbeing of these people flooded her heart.

Fleur did not know what was happening, but she knew this was not a dream. She was not a passive observer; she was experiencing events and emotions as though *she* was the dream woman.

Dancing lights appeared in mid-air and moved towards her. Something tender at the side of her neck caused Fleur to reach for the spot of her crescent moon birthmark. She drew back her fingers upon touching a warm stickiness. She was bleeding.

At that moment, Fleur felt violated, drawn into a reality that was not hers. Her body tensed. Panting, she started to panic; she didn't know how to deal with the experience. The encounter left her disoriented and no longer at peace with the unfolding events. She wished to end the experience.

Once Fleur wished to break contact from the grip of this strange merging with the woman, it was done. She shook her head to clear her mind, not understanding what just occurred much less how it had happened. She looked around in awe at the quietness apparently restored to the circle of standing stones. She wondered if the experience or vision had happened at all.

Fleur was bone tired. She stumbled when she stood up, taking a moment to find her balance. Deliberately resisting the urge to dash away, she paced her leaving with respect, still considering the circle of standing stones to be a sacred space, though completely confused about what had happened in this place. For the moment, her fear was under control, but she knew that she would have an emotional reaction to the events which transpired at the standing stones. She hurried over the ridge and down the hill, eager to reach the safety of the Factor's House.

CHAPTER EIGHT

AN ISLAND OF THE HEBRIDES, AD 560

T'Eilin kept a vigilant watch the two months since the gathering, scanning the shore from dawn until dusk. She was relieved that there were no signs of strangers coming to Tobirie. The spring agricultural activity kept the people occupied, and T'Eilin was glad for the people to enjoy peace. Their lives were hard enough eking an existence from the rugged land.

T'Eilin consulted with Alcorat often during the time of waiting. She had great respect for Alcorat and confidence in his leadership prowess. He had provided purpose, direction, and motivation to maintain the warrior's readiness and had balanced out their restlessness from the lack of action. Alcorat likewise respected T'Eilin. He had often sent warriors to train with her in methods of alignment and mind-spirit focus. The warriors of Tobirie were renowned for their single-minded clear action on the battlefield, attributed to the training the tribe's intuitive provided them.

On the day before the Speaking Session, a forum for people to bring cases of disagreement before the Healing Mother for resolution, T'Eilin sought to talk with Alcorat about the tension she sensed building. There was a growing negative energy from Tonnick, and she was concerned how it might be affecting the warriors.

"Alcorat, how it is with Tonnick?" asked T'Eilin. "Is he still impatient?"

Alcorat acknowledged T'Eilin's assessment of the situation. "You know Tonnick well," he replied. "He resists the work you teach, which is unfortunate, as it would help him to learn patience and focus. He is not content to wait; he wants action. His brother Orgah has disciplined him on a number of occasions. Tonnick is determined to rouse the warriors whenever he has an opportunity. I'm sure you are aware of the tactics he uses, a sly word here and there. What concerns me is that he is more open now, saying disparaging things to his brother in front of Orgah's men. I have let Orgah deal with the situation, but I may soon need to step in. I am also concerned that Tonnick may cause trouble at the Speaking Session tomorrow. May I suggest we keep an eye on that together?"

T'Eilin was late for the Speaking Session. She had lost track of time gazing at the spectacular sunrise over the bay. It had been a clear and magical morning, with a pink, purple, and orange glow streaking across the sky in a pattern T'Eilin had never seen before. She bolted to the healing hut and entered as the first petitioner was speaking.

The group of people gathered in the healing hut appeared angry, like a general discontent directed to Naghaire. T'Eilin sensed something was wrong. The energy inside the healing hut was fraught with tension, like a fire about to leap out of control. She touched her grandmother, and received a warning signal that had nothing to do with her late arrival.

T'Eilin sat very still to gauge the origin of the negative energy. Everything appeared to be in order. The petitioners were lined up along the outer edge of the hut, with the people involved in the first case standing before Naghaire as they each described their side of the issue. In the first case, a farmer wanted compensation for a newborn lamb that had been killed due to negligence of his neighbor not mending his fence. While the case was ordinary, T'Eilin frowned, troubled by the fact that this case even appeared before Naghaire at all. Such a case was usually settled amongst the neighbors. Though Naghaire maintained her composure, T'Eilin saw her grandmother flinch in awareness of a negative force disrupting the balance of the Irie.

When Farmer Hinnian spoke, T'Eilin sensed her grandmother holding onto her composure. He was openly rude to the Healing Mother. "Why are we even speaking in front of you, woman? You know nothing about farming," he said. "Our cases should be heard and judged by a man. Maybe even a warrior, for a warrior would understand the ways of men, not you, woman."

T'Eilin held her breath, incredulous at the venom of his words. "Farmer Hinnian," said Naghaire with steel in her voice. "You well know our ways and have abided by them for more than 50 years. They are the ways of Source, not of men or of women. Nor are they the ways of warriors. The words you speak are not your words, but the words of another. It would be good for you to speak your own wisdom and truth. You know very well that what you are saying is a non-truth. The shame is yours alone for not keeping true to your own nature and speaking what you know to be right."

Naghaire's words and tone brought the negative energy into check, and the remaining cases showed no more edge of dissension. T'Eilin continued to scan the room for the origin of the negative energy, and her instinct told her that Tonnick was behind it. Sure enough, she soon spotted Tonnick smirking in the back shadows. T'Eilin concluded that the disruption of the Speaking Session was linked to the episode when Tonnick interrupted the healing ceremony she was doing with his name. She suspected that he was angry at her and at the Healing Mother, and this was his way of extracting his revenge.

As T'Eilin sat on the floor near her grandmother, she considered the idea that Tonnick might in fact be a stronger intuitive than she herself was. Maybe his powers of influence were stronger than hers. How else could Tonnick change the mood of so many people so easily?

Her grandmother had told her many times that all people have access to the power through training and practice. T'Eilin was training the warriors to use the power through the work, and was disconcerted by the idea that Tonnick might be using his power for ill intent.

The next afternoon, T'Eilin told her grandmother about a conversation she'd had earlier with one of the herders moving his sheep to new pastures. He had told T'Eilin that Tonnick had been talking to the men outside the Speaking Session against her and the Healing Mother.

"He said that we should mind women's things and stay out of men's business," said T'Eilin. "Tonnick's talk appeared to have disturbed the herder, so he moved away, but he noticed others were agreeing with Tonnick."

T'Eilin's grandmother wasn't at all surprised. "Yes, I thought as much," agreed the older woman. "It felt like Tonnick was behind the change of energy at the Speaking Session."

T'Eilin paused rolling a ream of cloth for bandages to observe, "Tonnick's power of influence is getting stronger. He displayed that power by changing the energy just by talking to people before the session."

"I fear you are right about Tonnick's powers. He has the discipline and practice it takes to be a powerful creator. This work is available to everyone, but not many take up the call. You and I live it daily by way of example to our people, but our people have not been that interested in doing the work.

T'Eilin nodded her understanding as she tidied up the hut. Her grandmother concluded, "People prefer to be lost in the ego mind, remaining asleep in the dream of life, rather than to embrace the powerful creative force of Source. Tonnick on the other hand has motives that propel him to take advantage of his power. That was evident in the persuasive energy that changed the tone of the Speaking Session."

T'Eilin was distressed by the thought of the ill will Tonnick showed. "Why would Tonnick use his power for ill?" she asked. "We set an example by how we live, our oneness with Source spirit being for the expansion of life, not its detriment."

"Now T'Eilin, you well know that there is no such thing as good or evil. All is the same," said her grandmother. "All of life's happenings are from the same Source spirit energy, and therefore cannot be good or evil. Those who come to this world with a mind set on a specific goal consider that their thinking is clear minded. They hold a strong belief in that. Therefore, how can we judge what is good or evil? All that happens is not accidental." T'Eilin's grandmother swayed, and held up her hand.

"I hear your words, but I see your frown," said T'Eilin. "Do you doubt what you are saying?"

T'Eilin's grandmother was distracted. "I just had a vision about Tonnick. Not a pleasant one, I'm afraid. A recurring vision since the day Tonnick was born. It may be a story I'm holding about him. We cannot hold a story about someone and still hold the truth. I must cleanse myself of this."

"What is it? Share your doubts to lighten your burden," said T'Eilin with concern.

Her grandmother leaned nearer to assure T'Eilin. "We know what the truth is," she said. "It is the one energy of love that is true. All else is a dilution of truth, a dream, unreality. Events that happen in life are not accidental."

T'Eilin's grandmother got up to move towards the back of the hut where her sleeping area was and continued to speak with a solemn tone. "I had a vision a long time ago about Tonnick coming to change the course of our ancestry – yours and mine. Some action he takes in this lifetime will cause what appears to be evil to us, but it will be just a part of the work that our ancestry must do in order to grow and expand."

"Yes, I feel it too," said T'Eilin. "Tonnick is going to impact events around the village that will undermine the work we do daily with energy and with love. Subtle things will interrupt the ordinary flow of life on Tobirie. As you always tell me, one conscious person can carry thousands of unconscious people as it applies to the work. Therefore, whether or not Tonnick is a powerful intuitive, his energy should not change the course of our own work."

"As within, so without," said Naghaire. "Let us not build up any more focus on Tonnick. We will remain alert, but we will not think about him. If we continue to focus upon Tonnick that attention would help the vibration of his energy to grow. Remember, T'Eilin, no one can undermine the work. Everything is the work. Everything is practice in awakening the spirit within us." With that, her grandmother bid T'Eilin good night and settled onto her sleeping mat.

T'Eilin and her grandmother were busy the following week dealing with accidents and injuries typical of the spring season. While her grandmother tended minor ailments, T'Eilin trained the chosen warriors on mind focus, and gathered herbs, roots, and plants to replenish the medicine cupboard left bare after the long winter months. The meadows and forests provided an abundance of medicinal plants. It was a time-consuming task to harvest and dry the plants used in the healing hut, but T'Eilin enjoyed it. The young Diiaan had apprenticed with T'Eilin from the age of five, when she displayed an aptitude for understanding the healing properties of plants. Now in her fifteenth season, Diiaan's curiosity, observational skills, and intelligence shone.

T'Eilin and Diiaan were gathering in the forest one cloudy afternoon, enjoying easy chatter about the betrothal preparations for the upcoming bridal exchange. T'Eilin delighted in discussing her task of preparing the brides. Her task was to ensure they were well versed in their own spiritual culture before they intertwined their ways with the ways of their new home.

"The betrothal girls are ready for the exchange," explained T'Eilin. "We're expecting the men from Cenel Lairon and Dal Raida to arrive any day. They are quite excited. Yesterday, the Janiin sisters were so distracted with the anticipation, they couldn't remember the four rules of birthing, confusing them with the rules of baking bread." T'Eilin's observation made Diiaan laugh.

"I understand the Janiin sisters are good friends of yours, Diiaan. Do you think they are ready?" asked T'Eilin.

Diiaan gushed her answer. "Oh, yes, Saania, Tanaai, and Liiani are ready to go. I wish I were chosen. But I don't want to leave Tobirie. I mean I'm ready for betrothing, but not to go away from here. I'd like one of our own to request for me. I'd love a warrior to ask for me, someone like Tonnick. He is so very handsome! And he talks so well."

T'Eilin didn't expect that bit of news. She must keep an eye on her, T'Eilin thought. Diiaan was innocent, and Tonnick might take advantage of her.

T'Eilin murmured a noise like agreement while she noted that Diiaan's words were almost the same as what the herder had said about Tonnick talking to people outside of the healing hut just before the Speaking Session.

Another moon cycle passed as the Irie people went about tasks. T'Eilin, tense and watchful, was aware when the wind held the vibration of the strangers approaching. The anticipation was building in her bones. Without warning, without drama, the strangers arrived as she knew they would, as she had seen them in her visions.

It was a fog-laden dawn two days after the Bhealtaine, a ceremony signaling the start of the summer season with the anointing to protect the animals from disease. The Bhealtaine fest had gone well, due to the intentions set by T'Eilin and her grandmother.

T'Eilin was on the shore earlier than usual, knowing that today her intuition would come to pass. T'Eilin trembled at the chilling tendrils of fog seeping through her wrap, but she didn't move. In her mind, she could see what the watch guards saw from their higher ground. When the guards lit the broch with one fire, fear welled up inside her. She must warn the warriors, T'Eilin thought. She needed to make sure the warriors didn't think there was deceit.

Running hard, T'Eilin reached the launching area in record time. Tobirie had a natural inlet that was deep enough for vessels of moderate size, and a narrow beach perfect as a landing spot. A number of the Irie people were already gathered.

She paused to catch her breath, and to assess the mood of the crowd gathered on the shore. The warriors were tense and ready for action, but Orgah had them under control, making sure the warrior's presence was a subtle show of force but not of aggression. The tribespeople gathered to watch the vessels arrive were eager to hear news from the mainland. Those with daughters leaving had mixed emotions, pride in their daughters yet saddened by their leaving. It was all a part of the pattern of life the Irie knew so well.

T'Eilin saw Naghaire making her way to the shore, holding onto the arm of Diiaan. She noted that Healing Mother was flustered, despite her outward appearance of calm. T'Eilin ran to her grandmother and took her arm. "Grandmother, you feel the confusion as I do and are concerned as well," she said. "This ship is bringing the foreigners. We need to make sure there is no misunderstanding when they land that the warriors realize that the strangers are amongst us as we expected."

Naghaire turned her sightless eyes toward her granddaughter and said, "Yes, they are coming. I think it is best if you have a word with Orgah and Alcorat about what you know about the strangers on board with the Cenel Lairon and Dal Raida."

T'Eilin went in search of the two warriors. They were giving their section leaders directions. There was to be no mistaking the intent of the leaders in terms of holding off aggression.

Orgah was the first to see her approaching and noted her urgency. "I see you, T'Eilin, and assume that you have something to tell us."

Getting straight to the point, T'Eilin spoke without the usual ceremonial politeness. "The strangers are on board the ship with the Cenel Lairon and Dal Raida men," she said. "Understand this, there is no treachery."

Alcorat nodded his comprehension of the situation. "As you say, T'Eilin," he said. "We will be aware of the strangers. Fear not, our men will not make a move until they are instructed to do so." T'Eilin appreciated that the words were spoken without questioning her knowledge, accepting it as fact.

T'Eilin walked back to the front of the crowd where her grandmother stood at the water's edge. They stood side-by-side facing the bay and remained until the men stepped on land to ensure that all was well.

As the ship came into the bay, the tribe's people had a better look at the fearsome prow design that signaled the twin tribe of Cenel Lairon and Dal Raida, the severed head of a ravaged man hanging limp and lifeless by his hair. The Irie men from shore pushed three longboats into the water to transport the men from the boat to shore. Several powerful strokes of the oars had the longboats alongside the vessel in no time.

On shore, the people strained to see the men descending into the longboats. It was easy to recognize the men of Cenel Lairon and Dal Raida, even from this distance, for they were swathed in red and green garments. The men who stepped off the vessel onto the third longboat were wearing long brown robes tied at the waist with rope.

The thought that the strangers were amongst them crossed T'Eilin's mind at the exact instant her grandmother clutched her hand in a grip that told T'Eilin she sensed trouble. A murmur ran through the crowd as one single word formed, "Treachery."

Exactly as T'Eilin feared, suspicion was cast on the vessel once the Irie saw the unexpected men descending into the longboats.

Before T'Eilin could send a murmured intention to Source to allow straight-thinking minds to prevail, Tonnick leaped from behind a boulder and shouted to the warriors on the beach, waving his weapons in the air and yelling, "Treachery is afoot. Do not let them land."

Heard above the rumble of the people, those words caused many of the warriors and the tribe people to move forward. Tonnick led the way, demonstrating his powerful influence. To T'Eilin's relief, Alcorat and Orgah anticipated the rash move and quelled the warriors and the tribesmen. Orgah stood in front of the crowd and admonished Tonnick.

"Warrior, stand down," he said. "We have known there are strangers on the Cenel Lairon and Dal Raida vessel. It is these men come as foretold by T'Eilin, our intuitive. Do you not remember the gathering and the task we have been given?"

Orgah continued in a loud and angry voice for all to hear, "Have you forgotten what the Healing Mother has asked of us? We will allow the strangers to come, understand what they are here for, and then make decisions on the course of action related to their appearance here in our midst."

Orgah then dragged his brother to the side and spoke in a deadly tone, the likes of which T'Eilin had never heard from the leader. "Brother, you are about to feel my wrath as never before," he said. "What is the meaning of flaunting such disobedience in front of the entire tribe? You've gone too far."

T'Eilin heard Tonnick snicker, showing his complete disrespect as Orgah declared loud enough for his warriors and the nearby tribespeople to hear. "Tonnick, you have disobeyed your orders as a warrior and disrespected your duty as an Irie to uphold the words of the Healing Mother," he said. "For that, you must be punished. You are to be stripped of your weapons and shunned for three months. Now leave, go to the mountains and do not return until you know the meaning of duty to your tribe."

Banishment was a severe punishment, and T'Eilin was concerned seeing Tonnick's absolute fury. She tried to follow Tonnick's movement after Orgah dismissed him, but she was distracted by the activity at the shore as the long boats landed. She counted twenty men in the group coming onto shore, with five men wearing the long robes that distinguished them as the strangers.

T'Eilin breathed in an intention of peace, "If they come to change my people's spirit, let it be for the good of all."

The men who jumped from the long boats walked towards where T'Eilin stood with Naghaire, Alcorat, and Orgah. Naghaire broke the silence as was her right. She said, "I am Naghaire the Healing Mother, and I welcome you to the land of the Irie. Some of you are here as expected, come to take away betrothing women as we agreed. Some of you are here as anticipated from a vision T'Eilin, our intuitive, had that you were coming. We do not know why you have come, but we know you do not do us harm. All are welcome."

Bordain, the Clan Chief of the Cenel, stepped forward to greet the Healing Mother, "Thank you, Naghaire. Your wisdom is appreciated," he said. "You bestow a great honor allowing us your women. We will protect and take good care of them."

Bordain continued in a more robust voice, "We thank you also for trusting that the fact we have given passage on our ship to your lands is not an act of treachery. It is a distinction to know you have faith in our friendship to your people."

Alcorat replied, careful in his choice of words, to let everyone know that
he had the situation under control. "Bordain, long have we known you and
your people," he said. "We trust you, but it takes more than trust to believe
you have not been overpowered or bewitched in some manner. It is a relief to
know our faith appears to be well-founded, but of course these things we will
need to judge for ourselves, with time."

One of the brown-clothed strangers stepped forward and spoke in an
authoritative tone that was strong and certain, yet at the same time as gentle
as a summer's breeze. "Elder Woman, we thank you for your kindness. My
name is Brendan, and these are my fellow monks, Kerial, Bodrig, Markul,
and Johnna. You are correct when you say we do not mean the Irie harm. You
can see for yourself that we are not armed, and we are too few in numbers to
do anything untoward. We are in service to Columba, traveling to spread the
love of Source spirit, and have come to serve the Irie in whatever way we can.
We hope you will allow us to stay amongst you for a while so that we can learn
from each other and spread the knowledge of gifts that Source has given all
of us."

T'Eilin stood transfixed. From the moment she saw this man who called
himself Brendan, she experienced heightened sensations. The earth's vibration rose up from her feet and echoed inside her chest as emanating from his
footfall; the scent of pinewood and sea salt wafting in the soft breeze through
his thick, black curled hair reached her nose; the deep yet soft rumbling tim-
ber of his voice penetrated her heart. She took note of his eyes; they were the
color of the deepest blue sea. She saw lifetimes of laughter and love reflected
in his eyes.

With a shake, T'Eilin realized that Brendan was staring back at her. T'Eilin wondered if he could feel the same intense emotion as she felt.

He must have been speaking, for the crowd was focused on him, awaiting
a response to what he just said. T'Eilin remembered the words, "spread the
love of Source spirit." She had to think hard to understand how a stranger
from so far away would speak like one who knew about the work of alignment with Source Energy as she taught to the warriors.

To T'Eilin, it looked as though Brendan was in disbelief. She sensed
that he felt her presence as he stepped on the beach, like a calling to his very
soul. Their eyes met. T'Eilin vibrated with the energy of connection running
between them. It was as though they had dreamed each other. T'Eilin experienced an instant vision. She saw him as a young lad before the Irish had

taken him away after the sacking of his village on the mainland. He was of her people, from a distant past, and he was of her ways. He knew this, and that knowledge could not be erased by any teachings he might have received later.

With that thought, T'Eilin became nervous, sensing Tonnick's eyes on her. He must be watching from a hiding place, waiting to see if he could spot any weakness to use against her.

Naghaire guessed what was happening to T'Eilin. Her granddaughter had fallen prey to a blinding strike of love. If the situation weren't fraught with uncertainty, Naghaire would encourage the reaction, which was a first for her granddaughter. However, at this point, the people could not afford for their intuitive to be in love with the leader of these men who called themselves monks. She was needed to assess the situation with a clear mind.

The situation was not just uncertain, it was dangerous. The air sparked with opposing forces: the anxious tension of the Irie people and warriors, the sensitive feelings of belonging to each other as shared by T'Eilin and Brendan, and the hatred Tonnick sent out into the world directed most specifically at T'Eilin.

Naghaire concluded it was time to disperse people from the area. With a clap of her hands that signaled a command, she spoke words that were obeyed immediately. "Monks, come with me to the healing hut while we sort out what to do with you," she said. "Men of Cenel Lairon and Dal Raida, you will be taken care of by your respective betrothal women's families. Go and prepare for the betrothal fest tomorrow."

As the crowd moved, T'Eilin and Brendan lingered at the shores' edge. Sparks of light erupted where their hands brushed together. They stood mesmerized, not speaking a word but communicating their sudden longing for each other.

Though Naghaire could not see with her eyes, she heard the sizzle of energy in the space between T'Eilin and Brendan. Her granddaughter had long questioned the nature of unconditional love. Naghaire had tried to teach her that love is everything, even those things that do not look like love. With Tonnick's negative energy pulling T'Eilin to question the all-encompassing nature of love, and the new experience of being the object of Brendan's love, T'Eilin would learn many lessons. Meanwhile, Naghaire needed to figure out how the monks would change the spirit of the Irie people. Could it be the beginning of a time of expansion for the tribe, or its complete ruin?

CHAPTER NINE

ISLE OF MULL, SCOTLAND, 1987

Breathless and lightheaded from her experience at the standing stones, Fleur rounded the corner toward the front of the house as Matty parked the car, back from her day of sightseeing. Fleur stepped off the gravel walkway as Matty jumped out of the car in a rush to tell Fleur about her day.

"Great timing," said Matty. "Let's go inside, I have lots to tell you."

Fleur looked at Matty, still distracted by her thoughts about the standing stones. "What happened?" asked Matty.

Fleur was unsure if she should tell her friend what had happened. "I must have fallen asleep in the sunshine, I'm feeling drowsy still, that's all." She knew she wasn't fooling her friend, but at least Matty didn't push for more information.

Fleur smiled at her friend's exuberance as she followed Matty down the hall and into the kitchen. Auntie G. was putting the finishing touches on a moist-looking Battenberg cake.

"Sit and eat before you tell us about your day, Matty," she said, having heard the ruckus.

"Auntie G., you were right about all the characters in the village," she said. "The lady from the bakery had me in stitches about the runaway goat who dashed into her store. The goat's owner was upset because his prize stud goat ate a lot of sugar, and also the plastic display stands. He was going to sue the bakery for leaving their doors open, imagine that. His wife talked him out of it because the previous year, the same goat ate the judge's laundry off his line."

Fleur laughed, imagining a court case over a runaway goat. Matty waved her hands, she wasn't finished. "That's not all," she said. "Here's the best part: by the time the lady at the bakery got to finishing her story, there was a crowd of people standing in the store adding to it. Like it was some type of communal memory."

"Yes, that's the way it is around here," Auntie G. said. "Stories are the backbone of our connections with each other. There's nothing like a good story about having your knickers eaten by the local stud goat to keep you humble."

Fleur was pleased Matty had a successful day. Her friend enjoyed collecting stories on her travels. "This is why I love the work I do," said Matty. "I get to find out the real stories about a place."

Auntie G. served up the cake, and Fleur settled in for what she presumed would be an elaborate tale. "My first stop was the library, where I always find the best gossip," said Matty. "The librarian gave me a quick history of Mull, which is quite dramatic. The early settlers came from the North through Ireland, and are believed to have been Picts."

Auntie G. added to the tale, "There is very little known about Pictish culture. When the Scots arrived, the Pict identity was soon forgotten. But you'll find examples of Pict architecture around, like stone Cairns."

Matty continued. "Yes, the Scottish clans came and fought the Picts. Then Norsemen fought them. Even the Romans tried to invade, but didn't succeed. Of course, there were religious sects such as the Druids, and this other ancient sect called Culdeeism. Most recently, like more than five hundred years ago, there were the Clan wars and supporters of Robert the Bruce all over Mull. When he won, the island was given to his greatest supporter, a guy named Angus Og MacDonald. This place has a very dramatic history. It's hard to believe looking at the peacefulness around us."

Matty was on a roll. Fleur finished her cake and poured more tea. "The Highland Clearances happened right here too. It sounds like the Laird of Dowart was a cold-hearted Laird of the land," said Matty. "Not the Laird who gave you the Factor's House, the previous one."

Fleur's attention perked up at the mention of the Laird. "Did the librarian have information about the Laird?"

"She showed me a book of paintings about the Highland Clearances. There in full color were paintings by a famous artist named Fiona Kintrell. She used her paintings to tell the world about the injustice that was happening in Scotland during that time." Matty looked at Fleur, who in turn looked at her grandaunt for a sign of recognition about the book. "It's the artist from the gallery. The person you wondered if she could be your great-great-grandmother." Matty added. Fleur wondered if her grandaunt had a copy of that same book in the house.

Sure enough, as though Auntie G. heard Fleur's thoughts, she got up and beckoned Fleur and Matty to follow her into the living room. She rolled the step ladder towards the bay windows, climbed up, and took down a large ancient leather-encased volume from the top shelf.

"Ah yes," said Auntie G., passing the book to Fleur. "Here it is."

Fleur held the book with trembling hands. She gaped at Auntie G., who said to her, "Don't look so surprised. I know that you need to make the connection between the Laird of Dowart and yourself in order to settle the case for your inheritance claim. I'm sure you have many other questions. Sit down and get comfortable. I'll tell you the story about your family."

Those were words Fleur never expected to hear. "I would love nothing better," she said. "As a young girl, I dreamed of hearing stories about my family, but I thought I didn't have any one else other than Grana and Papa Joe. It's like you said earlier, stories are the backbone of our connection with each other. I didn't have many such stories growing up."

Glenna smiled as she gathered her thoughts. "Well dearie, let me start with my birth, though the story starts before that, but we'll get to that soon enough," she said. "Seventy-seven years almost to the day, right here in Dowart Factor's House, I came barreling into the world. My Auntie E. who raised me said I made my presence known."

Fleur asked, "Was your father the factor?"

"Yes, my father, Ian Currie, was the factor of the estate at that time, just as my grandfather had been a factor before him, and so on down our family line. I never met my maternal grandparents, Fiona and Jamie Kintrell. My grandfather died as a young man, which was why there was only one child from their union. I heard the story about him being crushed by a falling barn beam many times, but no one talked about my grandmother, Fiona. As a young one, I sensed there was something not right, especially after I came across this book with her paintings. I always wondered why such an important ancestor would disappear, and no one speak about it. Did it have something to do with her work about the Highland Clearances?"

Fleur chewed her lower lip. "Auntie G., my Grana suspects that perhaps her grandmother Fiona Kintrell took her as an infant to Canada because she might have been born to Moira out of wedlock. Do you know anything about that?"

Glenna looked into Fleur's eyes. "Aye, it's possible," she said. "Having a child out of wedlock was a huge shame in those days. But I think there was more to it than that. I believe that the problem lies in who might have fathered your grandmother."

Matty couldn't help herself. "Do you think it could have been the Laird, or maybe his son?" she asked. "Do you think he and Moira were in love, but because of her lowly station they couldn't be together, like Romeo and Juliet?"

Auntie G. adjusted her cushion as she considered how to answer Matty. "I'm not sure about that, there are still many unanswered questions," she said. "Why would she leave her only daughter here at the Factor's House? Why didn't she take Moira with her to Canada along with the baby, my half-sister Eileen? She could have arrived in Canada with a story to avoid the judgment of having a child without a husband. But then, if that had happened I wouldn't be here today, would I?"

Fleur considered what Auntie G. had said earlier. "You had an interesting point about Fiona's work," she said. "It could be possible Fiona left because she was threatened. From what my Grana told me, Fiona continued her work in Canada through her association with the St. Francis Xavier University in Antigonish to document the Highland Land Clearances. She did so for many years, through her paintings as well as recording live histories of the people fleeing to Nova Scotia in Canada."

The dusk shadows were coming across the library bay windows when her grandaunt murmured, "Yes, Fleur, that is possible."

Getting up from the settee, Auntie G. bid the friends good evening. "That's it for me, dearies. I think it's time to have a wee bowl of soup before heading off to bed." She threw a suggestion over her shoulder as she left the room, "There's some Italian red in the larder, help yourselves. And Fleur, feel free to use the telephone to call your grandmother. Give her my love. Tell her I'll speak with her myself tomorrow. Let her get used to the idea of having a half-sister first."

Matty followed Auntie G. to fetch the bottle of red wine and a couple of large goblets. Handing a glass to Fleur, Matty was the first to break the silence. "Doesn't that beat all," she exclaimed. "I don't know about you, but my head is spinning. It must be wild to go from not knowing where you come from to having a whole dramatic and romantic history in your family."

Too agitated to sit, Fleur got off the settee and paced between the fireplace and the bay window. She wasn't sure if she agreed with Matty about the story being romantic, but it sure was dramatic. Her unfolding family history left her in awe as she began to have a sense of belonging and connection with the past.

Matty wanted to chew on the story some more. "Poor Moira Kintrell. Imagine her as a fifteen-year-old country girl infatuated with the handsome dark-haired son of the Laird. This son and heir of the evil laird of the land impregnated poor innocent Moira. Her mother, Fiona, takes the newborn infant far away from the evil laird trying to silence her from exposing the injustices of the Highland Clearances," she said.

Fleur laughed at her friend's imaginative conclusion. "That's a bit of a leap," she said. "We know that Fiona Kintrell left her homeland with her grandchild. We don't know why, and perhaps we never will. From the stories Grana had told about Fiona, I believe she must have had a good reason for leaving Moira behind."

Feeling hungry, Fleur went to the kitchen and returned with a plate of cheese and crackers. "The part about my grandmother being an illegitimate child might put a different perspective on things," she said. "I wonder how Scottish law views illegitimate children. Surely, the Hayden brothers are the true heirs, direct descendants of the laird, so that would automatically put me out."

Matty jumped up and squealed, causing Fleur to cough up wine she was swallowing at the same moment. "I just remembered something I found out about the Hayden brothers," she said. "The evil laird had one son, who became laird after him, and one daughter. That son, who we now know to be the impregnator, I mean your grandmother's biological father, well he never married. The evil laird's daughter, Catherine, left for Ireland to marry a baron. She had two sons, Thomas and John Hayden, who are the current heirs of the castle. I wonder if that makes the Hayden brothers barons?"

"Where does that leave us?" asked Fleur. "It's a bit of a jigsaw, but the pieces are falling into place. I need a piece of paper to write this down so I can make some sense of it."

Fleur found a tablet on the library desk and began to recap what they knew. "Let's assume my grandmother is indeed the illegitimate daughter of the Laird's son. I'm looking at it this way, because it's the only thing that makes sense as to why the Laird would name me as benefactor."

She continued to run through the scenario out loud. "We have the Hayden brothers, who had to have inherited the Dowart Estate from their mother, Catherine, the sister of the most recent Laird of Dowart." Fleur paused to consider the logic. "Wait a minute, that doesn't make sense. I thought the brothers inherited the Dowart Estate from the Laird. Do we know his name?"

Matty frowned, trying to remember what the librarian had told her. "You mean the impregnator?" she said. "I think his name was Mackenzie. Nicholas – yes, that's it. Nicholas Mackenzie."

Fleur wrote that down and continued talking through her thought process. "Assuming that Nicholas Mackenzie is my grandmother's father, we can add Moira as my grandmother's mother. Moira's parents were Fiona and Jamie Kintrell. Sometime after Moira gave birth to my grandmother, she married Ian Currie, and subsequently gave birth to Glenna Currie."

Matty made a connection. "Currie. Auntie G.'s name is Currie. We didn't ask, but Glenna must not have married. So how come she lives in the Factor's House? I thought it was just factors who lived here."

Fleur sat back on the settee. "I guess that side of the story will be revealed as well," she said. "Right now, the question at the top of the list is how did the Laird know about me? If he knew enough to name me benefactor, why didn't he contact me while he was alive? For that matter, why didn't he contact his only child? And why didn't Fiona contact her own daughter?" Fleur could feel the emotional aspects of the situation grip her once more. Her Grana's childhood was much like her own, no parents or extended family.

"Slow down, Fleur," said Matty. "You know your Grana didn't do badly by having her grandmother raise her. Look at the big picture. Those were different times, very difficult times. We can't judge the behavior of people in those days compared with our standards today. You'll find out what you need to know. It will all work out." Matty knew how to say the right things.

Lifting her hair away from her neck to recline on the settee, Fleur allowed the red wine to relax her. She closed her eyes for a brief second, only to be startled by a sudden yelp from Matty.

"Goodness, you were bleeding! What happened to your neck?"

"I must have been bitten by a mosquito," said Fleur, holding her hand over her blue crescent moon birthmark. She wasn't ready to tell Matty that her birthmark started to bleed after she had gone into some type of trance, sitting in the middle of the standing stones. The family story Auntie G. told them pushed all thoughts of that experience from her mind.

There was a lot to digest, with more questions arising than answers. Fleur wondered about the meaning of the circle of stones at the top of the hill, and why she was drawn to that particular spot. All day, she had a feeling the path she had taken was familiar, though she had never been there before. She wished her Grana was here so she could talk to her about the standing stones, and ask if they were related to the dream about the woman.

Fleur remembered her intention to telephone her grandmother and exclaimed, "Oh no, what time is it?" With the five-hour time difference, it was the perfect time to telephone her grandmother before she sat down for her afternoon tea.

The overseas operator connected Fleur in a matter of seconds. Fleur held her breath with each click of the telephone exchange, and strained to detect if any of the voices on the line were her grandmother's. Her grandmother soon answered with strong and distinctive voice.

"Is that you, dearie?" she said. "I've been expecting your call."

Fleur wasn't surprised, given her grandmother's intuition. "Yes, Grana, it is me. How are you doing? I miss you so much."

"I miss you too. I sense there something you need to tell me but don't know how to say it," said Grana.

"Uh yes, it's fantastic news in fact. Glenna Currie is your sister. Your mother, Moira, had a child with Ian Currie several years after you were born. Auntie G. is a kind and wonderful person. She's so like you, I feel right at home here."

"Who would have ever thought it? Please give her my love." A brief pause, and her grandmother continued, "This telephone call from Scotland must be costing you a fortune, so let's get straight to the matter at hand. I hear in your voice you are troubled. What is bothering you?"

Fleur didn't hesitate. "I went out for a walk this morning, and saw a waking vision of the women from my dream. She led me to a circle of standing stones. I didn't see her at the stone circle, but I felt her presence. Then I fell into what I can describe as a kind of trance. I'm not sure how, but I then experienced things I believe the woman must have experienced with her tribe. It's like I became her, though I still felt like myself. I know it sounds strange. Do you think this experience is connected with the work I'm supposed to do? I haven't had time to think about it much, but it concerns me. I wasn't worried at first because it felt familiar. I became afraid when these lights came toward me, and the next thing I knew, my birthmark was bleeding. I think I blacked out."

"Are you feeling alright now?" her Grana asked, then continued when Fleur confirmed that she was. "Well then, this confirms you have been called to Scotland for a specific reason. You need to find out what that reason is.

It sounds as though you merged with a non-physical energy, the woman's energy, at the circle of stones. Likely so that you could understand life from her perspective. The ability to merge with non-physical energy is a great gift, and it tells me that you and the woman are linked in some way. I'm sure the experience frightened you, and you felt out of control. Don't be afraid, with practice you will be able to control what you allow to happen. Talk to your aunt. I have a feeling that she'll be able to help."

Fleur blinked twice after her Grana disconnected the phone. Her mind, buzzing with questions, didn't know where to focus attention. She was unsure if she should be anxious about what her Grana called a merging with non-physical energy. Grana talked about a potential link with the woman. She wondered what that could mean, and how she could possibly find the answer to that question. Fleur determined that she needed to concentrate on the immediate task at hand, which was to find out about her connection in terms of the inheritance.

Despite a restless night with little sleep, Fleur was eager to find out what her appointment in town would uncover. The friends set off after breakfast, and planned to be away the entire day.

Fleur savored being in the passenger's seat as Matty drove the western coast route to Tobermory. It gave her the chance to take in the views. For the first time in a long time, she wanted to pick up a paintbrush and encapsulate the utter tranquility of this land on canvas. She ached to paint the dramatic scenery and capture the contrast of colors between the rugged rocky brown, yellow, and green terrain with the aquamarine waters of the sea lochs.

Matty sensed her friend's yearning. "Are you doing that squinty-eyed thing you do when you see things that you want to paint?" she asked.

Fleur chuckled, "You know me so well. Frankly, I'm a bit surprised I feel the urge to paint. It must be this land working its magic on me. It's very inspiring."

Matty kept her eyes on the road and asked Fleur the question she'd been trying to get an answer to for a long time. "I don't get it. Why don't you paint anymore? Painting was your absolute passion. You've never told me what happened to make you so afraid to paint now."

Fleur had not had this kind of yearning to paint since Arthur had destroyed her last canvas. It was hard to speak about the feelings she had, because it sounded trite to blame Arthur for her fear of painting. Maybe it was the potential of discovering she wasn't good enough, like Arthur had told her over and over.

"I'm not sure I can explain why, but I get paralyzed when I think about painting. It's a physical reaction, like a panic attack. I get clammy and feel like I'm going to faint. It's strange I know, but I just can't control the reaction."

"Sounds like you need to *think* less and *do* more," ventured her friend, and left it at that.

They arrived in Tobermory by mid-morning, just in time for Fleur's appointment at Colomie & Sons. With a letter of introduction from Mark in hand, Fleur was focused on her mission to find evidence of Eileen Kintrell's birth, and to understand the rights of illegitimate children regarding inheritances. As Mark noted, they needed to make sure that the Scots Succession Laws were upheld in the Hebrides, and not superseded by some precedent set at a local court ruling or some local clan law.

Fleur left Matty to explore the array of colorful little shops on the waterfront, and of course to chat with the locals, gathering more stories and information. The friends planned to meet at the Delancey pub for a late lunch before taking a slow drive back to the Factor's House.

The law office was just off the main street. Mr. Colomie welcomed Fleur, exchanged a few polite words, and got down to business.

"Mark may have told you in Edinburgh, there is no deviation in law here on the island," he said. "Scottish Succession Law is under the Succession Law covering heritable property, being land and buildings. There is nothing to stop a landowner making a will that leaves his land and buildings to anyone he wishes, and that cannot be disturbed by claims from adult children or anyone else."

"Yes, Mark made that clear. The issue is that we don't have the original inheritance papers. He believes they were burnt in Mr. MacNeill's office fire. We're looking for a connection between myself and the Laird."

"I expect Mark was hoping there was something to link you directly as a descendant," said Mr. Colomie. "It would solidify your case in terms of inheriting the Factor's House, and also discourage a counterclaim on any moveable property that might be involved. Since you don't know what the inheritance papers identified as coming to you, there may well be moveable property, such as money, shares, cars, furniture, and jewelry. In fact, you'd be in a position to counterclaim on the latter point, should you wish to do so."

Fleur nodded. "Can you recommend how to make the connection as a descendant of the Laird?" she asked.

"I would suggest you cross reference the Statutory Register for births, deaths, and marriages with the census around the time your grandmother was born to see if you can prove she is the daughter of the Laird. Your grandmother was born in 1901, you said? That happens to be the year that the census was taken. The registrar office is in this building on the first floor. Let me call my assistant, she can take you downstairs and get you settled."

Within minutes, Fleur and Mr. Colomie's assistant were walking down to the first floor.

The archive room was heavy with the mustiness of aged documents, causing Fleur to breath as shallowly as possible to avoid inhaling the odor. She startled when the administrator appeared beside her to place three leather-bound heavy books on the wooden table at the same time as the grandfather clock in the corner of the room clamored the top of the hour. Putting on the white gloves she was given to preserve the archival material, Fleur had an odd sense of reverence for the history that the old volumes represented.

She didn't expect the rising emotions when she started to read her ancestor's names, handwritten on the yellow-aged, heavy paper stock. Tears came to her eyes, and she had to blink to focus on the cursive script of the administrator, noting her Grana's name as the one-month daughter of Moira Kintrell. She choked up as she read the census record. *1901 Census of Isle of Mull – Castle Dowart Estate Factor House: Jonah Kintrell, factor, and Elizabeth Kintrell, wife of factor, Fiona Kintrell, wife of former Factor Jamie Kintrell – deceased; Moira Kintrell, daughter of Fiona and Jamie Kintrell; Eileen Kintrell aged one month, daughter of Moira Kintrell – father Neacal MacCoinnich.*

The last entry noted the name of her grandmother's father, and it was not the Laird Nicholas Mackenzie, as she expected. Fleur continued to study the records, and wrote copious notes so she could keep the story straight in her mind, and jotted questions on the margins for later. *Why did Fiona Kintrell still live in the Factor House after her husband had died?* Another question on Fleur's margin was about the baby Eileen. *Is this baby mentioned again in the next census in 1911?*

Fleur pulled over the 1911 census records and saw the household names changed slightly. *1911 Census of Isle of Mull – Castle Dowart Estate Factor House: Jonah Kintrell, Factor, and Elizabeth Kintrell, wife of Factor; Ian Currie; Glenna Kintrell Currie, daughter of Ian and Moira Currie.* Fleur wondered why there was no Moira Currie listed, then remembered her Auntie G. had said her mother died giving birth to her. She must have been raised by Elizabeth Kintrell. Fleur made a note to check with Auntie G.

There was no mention of either Fiona Kintrell or Eileen Kintrell in the 1911 census. Fleur cross checked other houses in the area, and none mentioned either of those names. They disappeared after the 1901 census.

The Statutory Registry confirmed the information of the census, and the birth date of Eileen Kintrell. Fleur was satisfied that the records cross referenced accurately, but disappointed at not seeing proof of the Laird fathering her grandmother.

Fleur was still distracted thinking about all she had learned when she entered the pub to meet Matty. Her friend was already seated near a fireplace in the corner. She waved at Fleur and flagged down a waitress to order drinks.

"Girl, you look like you could use a glass of wine. Or do you want a pint of beer?" said Matty. "Were you not successful at the lawyers?"

Fleur admitted to feeling worn out. "I managed to find great information. It was quite emotional, seeing names of family I found out about in the last two days. It's a bit confusing, but I took notes. Basically, Grana's father is not listed as the Laird's son's name."

Her friend patted her hand. "No worries," said Matty. "It's normal to feel tired with all the things you've learned in the past few weeks. Let's order something hot and delicious, and you can tell me about your research."

While they sipped their wine and waited for the food order to arrive, Fleur told Matty the details of her findings. She read her notes on her Grana's parents' names as listed on the 1901 Census. "The listing for Grana says, 'Eileen Kintrell aged one month, daughter of Moira Kintrell – father Neacal MacCoinnich.' But the Laird's son's name was Nicolas Mackenzie. Maybe the name listed is a fake name to avoid embarrassing the families with an illegitimate child? I wish someone would just tell me Grana's father's name."

The waitress, hovering in the background with their food in hand, set the plates down, straightened her back, and looked up to clarify a point she overheard. "Well there, don't yea be knowing then that the name, 'Mackenzie,' is the Anglicized surname for the Gaelic, 'MacCoinnich,' and the name Neacal is the Gaelic for Nicholas. So Neacal MacCoinnich is Nicholas Mackenzie, that it is. Oh – does that help yea then?"

Matty looked at Fleur and grinned. "Now we're talking," she squealed. "Your wish came true, like it always does. Someone did indeed tell you your Grana's father's name. Won't your Grana have a field day wearing the queen's crown?"

Fleur laughed out loud at her friend's joy. She was elated with this new information. Finally, she had proof of connection with the Laird.

"Queen's crown? Where do you get this stuff from, Matty?" asked Fleur. "Grana couldn't care less about crowns or wealth, though I can imagine it would be a godsend for her to know her father's name."

The friends arrived home to find two men at the kitchen table having tea with Auntie G. Matty didn't miss a beat, turning into a femme fatale the minute she laid eyes on the attractive sight. It wasn't difficult to conclude these handsome men were the Hayden brothers. The two were obviously twins, sharing the same dark hair, deep blue eyes, and chiseled facial structure.

Fleur entered the Factor's House carefree from the day's outing and called out a happy greeting to Auntie G. from the front entrance. Now, she stumbled to an abrupt halt behind a seductive Matty, completely taken about by Matty's sudden transformation. Fleur bristled at the utter nerve of the Hayden brothers. How dare they sit there, having tea with Auntie G. as if they were great friends, and not the arbitrators of a legal case threatening to oust her from her home?

The identity of B. Thomas Hayden was confirmed. He was indeed the same Thomas Hayden who had walked out on Fleur during their coffee date this past winter. The hurt came to the surface. Fleur tried to gulp it away, not wanting to seem peevish, though she wanted to glare at Thomas Hayden until he confessed.

Meanwhile, Matty slunk around the kitchen. "Why Auntie G., looks like you had better sightseeing than we did. We saw lots of sweet lambs, but the sight in your kitchens is best for the foxes."

This type of flirtation was a habit of Matty's, but in that moment her friend's apparent betrayal made Fleur frown. She wondered how Matty could possibly flirt with the men causing her problems.

After introductions, Auntie G. waved Matty and Fleur to join them for tea. John Hayden raised an eyebrow at the sudden appearance of Matty, barely disguising how his imagination was captured by the thought of the fun he could have with her. Without missing a beat, John Hayden leaped to his feet, grabbed Matty's hand proffered for a handshake, then turned it over and kissed the back of her hand in the manner of a seventeenth-century gentleman, which made Matty laugh. If he were astute, which Fleur doubted, John Hayden would be able to see through Matty's femme fatale role to the real Matty – a funny, sweet, and courageous adventuress.

Fleur noted that Thomas was watching her reactions from the minute she stepped into the room. He knew who she was. Maybe he had always known. The thought that he might have known that she was the person who inherited the Factor's House made Fleur gasp. Not for the first time, she wondered if he could be that devious. Fleur took a second to assess the situation and stared at Thomas. She wasn't going to be the first to acknowledge that they had met before. She wanted him to say something.

Her indignation turned to angry bewilderment when she saw Thomas staring at her neck. Though her birthmark was hidden behind a low ponytail, he looked at the spot on her neck as though he were looking at something familiar, but couldn't understand the meaning of it. Fleur focused on appearing calm. She wanted to run away from Thomas before she embarrassed herself, but manners meant everything to her, so she stayed and smiled at the two brothers.

"Excuse my brother," said Thomas. "He is a bit of a showman. Apologies for us dropping in unannounced, we wanted to let you know that we are available anytime, should you wish to meet and discuss our position." It was apparent that Thomas would not acknowledge having met her before. Fine, Fleur thought, two could play that game.

Meanwhile, John let go of Matty's hand, but the two of them stood close enough to touch.

Fleur announced her displeasure at Thomas' words. "Your position? Do you mean the lawsuit against me? I think it would be best if you speak with my lawyers. Now if you'll excuse me." With that, Fleur left the room with her head held high.

Alone in her room, Fleur breathed from deep within her chest to calm herself. Seeing Thomas Hayden again had been overwhelming. She was disappointed with herself for not having the courage to hold him to the light of truth. This was a lost opportunity to find out what had happened in Antigonish. She had liked him when she met him in her hometown, and she sensed he had liked her too.

Fleur didn't mean to nap, but when her nerves settled, she fell asleep at the window seat, the dusking light filtering across her face. Despite her state of turmoil, she dreamed a loving dream about the tribal woman and a man who was the dream woman's once-in-a-lifetime soul connection.

In the dream, the tribal woman stood at a shoreline, watching men row towards land. She was focused on one man in particular. The man's eyes sought out and found the tribal woman in the crowd. The two stood locked in a knowing gaze. They were meant to be together. While Fleur couldn't distinguish the features of the two people, she could see the lights sparking between them. She saw herself in the dream as an observer on the beach, hiding behind a rock. She watched with fascination as the tribal woman and the man turned to walk towards her.

She saw the man's face first. Not surprising, given the recent events, the man was Thomas Hayden. She then turned her attention to the woman, whose regal bearing indicated an abundance of self-confidence. The woman turned around; it was herself.

In her dream, Fleur then turned to see if she was still crouched behind the rock. She gasped to see an unrecognizable male in the exact place where she had been at the beginning of the dream. The man showed great malice, vivid and horrible in contrast to the energy of love between the tribal woman and the man from the boat. Fleur jerked awake, chilled from the dampness of the sweat of fear.

CHAPTER TEN

AN ISLAND OF THE HEBRIDES, AD 560

T'Eilin kept a close watch on Brendan and his fellow monks. She told herself her people depended on her noting their every movement, but in truth she couldn't stay away. She wanted to be near Brendan, both physically and spiritually. It was disconcerting, T'Eilin had never felt like this around a man.

During the first two weeks since they arrived, T'Eilin observed how Brendan and his fellows became self-sufficient. They embraced physical labor as an honor and bartered for their basic needs. They built a shelter and an enclosed planting area to keep their crops safe. The monks were attentive to the people's interest in their techniques, since their method of constructing shelter was different from the Irie's roundhouses of wattle and daub. The monks had been happy to demonstrate how their large-framed rectangular single-dwelling housing was constructed, and to assist in building similar housing for others.

T'Eilin was well-pleased that the monks were contributing to the tribe. Brendan had endeared himself with the Healing Mother. He shared knowledge he learned during his extended stay with an Islamic physician, known to be advanced in the healing arts. T'Eilin had at first been suspicious of Brendan's motives. Though he had been invited to work with them in the healing hut by her grandmother, she wondered if he had been ingratiating himself with the Healing Mother to obtain information about the people and their ways to use for his own purposes. However, something she discovered about Brendan within the first week resolved that concern.

She and Brendan had been left alone to clear up after a day of administering remedies. T'Eilin had been watching Brendan, fascinated by the fluidity and grace of his motions. She spotted a blue tattoo on his neck when he pushed away a lock of hair that fell across his eyes while leaning over. Forgetting her shyness, T'Eilin approached Brendan, staring at his neck. Brendan acknowledged her discovery. "Ah, you have noticed my mark," he said, eyes glittering with humor about how tentative T'Eilin seemed to be when near him.

"That is the mark of mastery," said T'Eilin. "How can that be?"

Brendan smiled at the confusion on her face. "I bear the mark of my lineage," he said. "My ancestors are the same as yours. I had been taken from my family during an invasion at the age of eight summers, old enough to remember the ways of my people. They are the same as your people, the same beliefs, the same sacred connection with Source Energy."

While Brendan told her his story, T'Eilin stood close enough to smell the earthy scent of him. His soft, deep voice mesmerized her. Her knees trembled from the strong urge to touch the mark on his neck.

"But you were too young to reach the mastery level in the work. You must be very special indeed." She whispered the last few words. Feeling silly, she gave voice to her understanding in an overly confident manner.

"So that is the reason that our people have been so open to you and to your teachings," she said. "Not just because you speak our language, but you understand them. You have gained their trust. With their trust, you can complete your purpose for coming here."

Brendan noted that T'Eilin was not objecting, she was merely making an observation. "You understand the situation and seem not to be concerned. That pleases me," he said, and stepped closer to T'Eilin. She stepped away from him, as though his touch would burn her. A slight frown of disappointment etched his face when he noticed her backward step. "Most people seem pleased that we are here to teach them different ways. However, there are one or more persons who do not wish us to be here."

T'Eilin arched an eyebrow, and wondered if he were speaking of her.

She nodded her realization that Brendan was talking about the attempts to sabotage the monks' work. She too had noticed a number of times their efforts had been upset by odd occurrences. A few days ago, their freshly planted food garden was trampled, and their container of fresh water was mysteriously spoiled. Other instances of irritation had occurred as well, but nothing major.

"I asked Alcorat to keep an eye on the situation," said T'Eilin. "If anyone can find out who is attempting to impede your progress, he certainly can."

T'Eilin had been watching Diiaan for some time. The assistant disappeared before each of the mysterious events happened. T'Eilin was starting to make the connection, and wondered if Tonnick was using Diiaan to do his bidding. He was the only one who would do such things. He must be upset by his banishment. Perhaps he saw the monks as the cause of his punishment. Alcorat had agreed that it seemed like the work of Tonnick. Time would tell.

With each day, her enchantment with Brendan grew stronger. Only two weeks passed since the monks had arrived, but T'Eilin felt she had known Brendan forever. Each time she saw him, her desire to be near him, to touch him, increased. This troubled her. T'Eilin wondered how she could be of service to her people when so distracted.

On a day Brendan was not with her and her grandmother, treating the tribe's minor injuries, she mentioned her concerns to the Healing Mother. "May I speak with you about my emotional state?"

Clearly Naghaire was aware of the conflicting thoughts her granddaughter had been experiencing. "You are troubled by your feelings for Brendan," she said before T'Eilin gave voice to her concerns. "You are equally doubting whether you should follow your desire to be with him or whether you should stay true to your work for the people. You have been taught that split energy around any topic is a form of resistance, and blocks wellbeing flowing from Source Energy. You must clear this split energy one way or another. It is all up to you."

T'Eilin understood what her grandmother said, but it wasn't that simple. She was aware Brendan struggled with the same feelings. The spark between them was pulling her. It wasn't just her intuition; it was an energetic sensation in her physical body.

The work of alignment was important to T'Eilin, and she needed not to be swayed by Brendan's desires, though it was tempting to let go of control. She decided she could learn how to clear her divided feelings toward Brendan by connecting with the circle of standing stones. She left the healing hut after telling her grandmother of her intention, and headed to the hilltop. She would spend the evening in meditation in the middle of the stone circle.

The pre-dawn light cast a soft halo upon T'Eilin's hair as she sat in the middle of the stones, completing her nighttime vigil. She had seen visions of Brendan throughout the night, and expected him to join her any minute.

T'Eilin sensed his restlessness. She understood that he feared his feelings for her would jeopardize his life's work and the conversion of the Irie people. He wondered if meeting T'Eilin had been a test given by God. In her vision, she saw him walk away from the village to be alone to contemplate and to pray. The full moon guided him towards the highest hills, and now he was here, not knowing that T'Eilin was just a breath away.

Brendan stopped when he came upon the circle of stones. "You are acknowledged, Brendan of the Columba," said T'Eilin, the even tone of her voice belying the tremor in her heart. "What you seek cannot be found with the mind. The answers you look for are within your very nature. You are seeking a way to be true to yourself."

Brendan froze, clearly not expecting to find anyone in this remote place at this hour of the morning. It took him a minute to recognize T'Eilin as her features were unclear in the dim light. The slight tilt of her chin to the left when she was deep in thought gave her away. "How do you know what I am thinking?"

T'Eilin opened her eyes, fully aware of him. She spoke as though they had pre-arranged this meeting.

"I see you, Brendan," she said in a strong voice that she willed not to quake. "I know you, we are one in spirit."

He sat down on the ground beside her before he spoke, maintaining a safe distance to prevent himself from touching her as he desired. "T'Eilin, I now know that you have summoned me," he said in a gentle tone that matched his soft spoken nature. "Are we to speak about making peace with these feelings we have for each other? You believe as I do that we cannot have these desires and also accomplish our life's work."

T'Eilin showed no surprise at this confirmation. "You speak well," she said. "We must align ourselves with who we are and our life's purpose. We cannot live authentic lives if we hold split energy inside us. We will need to be true to our obligations. Mine is to my people, and yours is to your calling."

"You are right. We cannot give way to the physical desire we have for each other. There is a bigger cause for us to attend." A quiver of disappointment ran through T'Eilin at his words.

She held his gaze, understanding that his words went against his heart also. But his chosen path followed a greater destiny, just as hers did. She sensed his turmoil and sensed the moment he decided to pour his love for her into feeding her strong need for knowledge. She bowed her head, humbled by this evidence of the intensity of his unconditional love for her.

Knowing it was time to leave Brendan alone to find his peace of mind, she stood up, gave her respect to the circle of stones, and left.

A week had passed since T'Eilin and Brendan met at the standing stones. They were both conscious of the pact they had made to respect each other's work. They carried out their chores and were polite whenever they interacted, but the strain of their desire for each other continued to build. The pressure of the effort soon became evident.

They were alone, tidying up the healing hut. T'Eilin had been contemplating a question ever since she had seen the mark on his neck. "How were you able to achieve mastery at such a young age?" T'Eilin asked, barely restrained from reaching out to touch the blue inked image on the soft skin of Brendan's neck. The urge to wind her fingers around his coarse dark hair was so powerful, it left her breathless.

Brendan looked at T'Eilin, eyes darkened by his own desire. "Do not tempt me, T'Eilin," he said in a steady voice. "One touch from you, and I am undone."

This unabashed display of Brendan's desire quickened her breath. She withdrew her hand. Turning her back on Brendan to steady herself, she steered the conversation back to the discussion of their spiritual journey. She was interested to learn another perspective. "As one who has attained mastery, you know the power that Source Energy holds," she said. "You know that we all have access to that power, if we do the work. How can you teach something different?"

Brendan frowned in concentration, determining how to best answer. "I have not forgotten," he said. "It is through the knowledge of Source Energy that I come to understand this new way. It is about love, and the power of love. One of my first memories is of my mother, who was our tribe's healer, saying the wisdom words, 'As above, so below. As within, so without.' Those words hold true for Christianity."

T'Eilin shook her head. "I don't understand how love can be all there is," she said. "What of the great effort to survive in this world, how is that love? What of the evil that men do to each other when they kill and take what belongs to another? How can that be love? You yourself were taken from your family by invaders. How can you believe that is love?"

T'Eilin breathed through flared nostrils to still her racing heart. She was surprised at the intensity of her asking. These were not new questions. She had often raised these same points with her grandmother.

Brendan touched T'Eilin's arm to calm her. "You know of the power of the energy you call Source, and I call God," he said. "That is the Oneness."

T'Eilin's eyes lightened in recognition. Encouraged by this, Brendan continued to explain. "God's son, Jesus, came to earth to remind people about the Oneness of all in Source Energy," he said. "His teachings are solely about love. When people stood before Jesus dripping with illness, he saw them as whole because of his great love for them. Through his work of mastery, Jesus saw people through the eyes of Source Energy, and so they could only experience wellbeing, not illness."

"I can understand that a son might come to teach his father's work," she said. "But Jesus did not walk amongst my people. So why do you come to the Irie if Jesus does not know about us?"

Brendan nodded his head. "You and the Healing Mother are wonderful models of the old ways, teaching the people about Source Energy and the Oneness of all with the ancestors," he said. "You have rituals and tools to help the people know of the Oneness. But, as you have experienced, the people forget, and need to be reminded in structured ways. There will always be negative energy from some people or groups of people. Jesus came to teach us that all things are the same thing. All is love, or a call for love. He came to remind people, to connect them to the Source of love within themselves."

T'Eilin found the fact that Brendan was speaking about love to be very disturbing. How could he talk with such passion about love, yet insist they deny their love for each other?

She stopped the conversation, leaving Brendan with a bewildered look on his face. It pained her to see that look, but she couldn't tolerate another moment of this talk about love being all when she and Brendan denied their love for each other.

When the first moon cycle since their arrival completed, the monks sent a message to all the Irie to come to a ceremony to bless their two dwellings, one where they lived, and one where they prayed. The people were eager to attend, for they enjoyed spiritual ceremonies and the festivity that went along with them.

Brendan came to the healing hut on the morning of the ceremony. There was special work to do there. Four days previously, Brendan had performed a procedure on Naghaire's eyes. Today they would see the results.

T'Eilin had been present when Brendan told her grandmother her blindness was not permanent. Brendan explained how a cloudy film obscured her vision. The cloudy film could be pushed to the bottom of the eye using a sharp instrument to allow the light in so she could see again. Brendan had learned the procedure from the Islamic physician with whom he had spent a year studying. He had performed the procedure many times with success.

T'Eilin had been fearful, but Naghaire had been excited at the possibility of seeing again.

This morning they would find out how successful the delicate procedure had been. Brendan greeted them. "Greetings Healing Mother, I see you. Are you ready to see me?"

T'Eilin was anxious. "Don't you think that we should wait a bit longer? It's only been four days."

Brendan leaned in to comfort T'Eilin with a pat on her arm. She startled at the fiery contact of his hand. There could be no denying how heightened her senses were when Brendan was near.

"Do not worry," said Brendan. "You'll soon know that your grandmother is well."

Brendan motioned to Diiaan to close the entrance covering. He explained the need to block out all light before he removed the bindings because her eyes would be sensitive. Brendan kneeled closer to Naghaire and explained everything he was doing. He asked her if she was ready before he began.

"I am as ready as I will be," said Naghaire. "Let it be as it is."

With T'Eilin's help, Brendan removed the bindings. T'Eilin held her breath as Naghaire's eyes were exposed, and she fluttered them open. Although there was a great deal of stickiness around her eyes, it was obvious the cloudiness was no longer visible.

Naghaire appeared to be looking around the room. "What can you discern with your eyes?" asked Brendan.

Naghaire replied calmly enough, though her words had T'Eilin breathless with joy. "How remarkable," she said. "I had forgotten how well the colors of dawn are reflected in this room."

"Grandmother, does that mean that you can see?"

Naghaire turned to her granddaughter. "My beautiful T'Eilin," she said. "Look at how grown you have become, a woman in every aspect."

While her grandmother was calm about regaining her sight, T'Eilin was animated with joy. She grabbed her grandmother and hugged her tight. This was powerful healing.

Within an hour, her grandmother prepared to leave the hut to attend the monk's blessing ceremony. T'Eilin tried to dissuade her grandmother. "Do you think you should go to the gathering? Are you feeling well enough?"

Her grandmother was determined the people should know about the healing straight away. "This healing is proof that the knowledge the monks bring to our people is of benefit," she said. "It is a great example in fact. Let us go and tell the people."

The Irie people were gathered outside of the main dwelling house, enjoying the hospitality of the monks. The hum of voices fell as they noticed something different about Naghaire as she and T'Eilin approached. Within moments, voices murmured in the crowd. "Look, the Healing Mother is walking without holding T'Eilin by the arm. She is placing her feet between the stones."

Naghaire heard the mutterings of disbelief and called out in a strong voice, "Yes my people, I can see where before I was blind," she said. "This is the work of the powerful healer, the monk Brendan. I am healed, I can see."

Many of the tribe's people were excited by this news, and some were fearful of such a powerful monk. A few people spread harmful words that shifted the energy of the gathering. T'Eilin scanned the crowd to find the source of the person who started the words that incited the people to alarm. The sudden negative energy had the signature of Tonnick's handiwork.

She was glad when her grandmother raised a hand to silence the crowd. "You will recall that we spoke of this foretelling," she said. "We knew of strangers who would bring new knowledge of benefit to our people. What more proof is there than the healing of a blind person?"

Once again, there was a spike of dread in the air. T'Eilin searched among the people. At the edge of the wooded area beyond the gathering she saw Diiaan talking with a man. It was Tonnick.

T'Eilin turned her attention back to her grandmother, who was speaking to the people. "We know the teachings of our ancestors," said Naghaire. "We are here for expansion and growth. We must be open to new ideas, new thoughts, and new ways of doing things. This healing is a sign for our people; a sign not to follow anyone blindly, but to open our eyes to new possibilities."

Her grandmother then motioned to Brendan to speak. "Thank you, Healing Mother, for trusting me," he said in a quiet voice. "It took great courage, and I am humbled by that."

Brendan turned to the crowd and bowed as he spoke further words of gratitude. "Healing Mother spoke wise words when she said, 'I can see where before I was blind.' My fellow monks and I felt the same when we heard the good news about God, or Source Energy," he said. "A cloudy film lifted from our eyes. But this is not the time to tell you. Today, we give thanks for our safe arrival at your shores, for you granting us your permission to live amongst you, and to thank you, the people of Tobirie, for helping us to create a home here."

Motioning to the monk Kerial, he said, "Let us commence the blessing ceremony to give thanks for our new house of prayer. This is to be the place where God, the Source Energy, will spread the good news to you, the great people of Tobirie."

Taking up a burning bundle of sage the monks had prepared and placed in a pot beside the entrance to the building, Brendan began to hum and wave the smoking sage around the inside and outside of the entire building. The people were amazed to see the monk Brendan use a smudging ritual, identical to the one the Irie used to bless their own buildings. Although the words that Brendan chanted were foreign to the Irie, the smudging was familiar.

Later that evening, T'Eilin spoke alone with her grandmother. There was much to talk about, especially the healing of her grandmother's eyesight. T'Eilin enjoyed her grandmother's childlike joy as she looked at everything around her with so much wonder.

T'Eilin raised the subject of the people who had said things that caused fear to run through the crowd. "It is certain that I noticed the negative energy," she said. "I saw Tonnick in the crowd with Diiaan. She seemed upset. I suspect that she has been doing his bidding while he is banished, causing all of the small annoying incidents to upset the monk's work here."

Her grandmother acknowledged her observation, "Those are exactly my thoughts. We need to take care of that."

At that moment, Diiaan entered the healing hut to bring back remedies she had taken to one of the homes. T'Eilin and her grandmother looked at each other, aware it was an opportunity to question Diiaan.

Naghaire motioned to Diiaan to sit beside her. Diiaan asked how she was feeling. "It is wonderful that you can see, Healing Mother," she said, and after a short hesitation continued. "May I speak with you and T'Eilin about a matter that is weighing on my mind?"

"I am happy about the return of my sight," said Naghaire. "Though even without eyes I can see you are bothered by not being true in your allegiance to my granddaughter and myself."

Wide-eyed with surprise, Diiaan understood Naghaire already knew what she wanted to talk about; how she had been helping Tonnick. "Healing Mother, forgive me," she said. "I thought I was in love with Tonnick, and I wanted to please him. He never asked me to do anything harmful. But I see that I was foolish. I see that he is not a nice person. I deeply regret letting him use me."

Naghaire looked at Diiaan. "You are a naïve child, an innocent who means no real evil. For that reason, I do not punish you. Tell me why he has asked you to help him. What did he say to convince you?"

Diiaan told Naghaire and T'Eilin everything she knew. "He told me the monks were bad for our tribe, and I believed him, he was so convincing."

T'Eilin wanted to know if Diiaan was responsible for the small occurrences that sabotaged the monk's work. "Tonnick told me what to do," said Diiaan. "He said they would leave if we made it difficult for them to stay."

"So you did his bidding," said T'Eilin. "That disappoints me. What changed your mind, why are you telling us now?"

"He has been watching you very closely and sees love growing between you and Brendan and it makes him angry. I believe he is jealous of you and your power. He wants to be powerful himself."

T'Eilin considered that, and it made sense to her given his attitude towards her all of these years. "What is he planning next, do you know?"

"I do not know, but he said he was going North," said Diiaan, sounding contrite at her part in causing T'Eilin to be disappointed in her.

In the silence that ensued, T'Eilin glanced at her grandmother, wondering if she too felt the vibration in the air, like a rift leaving empty space where before life had pulsed.

Naghaire broke the silence, "Diiaan, leave now and spend the night thinking about what you have done. In the morning, tell us how you will repair the damage of your actions."

When they were alone again, Naghaire turned to her granddaughter, and nodded her head in agreement with her unspoken observation. "I also felt that vibration," she said. "To me it was like a curse being uttered into the universe. I fear the foretelling is about to happen. We must be vigilant, for we do not know what form it will take."

CHAPTER ELEVEN

ISLE OF MULL, SCOTLAND, 1987

Fleur wandered into the kitchen, ashamed of her behavior the previous evening. Something had snapped when she saw Thomas and John Hayden drinking tea with her grandaunt, as though they weren't trying to kick her out of the Factor's House. She admitted to herself part of her upset was the confirmation that the person contesting her inheritance was the same man who had walked out on their date in Antigonish. Regardless, Fleur felt bad about her rude departure. It wasn't like her.

Matty gave her a cheery greeting. "You must be feeling on top of the world, and hungry too."

"Have a sit down, dearie, and eat breakfast," said Auntie G. "We saved you crumpets, eggs, and sausage."

Fleur appreciated their efforts to make her feel better. She hugged Matty and her grandaunt. "Thank you, yes, I am hungry," she said. "I feel bad about my behavior last evening. I don't know what came over me."

"I understand," said Auntie G. "You sit yourself down here and let me get you a cuppa."

Fleur was relieved Matty and her grandaunt didn't fuss about her behavior. "I heard you talking about the Hayden brothers. Did they stay long after I left?"

Matty couldn't wait to tell Fleur. "Oh yes, they stayed quite a bit longer, and we had a great time," she said. "John even cooked us a gourmet meal. It was no problem, you see, because he owns a fancy restaurant in Dublin. A popular one, and it's French. John is so talented."

Matty preened when talking about John. It was clear to Fleur that her friend was infatuated. "Then after supper, we played a game of cards, what was it called, Auntie G.? Wishing, or something like that. It's a British game. Of course, I would rather we played stripping poker with John."

Auntie G. smiled and corrected Matty. "The card game is called Whist. You're right, it's an old British card game. We had a very pleasant evening."

It was clear that Matty would talk about John all day if given the chance. Even her grandaunt had an opinion about the brothers. "John is quite the live wire, he is," she said. "He kept us entertained with hilarious stories about his adventures. Thomas is quieter, but nice. He seemed to be lost in thought after you left. "

Fleur contemplated Thomas being preoccupied last night, and wondered if he was remembering their date too.

"Did they talk about the case?" she asked, changing the topic. She was a bit jealous of the fun Matty and Auntie G. had last night.

Matty scrunched her face in concentration. "Yep indeed, we did," she said. "I brought up the subject. I told John and Thomas they don't have a cement case, because we found out you are related to the old Laird. They didn't know about your grandmother. Blew them away to find out that you were related to them. Of course, we hadn't had enough time to tell Auntie G. since they were here when we arrived home from Tobermory. So, I had to go into all of the details for her benefit."

It hadn't dawned on Fleur that she and the Hayden brothers might be distant cousins. It felt odd that she'd had feelings for Thomas when they met in Antigonish. To her surprise, she was disappointed by the possibility that they were related, even if distantly.

Trying to understand the details of their possible relationship, Fleur asked Auntie G. for clarification. "We must be third or fourth cousins, is that right?"

"The truth of the matter is that John and Thomas are not related to the Laird. They were adopted as infants, so they are not blood relatives." The distaste Fleur had at the thought of being attracted to a cousin vanished.

"Did they seem to think differently about their case with that piece of information?" Fleur recalled that adopted children were deemed to hold the same rights as legal children under Scottish inheritance law.

Her grandaunt turned around from washing the dishes in the sink. "It seems to me that the news that you might be family wouldn't deter them," she said. "They are set on reestablishing the estate to its original functioning, and need the Factor's House for that purpose. What did you think, Matty?"

Matty paused in the middle of drying a large cast-iron frying pan. Her smile warned Fleur that she was about to gush about John again. "John is a dreamer," she said with a faraway look in her eyes. "He wants to turn the entire estate into a hospitality business, operating the castle as a hotel for people to experience the original way of life as a top wool-producing estate. Oh, and Thomas wants to restore all the buildings to their original condition. He's been researching the historical architecture of the castle for years. Great plans, but I think they can do all that and leave the Factor's House alone for you."

Fleur had a notion the brothers' plans to develop the property was not good for her case. She had read an article about the Scottish government supporting property development that encouraged tourism or increased jobs. According to Matty, the Hayden brothers intended to use the Factor's House for guest accommodations. If they couldn't win the case against her, Fleur then wondered what they would do to try to get ownership of the Factor's House.

"I'll call Terrence today to update him on developments and get his advice," she said.

"I forgot to tell you that Terrence called last night, after John and Thomas left," Matty said. "I told him everything that's been going on, and he said not to do anything, like sell or something. He figures if the brothers think they can't win the case, they might offer to buy you out. Terrence said he's still planning to come to Scotland, but doesn't know when yet. I wonder if he'll stop in Edinburgh, if you know what I mean."

Fleur smiled at Matty's romantic hopes for Terrence. Knowing that Terrence would come soon to Mull to help was a relief. She had every intention of winning her right to her inheritance. The Factor's House was becoming more and more important to her sense of self. She didn't know what she was going to do with her life, but she had a strong feeling that the Factor's House was a central part of it.

Fleur was helping to tidy up the kitchen after breakfast when a booming voice called out from the kitchen doorway and startled her. "Good morning to the house. Is my Petite Saut ready for the spelunking adventure of a lifetime?"

John rounded the corner into the kitchen, filling the room with his larger-than-life Irish manliness. Matty almost swooned when John leaned forward to kiss her hand after he had first greeted Auntie G. in a similar manner, and thanked the matron for her hospitality. He then turned to Fleur, gave her a wink, and asked her how her headache was this morning. Fleur wasn't inclined to apologize for her behavior, but feeling Matty's pleading eyes upon her, she went along with John's pretense.

"Thank you for asking, I'm feeling much better this morning. My head-ache is gone, although a slight nausea remains." She just couldn't help leaving that little dig in the air.

John grabbed Matty's hand, ignoring Fleur's comment with a smile. "Well, Petite Saut, now that we know your friend will survive my acquain-tance, away with us!"

Matty giggled and left to fetch her hiking boots, rucksack, and provi-sions. A picnic seemed to be in the cards for the day.

After Matty and John left in a flurry of laughter and good cheer, Fleur turned to Auntie G. "What else did I miss last evening?" she said. "He even has a pet name for her. Petite Saut means Little Jump, doesn't it? How did he get to know her so well in one mere evening?"

"Now, Fleur," admonished Auntie G. "You know better than to judge. You made a decision not to be open to the two brothers, so, you missed the chance to enjoy their company and get to know them a bit. Sure, one seems a little mad, but he is harmless and will be fun for Matty. The other seems a bit sullen, but I suspect still waters run very deep, true, and loyal."

As Fleur was about to protest, Auntie G. raised a finger to interrupt her. "I know you're embarrassed by walking out like that last evening, and I don't mean to add to your discomfort," she said. "You felt overwhelmed by your emotions and gave voice to that. You should celebrate the fact that you spoke up like you did, not feel embarrassed. It's a first step to remembering who you are, lass."

Auntie G.'s words and soft accent soothed Fleur's emotions. "Thank you," she said. "I'm so happy to know that you understand. I guess Thomas hurt me more than I thought." Fleur realized too late that she had never mentioned meeting Thomas when she saw Auntie G.'s puzzled look. She didn't worry though, for Auntie G. was too polite to probe.

Fleur looked around and felt Matty's absence. "It feels strange that Matty is gone. I had gotten used to being alone since the divorce, but I've come to rely on Matty so much lately. "

Auntie G. rose from the kitchen chair and motioned Fleur to follow her. "Come along with me, dearie," she said. "I've something to show you."

Fleur followed Auntie G. out a side door and down a long corridor lead-ing to a closed door. Auntie G. pushed the door open with a mighty shove and walked through the door ahead of Fleur. Stepping aside, she motioned Fleur into a bright room.

Fleur was astonished. The room was lined by floor-to-ceiling windows along one side, letting the fullness of the morning sunlight inside. The view from the windows was of a garden she hadn't seen before. It was a lush, private space, tended with obvious great love. Flowerbeds and fruit trees lined the perimeter of the garden. A path of white pebbles led from a heavy wooden side door to a wrought iron bench under a magnolia tree in the middle of the garden.

It was a secret garden, walled by thick stone seven feet high. Fleur could see that under an arbor of heavy wisteria there was an entry gate she had not seen in her tour of the property.

Her eyes moved away from the garden to the interior of the room itself. The space had not been used in a long time, although everything in the room was tidy and clean. Linen sheets covered a few pieces of furniture. There was an easel in the center of the conservatory with a couple of blank canvases leaning against it on the floor. Fleur guessed the space had been where Fiona Kintrell, her great-great-grandmother, had painted. It was a peaceful yet invigorating place for creative energy. She experienced the longing to hold a brush in her hand tug at her soul. Auntie G. sensed the yearning within Fleur, and moved towards the large cupboard in the corner. She pulled out a well-used wooden paintbox and a palette and handed them to Fleur, who stared at the items in her hand for a long while. When she looked up to speak with Auntie G., her grandaunt had already left the room.

She placed the paintbox and palette on the table near the easel. The name *Charles Roberson & Co. of London* was burnt into the wooden box. The strong smell of carmine and ultramarine pigment tickled her nose when she opened the box. She shut her eyes and lifted her face to the ceiling. The fragrance triggered memories of the happiest times in her life, the moments when she stood in front of an easel, her creativity flowing onto canvas.

Sighing, Fleur examined the antique box in her hand, fascinated by the rich history it held about the famous artist who had owned the paintbox. The neat wooden square sections contained pigment cakes in the deep hues that Fiona Kintrell had used to paint her masterpieces. In the second drawer under brass syringes of pigment, which Fleur knew were the forerunner of the collapsible tubes, a piece of parchment paper contained a handwritten color chart. Fiona Kintrell had written detailed instructions on how to mix the pigments to obtain each particular color denoted.

Tears spilled from Fleur's eyes as she returned the box to the shelf where it had rested undisturbed for years. She sensed the energy in the conservatory beckoning her to remember her true nature as an artist. It was a whispered reminder that she had her great-great-grandmother's talent in her blood. Fleur lowered her head, feeling the weight of shame. She wondered if she could push past her fear in this beautiful space.

In slow motion, Fleur lifted a canvas onto the easel. The desire to paint was strong. Time slowed. The rhythmic clicking of the trees outside the conservatory tapping the window in the breeze sounded like a timpani drum.

Fleur stood expressionless in front of the clean canvas. Nothing came to her mind. No inspiration. No images of what could be. Not even the usual whisper of excitement when she stood poised to create art.

Without warning, the saliva in her mouth dried and her breath became ragged. Her heart thrummed in her ears, and beads of sweat formed on her forehead. The harder she tried to control the panic, the worse the physical signs of distress appeared. She had one option, to get away from the conservatory.

Fleur hurried to the front hall, put on her hiking boots, and rushed out the door. Following her instinct, she strode up the hill until she stood in the middle of the stones. She believed she would receive a message there. Her desire for answers was much stronger than the residual fear from the last experience at the standing stones. Fleur sensed that by helping the dream woman she would also find a way to set herself free. She no longer wanted to be a captive to her fears. She sat in the center of the circle and raised her arms, feeling disconnected from her body. Within seconds, Fleur felt the stones reverberate and was compelled to chant in a voice that matched the pitch of the pulsation.

Thomas Hayden walked to the hilltop to clear his head. He hadn't gotten much sleep last night after his encounter with Fleur in Glenna Currie's kitchen. He had been surprised to see her, having no idea the woman who inherited the Factor's House was the same person he had met in Antigonish all those months ago. Seeing Fleur had brought up guilt about his leaving her at the café without a word of explanation. He had his reasons, and hoped he would have a chance to tell Fleur at some point.

Just like when he was a young lad visiting his grandfather the Laird, the view from the hilltop made him feel as free from worries as a soaring eagle. He resolved to speak to Fleur and explain what had happened in Antigonish as soon as possible.

As he turned to leave, Thomas heard a voice chanting from behind the trees. He ducked under the draping branches of the ash trees to investigate, and stood transfixed at the sight in the clearing. Standing silently in the morning sun was a circle of conical shaped stones. He couldn't believe he was seeing ancient standing stones. He had climbed this very hilltop many times and had never seen this circle of stones. He made a mental note to ask John but doubted his brother would have kept such a discovery to himself.

There were many such stone circles in various parts of the Isle of Mull, but not on the Dowart Estate, or so he thought. This was an astonishing discovery, not just from the viewpoint of being the owner of the property, but also from the perspective of his professional curiosity. He moved into the clearing to get a closer view of the circle of standing stones and saw a woman in the center. Thomas was stunned to recognize Fleur meditating, sitting cross-legged on the ground.

Fleur's eyes darted behind her closed eyelids as images flashed before her. People were gathered around a large bonfire enjoying a ceremony. Two figures stood in the middle of the group of people, a dark-haired man and a blonde woman. The couple were delighted with themselves, holding hands and smiling at one another.

The pleasant feeling of the ceremony vanished and turned to chaos. Shouting men on horseback thundered toward the gathering. A band of wild men brandished weapons and charged the people standing around the fire. A fierce and tattooed warrior led the group, roaring his hatred into the air.

"I will kill you and all you love, you wicked witch," yelled the warrior.

The blonde woman turned to gaze at the warrior, uncaring that he was charging his horse directly at her with his sword upraised. Her beloved, the dark-haired man standing beside her, pulled her out of the way and shielded her with his body. The woman flung her arms around the dark-haired man and called out, "Our love will save us." At the same time, the people gathered at the ceremony screamed and began to scatter. Too late to flee from the band of warriors, many in the group were slaughtered where they stood. Men, women, and children, none were spared. The peaceful ceremony turned into a bloodbath.

Thomas started to back away to leave Fleur alone in her meditation when she screamed. He sprinted to help her, unsure of what had happened to cause her to call out. Assuming that Fleur was daydreaming, he shook her to awaken her. Her long hair swung off her neck, and he saw that the blue crescent tattoo behind her ear was bleeding. That very mark was the reason he left during their first meeting in Antigonish.

As the horrendous scene started to fade from Fleur's awareness, the blonde woman turned around to look directly at her. "You must help us," she pleaded. "You are our only hope to save generations of lost daughters."

Fleur no longer knew if she was an observer or if she was merging again with the woman's energy, for when the woman turned around to look at her, she saw it was her own face. *She* was the blonde woman. The dark-haired man came to stand beside her. She sighed, and whispered words with warmth and tenderness. "Brendan, my love," she said as she wrapped her arms around him. "Hold me, our love will save us from this curse."

Fleur blinked and became cognizant of her surroundings. The tribal village was gone. She was sitting in the middle of the circle of stones. She focused and saw Thomas holding her in his arms, not the dark-haired man of her vision.

She pushed back from Thomas in alarm, and rasped, "What's going on?" She felt his disappointment; he had apparently been enjoying the tenderness she was showing. But those feelings weren't for Thomas, they were for Brendan.

Thomas answered her question, telling her that he had hiked to the hilltop and heard a scream. When he went to investigate, he saw her sitting in the middle of the stone circle.

"Honestly, Fleur," he said. "I wasn't going to disturb you in your meditation, but you screamed and started to shake. How're you feeling? Do you suffer from convulsions? Is there medication you need to take for your condition?"

"I'm fine," she snapped. "You must have imagined that. I've never had convulsions." Fleur attempted to push herself out of his arms. The movement was too fast, and sudden dizziness sent her tumbling backward.

"Wait just a minute, you'll feel better if you take it easy," he said. "The tattoo behind your ear is bleeding; maybe you hit your head." Thomas took his handkerchief out of his pocket to dab at the blood.

Fleur was confused. Brendan knew the mark behind her ear was a birthmark, marking her a one of the descendants tasked to do the work for the expansion of all. Why was he calling it a tattoo? It wasn't a tattoo, though others in the tribe did have similar marks. She had placed such marks on them herself when they completed mastery. "Brendan, you know this mark behind my ear is not a tattoo. It's a birthmark."

Fleur inhaled and froze. "Thomas, what's going on?" she asked, her voice trembling. "Why did I call you Brendan? Please help me."

A jolt of recognition caused Thomas' heart to thunder when Fleur called him Brendan. That name happened to be his own Christian name. In his professional publications, he used his author's name, B. Thomas Hayden. Outside of that, he used the name Thomas solely. He was unsure how Fleur could have known his first name as no one did.

What was happening to her, Fleur wondered as she looked around. She must have experienced a merging with the dream woman. It was clear that she still did not know how to handle merging with non-physical energy.

"Don't worry, everything is going to be alright," said Thomas with a soothing tone. "Let's get you home and make you some tea. Lean on my arm until you find your feet again."

As Fleur tried to stand, encircled by Thomas' arms, a light flashed across the western sky to illuminate the standing stones in an unusual manner. The splendor of the moment was not lost on her, and it caused her a brief moment of sadness to think about great love that was lost in time.

The lights moved around the standing stones and came to rest in front of her. Fleur stood transfixed by the sight, unlike the first time she came to the standing stones when the dancing lights scared her. She stepped towards the lights, reached out to touch them, and collapsed in a heap on the ground.

Thomas shook away the thoughts that Fleur might possess intuitive powers. She was clearly in distress and felt disoriented. His immediate concern was to get her home and in the care of a doctor.

CHAPTER TWELVE

AN ISLAND OF THE HEBRIDES, AD 560

T'Eilin approached her grandmother early in the morning, a week after the blessing ceremony. "Grandmother, you have spoken to me many times about the nature of Source Energy as love," she said. "You believe there is no evil in the world, only the absence of love. Why do some people want to harm others?"

Naghaire raised an eyebrow. She knew that T'Eilin was burdened by what Diiaan had confessed after the blessing ceremony.

Naghaire observed the instant flash of love between her granddaughter and the monk Brendan at their first meeting on the beach the day the monks arrived. That love was growing, and even though both denied it, it was destined to be. She surmised that Tonnick also noticed. Though he was banished, Naghaire knew he would not stop trying to exact his revenge upon T'Eilin. That too was destined to be.

Naghaire came straight to the point, as was her manner. "My beloved granddaughter, you are troubled because you are denying a very important part of yourself," she said. "There is no doubt about your devotion to your people, you take care of them well. But you are not being true to yourself. You are rejecting a love you have deep within your soul for the monk Brendan. I suspect that he is denying his love for you as well."

Naghaire could see this wasn't sitting well with T'Eilin. "Denying your love will bring you pain. If you allow your love, the work you do will be based on love, and therefore everyone you contact and teach will prosper."

Her granddaughter's comment spoke to her conflicted emotions. "Grandmother, you speak the truth about my love for Brendan," she said. "And yes, Brendan feels the same for me. We discussed this some time ago and concluded it best to put our work ahead of our feelings."

Smiling to acknowledge T'Eilin's words, though she thought them misguided, Naghaire kept any trace of judgment out of her voice. "There is no greater thing than love," she said. "It is the basis of all life. It is the pure energy that flows from Source. Embrace it, let it guide you always in the work you do."

T'Eilin fell quiet. "Healing Mother, do you know why Tonnick carries so much negative energy?" she asked. "It feels as though he won't be satisfied until he does harm."

Naghaire chose her words. "I have been observing Tonnick all his life," she said. "He is a very powerful creator, and would have made a good leader for our tribe, but he has always resisted wellbeing. He was trained in this pattern by the woman who raised him after his mother died in childbirth. She blamed me for the death of her daughter, and ingrained that hatred in Tonnick. He did not know a mother's love, only the bitterness of the woman who raised him. Now he turns that resentment toward you for spurning his misplaced affection."

Naghaire saw that T'Eilin was understanding what she said, but did not grasp the nature of all things as love.

"You see, no one comes into this world with evil intent," she said. "But in some cases, there is a severe absence of love that manifests as this evil, or negative energy. But it can be healed through love and through the alignment of split energy."

Her granddaughter nodded. "I hear your words, but what can I do to stop the split energy I hold?" she asked. "It is plain that Tonnick wishes me evil. I couldn't bear it if harm came to my people because of something Tonnick holds against me."

Naghaire shook her head. Her granddaughter was stubborn when it came to her duty to her people. That too came from a generational pattern. Her own grandmother had been like that, sacrificing everything for her people.

"T'Eilin, you know the work you must do," said Naghaire. "It is easier to tell others, but hard to see for yourself. It is always about alignment with your true self. Clear the split energy of your choice about Brendan by either accepting your decision fully or by joining with him. Clear the negative energy you attract from Tonnick. This is your work to do. Do not let Tonnick take away your power."

Naghaire knew she had work to do as well, to bring herself into alignment with the wonderful momentum of the good feelings she's had since her sight was restored. She knew her alignment impacted all those around her. Therefore, T'Eilin was bound to come into her own power again.

The days marched towards summer's end. With each passing day, T'Eilin's grandmother's message about the healing power of love came to fruition as she allowed small pieces of Brendan's love to seep into her heart.

One afternoon, when T'Eilin had completed a complex tattoo on one of the swordsmen, Brendan gazed at her with a contemplative look on his face.

"Brendan, what are you thinking?" she asked. "Do you not like this tattoo? It is quite a powerful spirit guide for a mighty swordsman, is it not? This man has honed intuitive skills to bring focus like none other I have met."

Brendan smiled at T'Eilin. "Quite the contrary," he said. "You are a master of the art of tattooing. It's a joy to see your passion. There is nothing more powerful than doing work you enjoy."

T'Eilin nodded her agreement, which encouraged him to continue.

"I was wondering if you would transfer your art to parchment," he said.

She hesitated to pronounce the unfamiliar word. "What is that word?" asked T'Eilin. "I have not heard of it – parchment."

Later that day, when Brendan and T'Eilin were alone, he showed T'Eilin a beautiful ream of precious vellum. He took one of the small wooden boxes the monks had brought into the healing hut to show her.

Brendan set the wooden box down in the middle of the room and opened it as T'Eilin leaned over his shoulder to look at the mysterious contents.

Brendan named each item as he removed and unwrapped the materials inside. "This is parchment, or vellum," he said. "It is made from calf skin, and acts like human skin when you apply inks similar to your tattoo ink. Using pigments, we can create pictures on the parchment that last longer than the tattooing on human skin, for it outlasts the human lifespan." Brendan unrolled a piece that had both pictures and words on it. "Parchment is used to write stories and to record histories of peoples, traditions, and cultures. Let me read you what these words say."

He read a passage from scripture, written in Latin. While she could not understand the Latin, she grasped the incredible power of the written word. Her excitement grew the more he read to her. She tapped her right foot in agitation as all the possibilities crowded her mind. Her fingers itched to put ink to this wonderful parchment.

She was relieved that Brendan understood what she was experiencing. "Would you like me to teach you how to write and read these words?" T'Eilin nodded her head, too eager to utter a word.

"I would love it if you could help me complete the illustrations for this manuscript," he said. "My skill as an artist is not very good. You would be able to do a beautiful job of illustrating these stories."

She was thrilled with Brendan's trust in her ability. And pleased that he understood her thirst for learning. From that moment, she knew their relationship would have a deeper connection as they explored new learning, and worked as partners to complete the beautiful manuscript Brendan had started.

T'Eilin proved to be an astute student, grasping the concepts of the written word. Painting on parchment was easy for her. In less than a month, the parchment manuscript was completed, including beautiful illustrations by T'Eilin. The figures were perfect in form. She had used the Irie women as models, and looked at her own reflection in a pond. She often added the blue crescent mark of mastery on the neck of a painted woman for sheer amusement.

By the autumn period, Brendan wrapped the completed parchments to send with two fellow monks traveling back to their monastery. Brendan told T'Eilin how proud he was of the part she played in bringing the collection of manuscripts to life.

T'Eilin and Brendan grew closer. Their daily routine of tending to the sick and teaching the people new methods of living brought them together for most of each day. There were many opportunities to exchange smiles and covert glances. T'Eilin never tired of watching Brendan tend to the sick elderly or young ones. He was so patient and caring of her people, it made her heart swell with appreciation.

T'Eilin was aware of how Brendan likewise watched her. He seemed delighted when she helped the people understand a complex topic by giving examples they could easily understand. She was supportive of his work, and that made him happy.

Gradually, they came to realize their contentment and how their feelings impacted the people for the better. Bit by bit, their resistance subsided, until one day they decided it was time to reinforce their love with a completion ceremony, the ceremony which bonded partners together for life.

The autumn solstice was nearly upon them when T'Eilin and Brendan requested a completion ceremony. T'Eilin was surprised by her grandmother's response.

"Well, it took you long enough," said the Healing Mother.

Preparations were made for the completion ceremony to be held fourteen nights hence, the night after the autumn equinox. The first mating, which according to Irie tradition took place on the night before the completion ceremony, would therefore occur on the auspicious night of the autumn equinox. The night of the autumn equinox held great powers of rejuvenation and replenishment for humanity and for the earth.

That two-week period before the autumn equinox was a special time set aside for reflection. During that time, T'Eilin contemplated her commitments to her people, as well as to her chosen life partner.

The evening of the completion ceremony was crisp and clear. A rising moon cast a cool white glow over the village. The earthen circle outside the healing hut was festooned with pine branches and a warming fire.

The people were excited that their beloved intuitive and healer was declaring her love for Brendan, whom they had come to respect. They anticipated this completion ceremony would be the start of great prosperity for the tribe. At the beginning of the ceremony, the Healing Mother would confirm the first mating consummated the previous evening, always a point of fun for those gathered to witness the completion ceremony.

During their first mating on the night before the completion ceremony, T'Eilin had been shy. She had appreciated the gentleness Brendan had shown her. It had not taken her very long to relax and to enjoy their union that evening, many times over.

T'Eilin was happy to see the people's smiling faces as she approached the circle for the completion ceremony. Coming further into the light of the fire, her footsteps faltered. Like a physical blow, she felt an evil presence. She looked in the direction of the hills to see if she could tell what caused it. She sensed that Tonnick had returned.

When she looked back towards the fire, Brendan beckoned her forward to stand beside him. His eyes reassured her.

The completion ceremony proceeded without interruption. T'Eilin relaxed at Brendan's side, holding his hand and smiling while Naghaire performed the ceremony.

Her face transformed into a mask of concern at the sound of yelling voices and thundering horse's hoofs coming towards them. She knew Tonnick had come to wreak his revenge. The scene around the fire became one of chaos and madness as the Irie people fled to safety, warriors took up defense of the people, and invaders yelled their war cries. Brendan shielded her with his body.

Above the bedlam, T'Eilin heard Tonnick screaming his demands. "Monk, hand over that whore witch T'Eilin or I will kill every man, woman, and child."

T'Eilin soon understood that Tonnick had consorted with Norse warriors to invade in a surprise attack. Shocked that Tonnick would destroy his own people to wreak vengeance on her, T'Eilin thought to sacrifice herself to save her people.

She made a move to go towards Tonnick, but Brendan stopped her.

"No, T'Eilin," he said. "Giving yourself to him would not stop Tonnick from completing what he has started here. Save yourself, in order that you might save your people."

Sure enough, T'Eilin looked around them and saw the Norse invaders well entrenched, fighting everyone in their path. T'Eilin realized the only thing she could do for her people was to save herself. She thought to run to the standing stones and ask the ancestors for assistance, but before she fled, she made Brendan promise that he would follow.

"Yes, I will fight Tonnick and come as soon as I can," he said. "You can hear that our warriors are fighting back, so all will be well."

T'Eilin turned to escape to the standing stones while Brendan fended off Tonnick. She would find refuge with the ancestors, and beseech them on behalf of her people.

As she ran into the darkness, she heard Tonnick screaming at her from the far side of the circle near the healing hut, unable to get to her as Brendan battled with him.

"T'Eilin, I curse you and your descendants," he yelled at her retreating figure. "Because you denied me love when you took up with a foreigner, I never knew a woman's love. Because your grandmother killed my mother, I never knew a mother's love. Your female descendants likewise will not know true love."

T'Eilin arrived at the standing stones, awash with exhaustion and fear. She tried to focus but thoughts of her people and of Brendan in danger overwhelmed her. If it hadn't been for her desire to be with Brendan, her people would still be safe.

An intuitive knowing that she and Brendan had conceived a child last night at their first mating pushed through her worry, and she knew the child would be a female. The thought did not bring her joy; rather it added to her remorse and feelings of selfishness. Tonnick's words rang in her ears. He had cursed her female descendants to never know true love.

T'Eilin cried aloud in great anguish. "No – I will not let him take away my power."

She felt great pain to think she was the cause of the curse, and threw herself on the ground to weep.

As T'Eilin lay in the middle of the standing stones, she heard her grandmother's voice speaking, "Do not forget who you are. Open your heart, be in the place of love where all creation happens. The illusion of time and space stops when you are in the place of love. All illusion of separateness stops. Then you can connect with the energy that creates life. Then you can do the work to be free. Do the work for yourself, do the work for your descendants ahead of you, and for your ancestors behind."

T'Eilin lifted her head to the heavens and vowed out loud, with the standing stones as witness. "I hear you, Grandmother. I will work in this life, and in the next life, and as many generations and lifetimes as it would take, to break this curse."

T'Eilin slipped into a deep trance. Her grandmother's voice whispered into the wind, "Find the one who is marked. She will do the work. She will set you free."

CHAPTER THIRTEEN

ISLE OF MULL, SCOTLAND, 1987

Glenna sat at Fleur's side. Her grandniece slept in peace for the first time in two days. Glenna was thankful the fever broke after the first night, but she witnessed a battle waging within Fleur. She had been restless, fending off the high fever as well as what she wrestled with in her dreams.

Glenna had called her half-sister, Eileen, in Canada when Fleur had come home from the standing stones. It had been a bittersweet conversation, as it was the first time Glenna had spoken to Eileen since finding out that she had a half-sister. Eileen hadn't been worried. She knew Fleur would pull through. Today Glenna called her back with the good news that Fleur was feeling much better, and would call in a few days when she felt up to it.

The curtains fluttered as a breeze wafted through the opened shutters. Outside, the morning was turning into midday, though the sun was still weak. Fingers of light filtered through the slates, casting shadows across the flowered comforter covering Fleur. She opened her eyes and looked around. Fleur rustled the covers and tried to raise herself on her elbow.

Glenna let Fleur know where she was. Her grandniece started to speak, but her voice was weak, and Glenna had to lean in to make out her words.

"Auntie G. I can't remember how I got here in bed," she said, wincing in pain. "Did I have an accident?"

Glenna smoothed Fleur's hair. "You've been sleeping off a fever these past two days."

Fleur was shocked at how long she had been in bed. "Two days! I don't remember anything." Glenna could see by Fleur's furrowed brow that a memory surfaced. "Did Thomas bring me home?" Fleur reached to touch her neck, and found her birthmark was covered by a bandage.

Glenna noted the involuntary movement and said, "Yes, you do have a bit of plaster on your neck, dearie. It was bleeding when you arrived home. The doctor couldn't figure out what happened, so he thought it best to protect it, in case you bothered it whilst you slept off the fever. Do you want to talk about what you remember?"

"It was like the first time when I found the standing stones," said Fleur. "I saw things, a vision or a dream. This time the vision was terrible. People were running and screaming." Tears formed in Fleur's eyes as she continued, "Men on horses killed people as they stood around a fire enjoying a ceremony. I didn't want to look, but it was as though I was there and couldn't help but witness it all. I even said things out loud that I didn't understand."

Fleur seemed to calm herself, and then she turned to Glenna and asked, "Have you ever been seen the circle of standing stones at the top of the hill, Auntie G.? Have you or anyone you know experienced visions there?"

Glenna's slight hesitation prompted Fleur to explain further. "You started to talk about this last week," she said. "We were interrupted, and never finished the conversation. Do you know about them?"

Glenna knew she was about to disappoint her grandniece. "I'm afraid not, dearie, I've never seen the standing stones myself," she said. "But I know they exist, and that they hold power for those who have the gift of being able to see them."

Glenna pondered how much she should share with Fleur, given the girl's current fragile state. "The standing stones reveal themselves to certain people at certain times," she said. "It is a wonder that you found them both times you approached the hill. I believe that is indeed significant."

Glenna recalled the stories passed down through the generations of her family. "Your own great-great-grandmother Fiona Kintrell had consistent commune with the standing stones over many years." Glenna saw this seemed to console Fleur, and make the experience seem normal. It reminded Glenna that Fleur was special, having apparently been chosen by the stones. She was intrigued that Fleur and Thomas both found the stones when she had a traumatic vision. She considered it must have been destined.

"Dearie, I accept everything as a gift, even when it doesn't appear to be a gift," said Glenna. "Like this experience. It is your gift. How marvelous, to be guided to the circle of ancient standing stones not once, but twice, and even to see visions. There is great meaning here." Glenna knew she needed to address Thomas in the scenario, and added, "Even the fact that Thomas was guided to the stones at the same time, there is a reason for that too." Fleur appeared comforted by her words, and Glenna waited for the girl to formulate her thoughts.

"Auntie G., there is something I had wanted to discuss with you after the first time I found the standing stones, but we never had the chance," she said. "At that time, you talked to me about the intuitives and the healers in our line of women. I wanted to tell you that this wasn't the first time I've had visions."

Glenna listened while Fleur told her of the recurring dreams about a tall, blonde tribal woman who looked like herself. She recounted how the Native Indian woman, Dante, came to her in a vision and said words that her own grandmother later recited upon concluding the true story of her birthplace.

"Now with all that's happened here, the same blonde woman from my dream appearing to me in visions at the stones, I know this must be connected," Fleur concluded.

Glenna was not surprised. She had her suspicions about why Fleur had arrived here on Mull. Glenna paused before she responded, careful not to prejudice her grandniece's journey. "There is no doubt in my mind you are on a path of discovery. The experiences are indeed linked to that path. I don't have the answers, for the work is different for every one of us."

Glenna saw Fleur's eyes fluttering and brought the discussion to a halt. "Dearie, it's past time for you to have a bite to eat and rest some more," she said.

Before Glenna left, her grandniece thanked her. "I'm grateful you stayed with me," she said. "Especially since Matty isn't back from being with John. It must have been a comfort for you to have Thomas downstairs, although I'm glad you suggested it wouldn't be a good idea for him to see me."

Glenna patted Fleur's hand in acknowledgment before she left the bedroom, trying hard not to show her surprise that Fleur knew all of that information. Glenna had not told her about Thomas waiting downstairs while she was ill. Neither did she tell Fleur that Matty was still away with John. Glenna had her suspicions that Fleur was in possession of great powers of intuition. Now she was convinced.

Fleur's physical stamina returned day-by-day, thanks to Auntie G. coaxing her to eat and rest. Before long, she was making short forays out in the garden, though she wouldn't go further. Emotionally, however, Fleur knew she wasn't doing as well. The events at the standing stones weighed on her mind, and she spent a lot of time mulling the vision she had seen.

Fleur was in a listless state in the garden when Matty arrived home. Rushing to Fleur's side, Matty exclaimed, "Boo, why are you looking pale as a virgin goat!" Matty inhaled and continued. "I leave you for two seconds, and you go and get sick. How'd that happen?"

Fleur smiled at her friend, tears streaming down her cheeks. Her suppressed emotions surfaced, and she wept with full shudders upon seeing her friend.

She was glad her friend knew how to handle the situation. Matty's joking did the trick. "I can't help it if John Hayden is such a hunk that the picnic turned out to be a full BBQ, meat and all," she said. "I should be the one crying about all the wasted years."

Matty leaned over to give Fleur a hug and said, "I know you are feeling low. Just let me know if you want to talk about it now, or later when you're more rested."

Fleur smiled; it was wonderful to have Matty back. "I think it will do me good to talk," she said. "But let me hear about your adventure first. Where did you go for five days, with John Hayden of all people?"

Matty smirked, aware of Fleur's procrastination. "Oh no you don't – that can keep," she said, for once not rushing into her story. "First, you tell me what happened. Auntie G. told me a bit, but I want to hear it straight from the camel's mouth. What's this talk about some visionary gripping your mind? "

Fleur loved to hear Matty's jumbled metaphors. She started by telling Matty about finding the circle of standing stones that first day, when Matty had noticed that her birthmark had been bleeding. When she described the most recent episode, she started to shake.

"It was so real," she said in a whisper. "I smelled the fear and the blood, and heard every slice of the blade through the people's skin. I can't get the horror of it out of my mind. I was there, Matty. I wasn't just observing. I was T'Eilin, and I felt her pain at the slaughter of her people. She blames herself, and she wants me to help her somehow."

Fleur stopped talking, overcome by emotion. It occurred to her that she must be scaring Matty, because her friend sat stunned, not uttering a word. She took a calming breath and continued her story.

"I must have come out of a trance a few times," she said. "That's when I noticed that Thomas was there. At least, I thought it was Thomas. I got confused and called him Brendan."

Matty breathed in. "Is T'Eilin the blonde tribal woman from your dreams? How do you know her name?"

Fleur remembered the beginning of her vision, before the fighting. "Before the invaders came, there was a beautiful ceremony, like a wedding. The woman was T'Eilin – the blonde woman of my dreams. The man, oh my goodness, the man's name is Brendan."

Later that afternoon, enjoying a cup of tea and homemade scones with Matty and Auntie G., Fleur struggled to make sense of the situation, of the experiences she had at the standing stones.

Auntie G. wanted to put her mind at ease, "Don't fret, dearie, I believe this was meant to happen so that you could resolve why you are here in Mull, and why you had those dreams."

Matty was curious to know how Thomas was involved, and asked the question that was at the top of her mind. "Auntie G., you said Thomas brought Fleur home unconscious. How do we know Fleur's condition isn't his fault?"

Fleur hadn't thought of foul play, and anticipated Auntie G.'s opinion.

"Based on his high state of agitation, I couldn't imagine he had harmed her," she replied. "Thomas was truly upset. Besides, his explanation was exactly the same as Fleur's when she woke up. Also, Thomas didn't leave the house the entire time Fleur was unconscious."

Fleur felt warm. "He's very polite, isn't he?" she whispered.

Matty shook her head, turned to her friend, and said, "I'd say he has feelings for you."

Fleur didn't want to entertain that notion, and stayed silent when Auntie G. explained further. "When he knew you were awake, he wanted to talk with you," she said. "But I wouldn't let him. I didn't know how you would react. He told me he needed to explain what had happened a while ago, and to apologize. I told him there would be enough time later. Now then, I'm going to do some gardening."

Matty gave Fleur a knowing look and said, "You'd better tell Auntie G. how you met Thomas in Antigonish. Then what he said to Auntie G. will make sense to her. It makes sense to me. Like I said, he has feelings for you."

Fleur didn't come down for breakfast the next morning. She didn't have the energy. The dreams were draining her.

Auntie G. came into her bedroom and found her huddled under blankets. "Dearie, you're making this more difficult than it needs be," she said. "Your life is mirroring your inner world, and you are living at the effect of your thinking. Fear and anxiety bring hopelessness. As within, so without."

Fluffing up Fleur's comforter that had fallen on the floor, Auntie G. continued to encourage her.

"You asked me if I knew what the work might be? I'll tell you," she said. "The work is about adjusting your energy to allow the universe to flow the best to you so you can realize your dreams."

Auntie G.'s words got through the fog of Fleur's brain, and she got out of bed with more energy than she'd had in the last few days. "You're right," said Fleur. "Grana taught me that miracles come from the heart, not from the mind. It's time I stopped overthinking this."

Matty peeked into the bedroom as Fleur was getting dressed. "I'm glad to see you aren't going to mope like a cow about to birth a moose anymore. Auntie G. is right. What are you doing with all of that contemplating anyway?"

Fleur grinned at Matty. "You have a point," she said. "Somehow I'm going to find out what T'Eilin wants. Meanwhile, I'm getting on with my life. What are you doing today, Matty, going for another picnic?"

"Yep, something like that," grinned Matty.

Matty proceeded to tell Fleur about her trip to the mainland with John. "He took me to Dublin," she said. "When we arrived, we had dinner at John's restaurant. It's an awesome place, and the food was amazing. Dublin is lively, lots of restaurants and pubs, and everywhere there's music. Oh, and I saw a picture of you."

Fleur frowned and asked for clarification. "John had to go to the university to pick something up for Thomas, and I was waiting for him to finish," said Matty. "This book on display showed a painted lady that looked familiar. The woman looked just like you, complete with a blue crescent mark on her neck."

"What book?" asked Fleur, a sudden twinge in her gut.

Matty told her it was the Book of Kells, and Fleur made a mental note to research it.

Matty's comment about the lady in the painting had to be a clue, but for now Fleur would spend the day in the conservatory to face her irrational fear of painting again.

The first time Fleur stood in this room, she'd been afraid to do anything. Now, she was determined to paint.

The familiar smells of the art studio excited her, and the natural light that streamed in through the windows was a treat. She positioned a chair in several places to become familiar with the nuances of the light in the conservatory. Her excitement mounted at the prospect of working in this exquisite environment.

As she was pulling out supplies, intuition told her to search the back of the cupboard. When she reached inside, her hand brushed against a latch. Leaning forward to see better, Fleur found a false backing that the latch released. Pulling her hand through the hidden space, she drew out a leather book. With trembling hands, Fleur examined the book. She knew it must be her great-great-grandmother's diary.

Her heart thumped. Just a few short weeks ago, she didn't even know she had family beyond her Grana. The prospect of reading about her ancestry through the eyes of her great-great-grandmother was remarkable.

CHAPTER FOURTEEN

Fleur read the diary well past midnight. Once she had gotten used to the penmanship and the oddity of speech, she devoured much of the earlier writing in no time.

She discovered that her great-great-grandmother had started to chronicle her life during her teen years. Even then, the young girl's words indicated passion to capture the suffering and joy of the human spirit on canvas.

Fiona had been the only daughter of the Factor. Her father's relationship with the Laird had been respectful, and when the Laird saw his daughter's talent for painting, he became her mentor. The Laird had built the conservatory for Fiona, and employed a tutor for her from the village.

Fleur learned about the tough and grueling life the crofters lived as they sought sustenance from the land. She also learned Fiona's father and mother had cared for the crofters under their responsibility, and Fiona learned compassion from their many examples of helping people. The most exciting part of the diary was a reference to what Fleur interpreted to be the circle of standing stones at the top of the hill. Though there was no specific mention of the stones, Fiona had written about a higher consciousness or an energetic higher power she called Lliam. Fiona had found guidance for her life's questions while at that location.

Sometime after midnight, her eyes could no longer focus on the small handwriting in the diary. Fleur went to the kitchen for a glass of water before going to bed. On the counter she saw an envelope with her name on it. Fleur's heart sank to see the return address. It was from the Hayden brothers' solicitors.

She read the letter several times. It referenced the historical relevance of the estate and the implication it would have to the case. She recalled that Matty had talked about the estate having ties with Bonnie Prince Charles. The letter stated that this historical relevance favored the Hayden brothers.

Fleur was livid. Her next thoughts were about Thomas. He appeared to be sympathetic at the standing stones, but was his intention to fool her? Thoughts of deceit and falsehood would haunt her all night.

The next morning, Fleur was still angry when she came down for breakfast. Matty and Auntie G. noticed Fleur's ill humor right away.

"You have monster black shadows under your eyes," said Matty with concern. "Couldn't be because of the Hayden brothers, they haven't been around. John's away on a business trip. I can't wait to give him his 'welcome home' treat."

"Actually, it *is* about the Hayden brothers," said Fleur. "That letter left on the counter for me, it was from their solicitors pressuring me to back down. Apparently, the property has enough historical significance that they could win the case." Fleur was distraught, "Matty, can't you see that John is using you?"

Fleur thought that Thomas had used *her*, that he had let her down somehow.

Auntie G. got up from her chair, stood behind Fleur, and enveloped her in a great big hug. "Now dearie, take three deep breaths and listen to the emotions arising. They are telling you that you are believing a non-truth."

Her grandaunt let go and stood in front of her. "Let's dig a bit to find out what is going really on," she said. "There is something bigger at play here."

Fleur nodded her head, but the frown on her face said otherwise. "Yes, Auntie G., please help me understand what's going on. I want to feel like myself again, to remember who I am."

Auntie G. smiled. "That has been your struggle for a long time, but you haven't been aware of it." The last words were murmured, almost in a whisper.

"Let's start with the offending letter. May I take a look?" asked Auntie G. as she picked up the envelope. "Ah, well then, there you go. This letter is postmarked well before you met John and Thomas here."

Opening the envelope, she perused the contents and pointed out where Fleur had misinterpreted the message. Fleur read the last paragraph, then uttered a sound of disbelief. "How could I have read this so wrong last night?"

Matty, who had been sitting without saying a word for once, took the letter and read the last paragraph out loud. "'In conclusion, as the evidence is irrefutable regarding your rights to said property, and notwithstanding clause XXv1F35 of the Historical Properties Act, we propose the above treatment to grant you surety regarding the Factor's House. Please contact us to advise your agreement with said.'"

Without waiting for Fleur to reply, Matty grabbed her friend and twirled her around in a jig. "Whoopee! This is a happy day." Fleur couldn't help being swept up by Matty's exuberance.

"Tis fine news indeed, Fleur. Don't worry yourself about how you missed that last paragraph. These things are what they are," said Auntie G., intuiting Fleur's thoughts. "Let's get back to what's troubling you. Let's see if we can find out what's behind your anger against the Hayden brothers."

Fleur decided she needed to tell Auntie G. everything about Thomas. "You're right, Auntie G., there is something else going on," said Fleur. "This isn't the first time I've met Thomas. We met in Antigonish about eight months ago. It was like we've always know each other." She had felt that same strong connection with Thomas at the standing stones.

"Yes, dearie, sometimes when we meet someone it feels like destiny, like we are supposed to meet them. What happened to cause you heartache?"

"I'm not sure why, but he bolted," said Fleur. "He left, never called me, never made any contact until I met him again in your kitchen."

Auntie G. remarked, "Ah, that's it then, why Thomas wanted so desperately to talk with you, to explain something, he said. He left after he knew you were well, saying he had to go to Dublin to do some research, and that he'd talk with you when he found the answer."

"Great, can I get back to having fun with my John, now that the Hayden brothers aren't such an evil lot after all?" asked Matty with a twinkle in her eye.

Fleur laughed. "Ah Matty, sorry I gave you a hard time about John. I'm pleased that you are enjoying each other's company."

"Right, now that's sorted, I'm off to the salon, dearies," said Auntie G. "Fleur, remember what I said, get out of your head, stop pausing your life, and take action. Oh, and don't forget to telephone your Grana, she's expecting to hear from you."

After Auntie G. left, the friends went out for a short walk to enjoy the fresh morning air. They were both surprised by Auntie G.'s abrupt departure. Matty said in a stage whisper, "Do you think my sexual innuendo-ing has sent poor Auntie G. to drink?"

Fleur looked at her friend for a moment, then grinned as she realized Matty had mixed up that word again. "No Matty," she said. "Auntie G. is going to get her hair cut. Salon, not saloon!"

Matty's lopsided grin was endearing. "I keep getting that word confused," she said. "Now that we're alone, what were you doing in that painting room all night? Did you actually paint?"

Fleur expected the question, but first commented on something she just remembered. "I wanted to tell Auntie G. what happened yesterday in the conservatory," she said, clicking her fingers together.

She shook her head and answered Matty's questions. "I'm getting close to painting. I was inspired by the way the daylight filters into the room. But when I looked for supplies in the cupboard, I found a leather notebook hidden in a secret drawer. It's Fiona Kintrell's diary."

Bending down, Fleur fingered the new blossoms on the rose bushes; the fragrance was intoxicating. She looked up to see Matty wide-eyed and speechless.

"I know, right. I couldn't believe it. Her hopes and dreams, her memories written in a notebook," said Fleur. "At first, I didn't feel comfortable reading her private thoughts. But I got over that, and I've been reading it nonstop. I'm finding out about my family. All the history about the Castle Dowart Estate and the Factor's House. It's incredible."

Leading the way to the chairs at the side of the house, Fleur sat down anticipating a ream of questions from Matty about the details in the diary. But she didn't expect the one question that Matty asked.

"Did the diary tell you what work you're supposed to do for your ancestors, like it said in the prophecy?" asked Matty.

She blinked twice before answering her friend. "Can you not use the word prophecy," she said. "I'll admit, it was spooky that Grana spoke the exact same words Dante said to me. It did kind of sound like a prophecy. But I don't like the idea of not having control of my own destiny." Fleur took a breath and continued in a calmer voice. "But to answer your question, I think the diary has clues about the standing stones at least. There may be a connection. Fiona doesn't use the words standing stones, but she writes about a place of energy where she contemplates and seeks to resolve questions about her life. That sounds like the energy that I felt in the circle of stones, like a healing energy."

Sitting in the sunshine was relaxing. Fleur suggested she get them both more coffee to enjoy outside. Matty got up from her seat with a wave, "I'll get it."

When her friend returned, Fleur was quite comfortable, enjoying the glow of the sun shining on greenery and flowers. She wanted a change of conversation, away from her issues. "I've been so wrapped up in my stuff, I haven't even asked you how things are going with you," she said.

It was the perfect thing to say. "Girlie, I'm falling off my red stilettos for John," said Matty.

Fleur smirked. She knew what Matty meant by her confused metaphor, but it would amuse her to hear her friend's explanation for this one. "Do you mean you have fallen head over heels in love with John?"

Matty's brimming smile said it all. "Oh, yes indeed. I've fallen off my highest heels, which of course are my red stilettos. For once it has nothing to do with my head. It's all in my heart! I've never felt like this before."

Fleur tried to keep incredulity out of her voice, "That happened kind of sudden, didn't it?"

She banished the thought when she saw how happy her friend was. "Ah, Matty, I'm pleased. Is it real? I don't want John to be taking advantage of you."

Matty hugged her friend. "That's sweet. Yes, it's real," she said. "I feel like I can be myself. We spend every minute together talking. I mean we both talk. It's a toss-up who can yak the most!"

Fleur chuckled. Having met John only briefly, she could imagine that he could give Matty competition when it came to chatter.

"Has he been in contact with you since leaving for Dublin?" asked Fleur. "Do you know how he feels about you?"

This made her friend flush uncharacteristically. "Don't you worry about that," smirked Matty. "John has plenty of feelings for me. He calls three or four times a day."

"What happens next?" asked Fleur. "You know you'll be going home in a couple of weeks."

Matty hesitated. "I may be going home earlier."

Fleur lifted an eyebrow in question, which prompted Matty to explain further, "You see, John is coming back from Dublin in a couple of days, and we're making plans. He wants me to help him rebuild the estate, to help make it a travel destination. I'm so glad the inheritance thing worked out, because I would have felt awful, like a traitor if it hadn't. Anyway, I'm going home earlier to sort things out, and then coming back here to be with John."

That last statement was a shocker. How could she have been so out of touch not to see Matty's relationship with John had gotten that far?

"Don't worry," said Matty. "This is a very good thing for me. You might even still be here when I come back, you never know."

Maybe she would still be here at the Factor's House, though Fleur wasn't sure what she would decide to do yet.

"I'm going to the village to find a cute welcome home outfit for John," said Matty. "Something with satin. Then I'm going to surprise him at the ferry terminal. He's coming on the early afternoon ferry. Want to come for the drive?"

Fleur declined. "No thank you, Matty," she said. "I'm going to telephone Grana, and then I might be able to get through the rest of the diary today. May even turn my hand to a bit of painting."

Fleur could hear the absolute relief in Grana's voice to hear from her. Though Glenna advised her grandmother she was on the mend, Fleur knew that her Grana wouldn't be satisfied until she heard from Fleur directly.

Fleur told her grandmother what had happened at the standing stones, just as she had explained it to Auntie G. Fleur sensed her Grana nodding in consideration as she spoke.

"Yes, I also believe your vision has something to do with the woman calling you, and maybe even with the curse," said her Grana. "Please ground yourself before you go to that place again. It has a tremendous influence over you. It sounds as though your Auntie G. doesn't know too much about the stones."

"I asked her, and she thinks that great-great-grandmother Fiona may have had interaction with the stones."

Fleur told her grandmother about finding Fiona Kintrell's diary. "It's like she is speaking directly to me, giving me advice," she said. "There are quite a few times when she mentions something or someone called Lliam. I believe it was the energy at the standing stones speaking to her and guiding her."

Hearing a soft inhale from her Grana, Fleur deduced she knew the name. "Grana, you've heard this name before, haven't you?"

"You found my grandmother's diary, how marvelous, I'm very happy for you," said Grana. "That is indeed a special gift. Yes, I have heard the name Lliam. My grandmother mentioned the name a few times. I had believed that it was a friend of hers. Now it makes sense. It must have been a higher consciousness guiding her, likely at its strongest when she approached the standing stones."

Her grandmother didn't like to spend a lot of time on the telephone, so she closed the conversation. "Well dearie, take care of yourself. All will become clear soon."

After her call, Fleur took her great-great-grandmother's diary outside. She made herself comfortable on the wooden bench at the front garden. Three plump black sheep that her Auntie G. called the Three Sisters chewed away at the hedgerow in front of Fleur. She settled down to read, excited that she was coming to the conclusion of the diary. The writing was not as legible in the last chapters, as though Fiona were rushed when she wrote.

Fleur deciphered that last entry in the diary. *I sometimes feel as though I have failed Lliam in the work to clear the ancestry, because I must leave this land. I must follow another call that I cannot ignore. I'm to embark on another journey of self-sacrifice, like generations of my line before me, taking my sweet infant granddaughter away from the land I love so that she can be out of harm's way.*

I trust Lliam, that this is the work I'm to do, though it breaks my heart to leave my family and this land. My heart remains open to possibilities and miracles. My energy is aligned. There is no split energy in my heart. I trust this action will lead eventually to the one who will do the work, and maybe it is my work to go to another land to start the process. One of us will clear what needs to be cleared. If it is not to be me, another will come behind me to do the work that will set our ancestry free. She will bear the mark of our ancestry, that is as foretold. She will find the key for if it is meant to be, all will be revealed to her.

Fleur puzzled about those words, and concluded that the reference to the work and to split energy was of significance to her own journey. She was more certain than ever that she had been called. Her job was to trust that all would become clear in time, just as her Grana said.

While she was disappointed her great-great-grandmother didn't tell her what to do, reading the words handed down from the past gave her a feeling of solidarity and connection. Directing those positive thoughts into her heart deliberately, Fleur fell asleep in the glorious sunshine.

Upon his return from Dublin, Thomas made his way to the Factor's House as soon as he could. He had information from his research he wanted to share with Fleur, if he could find a way to get her to listen. It would explain his actions in Antigonish, and might help Fleur to understand what she experienced at the standing stones. It was dawning on Thomas that he was drawn to Fleur. Perhaps it was because he had seen her so vulnerable at the circle of standing stones. He needed a bit more time to explore his growing feelings for her.

Walking up to the front door, Thomas saw Fleur asleep on the bench beside the wisteria. He didn't want to disturb her slumber, but she was sliding into an awkward angle, and it looked as though she were about to fall off the bench. Ever so gently, Thomas shook Fleur's arm and whispered her name.

Fleur opened her eyes and smiled at him as she had at the standing stone, and spoke in a gentle voice. "Brendan, you are back. All is well," she said.

Thomas felt his heart squeeze at her soft words and demeanor, which changed when she realized who was shaking her awake. She leaped from the bench and dropped the book resting on her lap. "Easy, there, Fleur," coaxed Thomas. "I didn't mean to startle you."

He continued, "I need to explain about our first meeting in Antigonish, and my reactions since meeting you here. It's all tied into why I went to Dublin. I have something to show you that may help you understand." Thomas held out an old book as he spoke the last words.

"Thomas, I don't want to talk right now," said Fleur. "But I'll take a look." Fleur took the book he offered without looking him in the eye. Thomas raised an eyebrow, watching her as she turned her back to him and went inside the house. No doubt she was embarrassed at calling him Brendan yet again.

Shaking his head, Thomas wondered if she would look at the book. He knew that if she did, she would want to find out more details.

CHAPTER FIFTEEN

Fleur was in the library, out of sorts with herself for running away from Thomas yet again. She felt nervous and paced the room before coming to a standstill in front of the expanse of bay windows. Fleur stood there deep in thought, unknowingly creating a beautiful gilded picture as she was framed by the golden light of the sun. She heard the slight intake of breath from behind her, and turned around to see Thomas gazing at her with a distant look in his eyes.

Thomas raised his hand and extended the book that was in his hand. "You dropped this," he said, handing her the notebook she had been reading outside. "It looked important." From his manner, it was apparent that Thomas knew Fleur was sensitive about him. Boldly he continued, "I couldn't help noticing that this looks like a diary. Was it written by someone in your family?"

Turning the notebook in her hand, Fleur answered Thomas. "Yes, this is my great-great-grandmother Fiona Kintrell's diary."

Fleur was secretly delighted that Thomas had come after her. She made up her mind in the moment that enough was enough. She was going to start over with Thomas. Perhaps that was what her Grana, her Auntie G., and even her great-great-grandmother meant when they talked about "opening your heart."

Fleur smiled, swallowing the nerves threatening to engulf her. "Thomas, I'm glad you came in," she said. "I don't know what's the matter with me. I'm not usually so rude. It would appear every time our paths cross lately, something in me snaps and I can't help myself. Please accept my apology. I'm quite embarrassed by my behavior."

Thomas appeared surprised and happy to hear Fleur verbalize her feelings. "None of this makes sense," she said. "I'd appreciate hearing your perspective about the incident at the standing stones."

As Thomas stepped towards her, Fleur's skin tingled. She noticed that Thomas held his hands by his side, as if he didn't trust himself not to reach out and touch her. "Please don't apologize," he said. "I'm as much to blame.

My behavior in Antigonish needs explanation. I know it must have confused you. We were having such a great time, and I ran out on you without a word."

"It's what I have most wanted to talk to you about since I saw you in Auntie G.'s kitchen," he said. "But there never seemed to be a good opportunity to be alone with you. Would you mind if we talked about it now?"

To hide her fluttering heart, Fleur motioned to the chairs nearest the bay windows, "Please, have a seat."

"Let's talk about Antigonish first. I think it will give a bit of background to all of the rest," he said. "I want you to know that I enjoyed our short time together at the Thirsty Duck, wasn't that the name?"

"Yes, that's correct, best pub in town," she said. "You have good recall."

Thomas smiled at the memory. "I remember how lovely you looked in a kelly-green cardigan and black jodhpurs," he said, exaggerating his Irish accent. "I'm rather partial to kelly-green, being from the Emerald Isle myself."

Thomas' grin and lilting accent when he said the words "Emerald Isle" caused Fleur's stomach to flutter. She was impressed that Thomas remembered what she was wearing. She could still close her eyes and picture Thomas, looking a bit disheveled in his tan blazer with the leather patches on the elbows and his hair blown across his forehead. It had given him a boyish look that Fleur found appealing.

There was nothing boyish about the intensity of Thomas' navy-blue eyes as he stared at Fleur with a longing that her intuition said was partly wanting her to forgive him and partly lustful thoughts of desire. She blushed seeing his gaze, cleared her throat, and moved the pillow that was in between them aside, a telling sign of her unconscious desire to be nearer to him.

"I guess as a historical architect you would need to have a good memory," she said.

Thomas adjusted his collar, looking like he needed more air. "Yes, a good memory does help in my field," he said. "Sitting across from you at the pub, I wondered what it would be like to get to know you better. But then, at the exact moment, you flipped your hair back and I glimpsed the mark on your neck. It's hard to explain, but seeing the symbol on your neck upset me."

Fleur's suspicions had been right. "I wondered if that was the reason," she said. "Were you grossed out by my birthmark?"

Thomas shook his head. "Not at all," he said. "I thought it was a tattoo."

Fleur didn't see what difference that should make. Tattoo or a birthmark, his reaction was still very odd.

"Let me try to explain," said Thomas, seeing her puzzled look. "I've been researching the Dowart Estate history for many years. My goal is to restore the place to its original state. I researched every historical document I could find, hoping to piece together the full context of the entire history of the region and the people associated with the estate."

Fleur saw Thomas glance at the diary he retrieved, which was now resting on the coffee table. She imagined it would be very exciting for Thomas to read the diary, as it might provide him with a wealth of information on the estate from a first-hand account.

"Years ago I had discovered an image of a beautiful woman from the Middle Ages. There is something odd about how the woman is painted. Her clothing and hair are correct for that period of time. Her facial features, however, do not match those of women painted similarly for that era."

Fleur focused on what Thomas was saying. The mention of a painting grabbed her attention. "Where was this painting of the woman located, and who is she supposed to be?" she asked.

"Have you heard of the Book of Kells?" asked Thomas. "It's a biblical book from the Middle Ages, said to have been created by the monks of St. Columba, who founded an abbey in AD 563 in Iona, a sacred island not far from here, from which the Christian conversion of the earlier Scots tribes started.

"The Book of Kells is housed at Trinity College in Dublin," said Thomas. "It is kept safe in the library's vaults, but a few pages are displayed under glass, which is how I came to know it so well. The library has replica copies that can be studied. The Book contains the four Gospels of the New Testament. The illustrations and ornamentation of the section that is on display far surpass any other illustrated Gospel books in terms of extravagance and complexity."

Fleur was captivated with Thomas' descriptions of the illustrations in the book. "It sounds amazing," she said. She held her breath, wondering if Thomas might also say what Matty said, that the image looked like her.

"Yes, there is something odd about the blonde woman in the Book of Kells," said Thomas. "Her attitude makes her stand out, as do her looks. She shows strength, wisdom, and an otherworldliness, unlike other women of that period.

"Not only that, but she has been depicted with a mark behind her ear," said Thomas and paused for effect. "Can you guess what the mark is? A blue crescent moon, exactly like yours."

Fleur was confused. Thomas didn't say the image looked like her, but he did say that it had a tattoo behind her ear. "So why would that make you run out of the Thirsty Duck like it was on fire?"

Thomas chuckled and raised his hands in surrender. "Yes, I see what you mean. Let me try to be clearer," he said. "I developed a theory from my years of research. I think the blonde woman depicted in the Book of Kells, Chapter XXIV, Section III, is a woman of the Scots tribes, not a lady from the high court of the Middle Ages. Perhaps she had even been a Pict, because of the tattoo. We know that Picts had inhabited these Hebrides during that time frame."

Fleur was fascinated to hear Thomas speak about that era. "Are there examples of what Pict women looked like?"

"Not really, it's more by process of elimination of what Scots women of the time looked like," said Thomas. "I also think the artist who painted that particular image was a woman."

Fleur raised an eyebrow, quite interested to hear more about his theory.

Thomas explained when he saw Fleur's eagerness to hear more. "Granted, it was unheard of for women of that era to paint anything of substance, especially to paint a book of such importance, one that would only have been handled by the monks. I don't know, it's something about the way the figure was painted. It captured the essence of the woman. I don't think men do justice to putting into art the inner thoughts of a woman, quite frankly."

"Very interesting," said Fleur. "Now I'm intrigued. It might be fun to visit Dublin and have a look." She wondered if the people in her visions had been Picts.

Fleur wanted to be more open with Thomas, and she had a need to make amends for her earlier rudeness by showing her interest in getting to know him better. "It's a surprise to me that you would need an intimate knowledge of art to be a historical architect."

Thomas grinned. "You'd think those crumbling buildings were enough, wouldn't you," he teased. "But there's quite a lot of investigative work in my profession. To authentically bring the past back to life, you need to be knowledgeable about all details of the time period."

Fleur used the opportunity to turn the conversation back to Antigonish. "Which brings us back to why you ran when you saw my birthmark." It felt so natural to tease Thomas. There was indeed still a connection between them.

"Yes, I can see you won't let me live that one down," said Thomas with a fake look of pain on his face. "Let me show you something. It's a copy of the blonde woman in the section of the book." Thomas flipped through the manuscript he had given Fleur earlier, and handed an opened page to her. She looked at the image on the page and froze. After a pause, she looked up at Thomas with wide unseeing eyes.

"The likeness is remarkable, isn't it?" asked Thomas. "It's you, down to every small detail. Your hair and eyes, and even your stance. I'll admit my reaction was dramatic, you see, because I thought you were joking with me. Not only did you look like this image, but you also had the mark in the exact same place." Thomas stopped speaking when he noticed that Fleur wasn't responding.

Her body rigid with shock, Fleur whispered more to herself than to Thomas. "It's the woman in my dreams," she said. "The one calling me. It's her, it's T'Eilin."

Fleur whispered the last words, stunned by this development. She found it hard to focus with Thomas so close to her. She got up off the settee and moved to pace in front of the window, far away from Thomas. He wouldn't know anything about the dreams of the blonde woman, and clearly he needed to.

"Thomas, there's a long story I need to tell you," she said.

Fleur sat down on the armchair away from Thomas, who remained seated on the settee. She took her time to tell Thomas all the details from the beginning, when she started to experience the dreams about the tribal women beckoning to her. She also told Thomas about Dante appearing to her with a prophecy, which were the exact words Grana had spoken. She finished telling him about what had happened before he found her at the standing stones, the vision of invaders attacking the tribe's people, and all of the bloodshed. During the entire time Fleur was telling Thomas all these things, he sat very still, absorbing the details of her story.

"The blonde woman in my dreams looks like this image of the lady in the Book of Kells," said Fleur. "Her name is T'Eilin, but I don't know much more about her. When we were at the stones, the vision I experienced was horrible. I can't help feeling like the past is trying to correct a mistake now."

Thomas was quiet, amazed by the story Fleur told him. He had seen mysterious occurrences during his career, so he was open-minded to all events. Fleur's question to him about the past correcting a mistake was a possibility.

He took a measured breath before he said anything, well aware that Fleur must be feeling vulnerable after sharing her story with him. "Thank you for telling me all of this, Fleur," he said. "That couldn't have been easy." Thomas paused to see if she had anything to add.

"To answer your question," continued Thomas. "I believe our actions ripple through time, and it is possible for a situation in the past to be resolved in the present."

Thomas gestured back to the woman in the Book of Kells. "The woman in the image looks like you, can you see the resemblance?"

Fleur paused. "You're right," she said. "I think that is the part that has me most concerned. At the start of this adventure, I was intrigued. Now, since finding myself a part of it all, I'm scared. At least now I know what Matty was talking about." Seeing Thomas' puzzled look, Fleur added, "Matty told me yesterday that she had seen an image in the university that looked like me. She and John visited the university when they went to Dublin."

Thomas knew that John and Matty had traveled to Dublin. John was on a mission to get this very manuscript for Thomas. He then turned to the topic of the diary. "The book you dropped outside, was there anything in it about the standing stones? They appear to be a link between the past and the present in your story."

This astute observation seemed to impress Fleur. At least it gave her confidence to talk about the diary. "My great-great-grandmother started writing her diary when she was a young girl just beginning to show a real talent for painting."

Thomas, glad to have broached the subject, listened to Fleur with great intent. "Fiona's story about life in the Factor's House and on the estate is very detailed, and one day I'd love to share it with you," she said. "She did talk about the standing stones, although she didn't mention seeing them specifically. It was more about how they impacted her life. I'm not sure I'm ready to talk about that yet."

Fleur picked up the diary sitting on the coffee table to put it out of the way. Her hand bumped the edge of the chair and knocked the book to the floor. Thomas picked it up and handed it to Fleur. As he did so, a page fluttered to the floor. His hand stilled in midair as he was handing the page to Fleur. The page was filled with black and white ink illustrations of symbols or marks that Thomas recognized as runes.

Thomas looked at Fleur. By her puzzled look, it was clear she had not seen the page before.

Fleur flipped the diary open, examined the covers, and showed Thomas there was indeed an overleaf. It appeared to be stuck together, holding the loose page until this moment.

Fleur took the page from Thomas and puzzled over the images. "Do you know what these are?" she asked.

While Thomas recognized the image to be runes, he wasn't sure what type of runes. The runes on the loose page did not exhibit the typical letter shapes and standardized form of bind runes.

"These images are runes of some description," he said. "The runic alphabet was used to write various Germanic languages in the first and second century AD. But earlier runes were not used very much as a writing system but rather as magical signs, and some say for divination."

Thomas gave Fleur a few minutes to digest the implications of finding an illustration of runes in her great-great-grandmother's diary. "This is very interesting," he said. "It might be the key to solve the mystery of the woman beckoning you from the past. Do you remember seeing inscriptions on any of the stones? Perhaps there is a set of runes etched in the stones?"

She shook her head. "No, I don't recall seeing anything like these images," she said. "I must tell you, not everyone sees the stones. There is significance in the fact that you can see the stones as well."

Thomas had not considered this possibility, but it would certainly explain his astonishment at discovering the standing stones the day he found Fleur sitting in the middle of the circle of stones. He had never seen them before in all the years he and his brother explored the entire area.

Before Fleur could ask more questions about runes and their meaning, an enormous bang sounded from the direction of the front door, followed by an excited ruckus. Matty must be home. Sure enough, as Fleur and Thomas composed themselves after the excitement of finding the page of runes, an exuberant Matty, with John and Auntie G. in tow, filled the library with laughter.

"Well, hello you two," crooned Matty. "What do we have here? Looks like the cat amongst the pigs, if that guilty look tells me."

Matty kissed Fleur and Thomas on both cheeks and plunked herself down on the settee with a smirk on her face. Fleur had little time to recover from the emotions of the afternoon, but seeing Matty splayed out on the sofa, she couldn't help but smile.

John popped out to the kitchen for a bottle of wine and glasses, and Auntie G. bustled in with a large tray of snacks. The evening had the makings of a great gathering. Conversation revolved around what Matty had done with John during their time in Dublin. John chuckled recounting the story of Matty's enthusiasm on their tour of Dublin Castle. "She called everyone she met 'your Highness' or 'your Excellency' depending on the person's gender," said John.

Fleur chortled, "That's Matty, she couldn't wait to see royalty when we arrived in Scotland."

Fleur noted that even Thomas, who she suspected to be more reserved in the boisterous company of his twin brother, told his fair share of amusing stories about his summer internship at an archeological dig in Orkney. By the end of the evening, Fleur was looking at Thomas with different eyes. She felt intrigued by this man who could appear to be aloof yet caring, shy yet charming with his self-deprecating stories.

The mantle clock struck midnight. When it was time to end the evening, Matty pulled John along with her, saying with a wink, "Come along then, John-man. You are staying here tonight. I have a welcome home present for you upstairs."

Auntie G. made her exit from the room with a twinkle in her eye and a nod of her head. "I'll be calling it a night too," she said.

Alone once more with Thomas, Fleur was shocked by the intensity of her desire to be in his arms. It has been a very long time since she'd felt such a physical attraction. Maybe it was the fun and relaxing evening of being in the moment and not worrying about the mystery of her circumstances. Or maybe those stirrings that had started in Antigonish were now returned. It didn't matter why, her desire was strong.

Thomas must have sensed the shift in Fleur, for he moved to be closer to her. "You need some time to process all of these feelings you are having right now. It's been quite a full evening."

Fleur was both delighted and disappointed. "Thank you, Thomas," she said. "It makes me happy that you would know that much about me, despite the short time we're known each other," said Fleur, then paused to choose the right words of appreciation. "I want you to know that I appreciate your kindness and your understanding."

Thomas smiled and said nothing. No words were needed.

Fleur moved to the door with little enthusiasm. She wished she could be easygoing as Matty was with John, but she knew herself. She would be upset in the morning if she succumbed to the desire of the moment and took Thomas upstairs.

Thomas stepped towards her, lifted her chin and leaned down to give her a slow kiss. The taste of him was as wonderful as she had imagined, and the slight inhale she heard from Thomas clutched her stomach. It took him a minute to ask Fleur, "Will you feel up to continuing our conversation tomorrow afternoon, do you think?"

Fleur nodded and opened the front door for Thomas. She would need time to sort out the jumble of emotions pulsing through her as Thomas closed the door behind him.

Fleur went to her room burning with longing to be with Thomas. When he put his arms around her to say good night at the door, the gesture was warm and familiar. She did not want the embrace to end.

She knew she would have difficulty getting to sleep. She decided to meditate in the conservatory rather than spend the night tossing and turning.

Fleur wondered if being in the room where her great-great-grandmother painted would provide a connection with Fiona Kintrell's spirit that would help ease her way back to painting once more.

Before Fleur switched on the lights in the conservatory, she gazed at the moon's silvery light spilling through the large windows creating the impression of daylight in the room. The evenings this far north were lighter at this time of year.

Fleur settled herself on the small settee near the center window. From that vantage point, she could make out the outline of trees and bushes in the secret walled garden shimmering with the light cast by the moon. Her thoughts drifted naturally to her ancestor.

"Great-great-grandmother," she called out to the empty room. "Did you find what needed to be cleared in our ancestry, and do you think I'm the one to clear it? Can you help me understand what is the work that I'm supposed to do, if indeed I'm the one?"

Not expecting an answer, Fleur settled to contemplate the energy in the conservatory. She sensed the spaciousness of time standing still, making room for limitless possibilities. The space clearly held Fiona Kintrell's creative passion for her craft. Settling into her meditation practice, Fleur allowed herself to be fully present; with the moment, with the room, and with the sense of perfect wellbeing that enveloped her.

Fleur slowed her breath and heartbeat to commence her meditation practice. An inspired thought came to her; she remembered a practice she had used many years ago but had forgotten. It involved centering her energy into her heart. Fleur decided to try that practice again now. Taking a slow, deep inhaled breath, Fleur held the breath and then exhaled in a slow and deliberate release, focusing on dropping her attention into her heart and filling her heart space with the comfort of the breath.

After a few such deep and deliberate breaths, a warm glow arose from her heart, bringing a sense of lightness and freedom. She smiled at the feeling and reveled in knowing it was all her doing.

Enjoying the sensation of pure bliss as she continued to drop her breath into her heart, Fleur recognized the feeling as her heart opening. Neither time nor space existed in this feeling place of the open heart. She allowed her heart to expand further with each deep breath until anxiety was no longer present, and love replaced her fear. It occurred to Fleur that this is who she really is, that she discovered her true nature as love at its source.

Smiling in that place of bliss she set for herself, Fleur picked up a brush, dipped it into the paint pots, and put the brush to canvas. Flowing on the wave of bliss, she allowed the energy to take hold of her as she placed one brushstroke after the other on the canvas. Her action seemed not to come of her own volition. It came rhythmically, purely inspired, like her experience at the standing stones before she became afraid. The thought that she might be merging with her great-great-grandmother's energy invigorated her. It felt natural, carefree, and passionate. It felt like pure love. Love for the present moment and for the details she was painting.

Hours passed in a flash. The dawn light had moved across the conservatory when Fleur at last put the brush down. Without looking at the canvas, she knew that her all-night session had produced more than a creative piece of art. It was a calling from her very soul. The work was not about painting, it was about embracing her life-force energy. She had found a way back to her joyful true nature.

Fleur went to bed, enjoying a sense of her oneness with her great-great-grandmother, with all artists, and with all of life. She felt connected with her Source Energy, convinced that the flow of inspiration she experienced this evening had come from spirit. She smiled to think that the total alignment she achieved with her true self might be the work she was supposed to do for her ancestry.

Fleur managed to get a couple of hours of dream-filled sleep after her experience in the conservatory. In the dream, she painted as effortlessly as she had that evening. When she was finished with the painting in her dream, she turned the canvas around to scrutinize what she had created. It was a scene at the hilltop with three people on the ridge looking down at the view The three people were T'Eilin, Brendan, and an older woman whom Fleur recognized as the one who had performed the ceremony before the invaders attacked the tribe's people.

While Fleur considered the artwork, T'Eilin spoke to her in her dream. "You are correct in your interpretation about what you accomplished here," said T'Eilin. "You found your alignment, you found pure love from your open heart. You were fully present in the moment of creation, and you loved each detail you painted. Your heart was wide open so that fear fell away. You were no longer in the grip of the illusion of fear."

"Did I merge with my great-great-grandmother's energy?" asked Fleur.

"Yes, you did," said T'Eilin. "You called upon her to guide you. It wasn't only her energy that helped you, but all artistic energy from all non-physical beings who surround you with wellbeing. The field of energy is always there. Physical beings can at any time call upon the energy of non-physical to assist them; we are always delighted to participate in your expansion."

"How do I have visions of you?" asked Fleur.

T'Eilin replied with a loving tone, "When you are completely in that feeling place of oneness and pure energy, the illusion of time and space falls away. There is only one energy, and when you tune into that oneness anything is possible. You can contact non-physical energy from that place."

"I understand," said Fleur. "But it isn't always easy to find that heart space. Most times the mind is in the way, thinking and trying to figure things out."

"You will learn with practice," said T'Eilin. "Each time you accomplish that feeling, initially by accident, then more and more on purpose, you will grow in confidence as all fear leaves you. Creation happens in that heart space, where there is no need or want. Story leaves, the illusion of separateness leaves, and only oneness remains. You are well, everything is working out."

Fleur was pleased when she awoke from her dream and remembered the conversation with T'Eilin. It inspired her to practice connecting more with her heart and to leave her fear behind.

CHAPTER SIXTEEN

Fleur found a note addressed to her on the counter when she wandered downstairs by midmorning. Written in her Auntie G.'s handwriting, the note said that she and Matty had gone into town to sort out Matty's return to Canada. Fleur had dismissed what Matty had told her about going home to sort things out before she came back to live with John as wishful thinking, but seeing the words in writing made it real.

Content to be left to her own devices, Fleur walked outside to clear her head. She felt no need to rush back to the conservatory to examine what she had painted last night. Her creative block had been released, that was all that mattered.

In this positive frame of mind, Fleur reveled in a sense of freedom she hadn't felt in a while, and her senses seemed heightened. The cool air lingered on her arms, and she heard the cry of pheasants in the distance. It felt as though she had no past, no future, only this moment, and Fleur was enjoying it.

She walked back to the Factor's House just as Thomas pulled his Land Rover into the driveway. Fleur approached to greet him, hoping that he would kiss her again. As if reading her mind, Thomas leaned in and gave her a kiss, then looked her in the eyes, and murmured, "You look as though you didn't get much sleep last night. Is that so, mo mhuirnín?"

Fleur suspected the word Thomas used was a Celtic endearment, and sensed it pleased him that she didn't ask what it meant.

"No, I didn't sleep at all," she said, leading the way into the house. "I spent the entire night painting in my great-great-grandmother's conservatory."

Waiting for the coffee to brew, Fleur felt peaceful domesticity sitting across from Thomas at the kitchen table. The sun was streaming through the roses along the windowsill, casting a pinkish glow onto the window panes. She could hear bumblebees humming, and appreciated the sound that reminded her of lazy summers in her youth.

"What medium do you work in?" asked Thomas, showing no surprise at learning that Fleur was an artist. "If I were to guess, I'd say you love the texture, vibrancy, and pliability of oils."

Fleur was pleased Thomas knew enough to ask that question. "You guessed right," she said. "I love to play with oils, sort of to speak."

Fleur had an overwhelming need to show him what she had worked on last night. She wasn't quite sure if the painting was any good, but it didn't matter. It surprised her that she didn't care what another person thought about her artwork because she had always been concerned about how others reacted to her work. Maybe from the years of Arthur's criticism.

"I'd like to show you what I painted last night, if you don't mind," said Fleur. "But be warned, it's the first piece I've done in more than a year, so I don't know how it turned out. It flowed out of me, if you can understand."

Thomas nodded. "I think so," he said. "It's the same with me when I'm researching. Time flies and I accomplish so much, but I don't feel I've had anything to do with the process. It flows from someplace else, like from a river of inspiration."

Fleur led the way to the conservatory, explaining the story of her great-great-grandmother who lived in the Factor's House and was a protégé of the Laird. Opening the door to the conservatory, Fleur felt pride in what her great-great-grandmother accomplished.

"Fiona Kintrell was an artist and a historian," she said. "She documented the Land Clearances through her works of art. I saw some of her paintings in the Museum of Art in Edinburgh."

Thomas remembered having seen the work Fleur spoke about. "I know the paintings well, though I didn't know that F. Kintrell was a female. Her work is very good, as I recall."

Fleur stopped, taking a moment to inhale the pungent smell of oil and turpentine. Thomas halted in mid-stride to gaze around the room. Fleur expected this reaction from Thomas; as an architectural historian, she expected that the room would intrigue him.

"Wow, look at this place," exclaimed Thomas, totally absorbed in the details of the conservatory. "This is an incredible example of eighteenth century Georgian-era conservatories, likely late 1700s or early 1800s. Look at the symmetry of the room. Oh my, a leadwork roof with lead detail on the clerestory panels. I've only seen one instance of that, and it was in Ireland. In fact,

I believe this particular conservatory was inspired by Palladian architecture. It was in the height of fashion then."

Thomas moved to get a closer look at the glass used for the windows. "Yes, the Laird spared no expense in building this room," he said. "Georgian conservatories did not have such an expanse of glass. They were mostly built of brick, because glass was expensive. Do you see the individual panes that make up the larger profile? There are six panes in total, three across and two down."

Fleur enjoyed watching Thomas wander around the room like a kid in a candy shop. She was intrigued by his descriptions and asked, "What is Palladian architecture?"

Thomas apologized, "Sorry. I didn't mean to throw around phrases you wouldn't know." He explained about the European style of architecture based on the designs of the Italian architect Andrea Palladio. Palladianism became popular briefly in Britain during the mid-17th century. The symmetry of this style of architecture made the exteriors seem quite austere.

Fleur found Thomas' description fascinating. Her artist's brain grasped the concepts of harmony and symmetry in the architecture, the system that Thomas referred to as Georgian Double Cube.

She loved the notion that Thomas could perceive something different yet complementary to what she saw. When she stepped into the room, she felt the creative energy it fostered, whereas he saw the intricacies of design and structure of the room itself.

Fleur walked to the canvas, intrigued to see what she had painted last night. She wondered if the dream she'd had last night about painting in the conservatory captured the actual artwork she had created.

On the easel was a painting of a scene both serene and yet charged with emotion. A man and a woman, sitting on a grassy knoll, gazed at each other with an intensity of energy sparking between them. The woman cradled one hand around a pregnant belly, and the man rested his hand on her stomach. The view in front of the couple, at a great distance in a valley sweeping to the sea, was a village with primitive-looking dwellings. Standing behind the couple was the silhouette of an older woman, like a loving presence watching over them. The entire scene was framed by the standing stones.

Thomas, standing next to Fleur, broke the silence with a quiet observation. "You've painted us," he said. "The woman is identical to the woman in the Book of Kells, which I think looks so much like you, and the man resembles me, don't you think?"

Fleur had difficulty speaking. She croaked a few words to acknowledge his observation, "I think you're right, though I didn't intend to. I painted this in a meditative state, summoning answers from my great-great-grandmother. Do you think this could be her way of answering my questions?"

Thomas studied the painting. Fleur could see that he contemplated all the possibilities. He was a logical person, but she suspected he had researched enough ancient histories to appreciate the unknown.

He pointed at the top edge of the farthest standing stone. "Do you remember painting a rune inscription on one of the stones?"

Fleur didn't remember painting anything specific, and the thought of being so disconnected brought fear hurtling into the pit of her stomach. She couldn't control it. Her breath was no longer accessible as she panted in her fear.

"Can we get out of here?" she asked, having difficulty breathing. She was disappointed with herself for forgetting so quickly her resolve to leave her fear behind.

"How about a drive?" suggested Thomas. "We could go for lunch. I know a perfect place not far away."

Fleur relaxed on the drive to the coast. She needed to speak of normal things, not about visions, runes, and mysterious standing stones.

"This is wonderful," she said. "I'm enjoying the drive, thank you for suggesting it."

The Tiroran Country House, overlooking Loch Scridain, was the perfect spot to distract her. The sunroom that served as the dining room was bright and airy, and provided a stunning view across the Loch.

Fleur wanted to get to know Thomas better and asked him many questions about his childhood while they waited for their meal to arrive. Thomas shared funny stories of the mischief he and John would get into growing up. His stories and his wry sense of humor pleased her. In turn, Thomas asked Fleur about her family in Canada. She talked about her close relationship with her Grana, the only family she had known her entire life, up until now that is.

"I owe Grana a great deal," she said. "Grana and Papa Joe raised me when my parents were killed in a car accident. Then my Papa Joe died of a heart attack when I was 12 years old, so it's been mostly Grana and me. Grana gave up a lot to raise me." Fleur was surprised at the sudden feeling of guilt about her Grana sacrificing her life to raise her. Tears came to her eyes with that thought.

Thomas put his hand over hers. "I know what you're feeling," he said. "There's a certain angst that you feel when you realize someone has sacrificed a part of their life for yours."

Fleur looked up at Thomas and saw compassion in his eyes. "John and I have a similar story," he said. "Our parents were also killed in an accident when we were two years old. We had no other family, but we were fortunate to be adopted by the Laird's sister Catherine, who lived in Ireland with her elderly husband, a baron. The Laird took us under his wing after Catherine died when we were eight years old. The Laird raised us as though we were his very own sons. He had no children. Ever since I learned about that, I've had enormous feelings of the debt that I owe him. John feels the same way, though I'm sure you might find that hard to believe. I think that's why we both have such a drive to bring back the estate to its former glory, to repay the Laird and to keep his name and legacy alive."

"I can appreciate your feelings of loyalty about legacy and heritage," she said, turning her hand around to lightly clasp his hand that rested on hers. "I'm sure this land was a source of pride and honor for the Laird. Do you think that is why you are so passionate about historical architecture?"

Thomas didn't hesitate to say, "This land inspires me every day. I've always been fascinated by the estate, and couldn't wait until summer holidays to come home. John and I had some great adventures here."

"I get what you're saying about owing something back for the sake of the land and the legacy," said Fleur. "I never had thoughts of indebtedness before. My Grana never did or said anything to make me think that way. That's the wonder of truly being loved unconditionally, isn't it?"

Fleur paused for a moment to allow the waitress to set down the fresh trout for their lunch. It gave her a chance to consider how much she was ready to share with Thomas. She took a sip of Pinot Gris and said, "Since my husband left and we divorced, I don't know what I'm meant to be doing. I feel like I'm a teenager, unsure about my life. Then the dreams and visions started, and the rest you know."

Fleur glanced to see Thomas' reaction. He was listening with such intent, she was encouraged to continue. "I hope that you don't think I'm strange with this talk of visions and the like," she said. "It's thrown me for a loop, especially yesterday when you showed me the image of the lady in the Book of Kells."

Far from feeling awkward, it felt natural to discuss these bizarre events with Thomas. It occurred to her that with his help, she might be able to solve the mystery of her ancestral curse.

"We didn't talk about what happened at the standing stones the other day," she said. "I wanted to thank you for coming to my rescue."

Thomas suggested, "What do you think about us going together to the stones to see if we can find the runes? How about we go tomorrow afternoon? I'll be there to support you, but if you are afraid, I understand."

Fleur put her shoulders back at the mention of being afraid. "That's exactly what we should do," she said. "Yes, I'm scared, but with you there beside me I'll be just fine."

Around noon the next day, Fleur stepped into the hallway to the sound of laughter from the kitchen and concluded John had arrived.

Sure enough, her friend hugged John, who stood in the middle of the room grinning from ear to ear. Auntie G. leaned against the counter with spatula in hand, grinning at Matty's enthusiasm.

Fleur grinned at John, pleased to see her friend so happy.

"Hello, dearie," said John, using Auntie G.'s term of endearment. "It's good to see your lovely smile."

"May I pour you some coffee?" she asked, reaching for the pot to hide her embarrassment. She knew John was teasing her, but it stung to be reminded about her earlier rudeness.

Seeing Fleur's sudden discomfiture, John grabbed Matty and whirled her around the kitchen to change the energy. "Matty, my Petite Saut, let's dance!"

With a grin, and a rushed, "See you all later!" thrown over his shoulder, John twirled Matty out of the kitchen.

Fleur looked at Auntie G. and laughed out loud. "Those two are meant for each other."

"I couldn't agree with you more, dearie," said Auntie G. "What have you planned for the day? Do you and Thomas have something planned?"

Fleur didn't hesitate, "We're going to the standing stones to see if we can find a clue to the mysteries of that place. You had mentioned that you believed Fiona Kintrell interacted with the standing stones."

Fleur needed to update Auntie G. about her discovery in the conservatory. "I haven't had time to tell you something rather exciting, Auntie G. I found Fiona Kintrell's diary hidden in the conservatory," she said. "She mentions Lliam as guiding her. From the descriptions, I believe it is energy from the standing stones that she is referring to." She proceeded to tell Auntie G. the details of the diary, and concluded with the news about how she and Thomas had found a page of runes.

"There's something else," said Fleur. "I painted a scene that must have some meaning. I painted it in a trance, right after I asked my great-great-grandmother to help me find answers." Auntie G. was calm listening to the remarkable things that transpired. She didn't seem surprised by any of it.

"I'm very happy for you that you finally broke through your fears and painted again. It sounds as though you are moving to your heart to find inspiration, not to mention love," she said with a knowing smile. "Listen to your Inner Being. You'll find all the energy guiding you to your true life from that place."

Thomas understood that Fleur would need to mentally prepare herself before she was exposed to the power of the standing stones again. He considered her to be very brave to go back to the place where she'd had such a horrible vision.

Fleur looked ready to go when he met her at the Factor's House. Her trusting smile warmed his heart and made him want to protect her all the more. The hike up to the hilltop seemed to take less time than when he went a few days ago. Thomas wanted to distract her, so he told her more stories about growing up on the estate.

Halfway up, she stumbled on a rock. Thomas caught her and lingered a moment before he let her go. The energy between them seemed to grow as they climbed the hill towards the stones. She was a sweet and endearing person with great courage, and he liked that she no longer guarded herself from him.

At the crest of the hill, Thomas took her right hand to keep her safe with his physical touch. They were thus connected as they walked into the middle of the standing stones. He felt her hand tremble, and squeezed it to assure her of his presence.

A tangible energy, akin to static electricity, caused the hair on Thomas' arms to stand up. He was unsure if he felt this in his own right, or because he was still holding Fleur's hand.

Fleur halted in the center of the circle, breathed as though preparing for a meditation practice, and spoke aloud with a voice that was strong and confident, "I am seeking to understand how I might do the work to help T'Eilin, Brendan, my ancestors, and my descendants."

Thomas flinched upon hearing the name Brendan. Fleur had told him that the name of the woman in her dreams was T'Eilin, but she hadn't mentioned Brendan. His senses were on high alert as he prepared himself for whatever action might be needed. Fleur gripped his hand hard, startling him. He looked around, but couldn't see anything to be concerned about.

When he looked at Fleur, he became alarmed. Her eyes were glazed, her body rigid. She must be having a vision, Thomas thought.

Fleur started to walk forward, fixated on one of the stones at the far eastern quadrant of the circle. Thomas walked next to her, allowing her to control the direction in which they moved, but never letting go of her hand. She stopped, pointed at a spot at shoulder height, and placed the palm of her hand flat on the stone.

As Thomas watched her actions, he saw shapes appear on the stone where none had been before. He blinked. The outline of several runes became visible, indented into the stone. He furrowed his brow. A memory of this scene was trying to push its way into his consciousness. Thomas pulled out the illustration from the diary to compare it to the markings on the stone. Identical.

Fleur stood still, unaware of Thomas' thudding heart as he thought about the familiar runes appearing. It was a few minutes before she jostled herself, turned to Thomas, and spoke for the first time since they arrived.

"Brendan, the answers are in the book," she said. "We have to go to Dublin to see the Book of Kells. Clearing the curse depends on resolving this mystery by the night of the crescent moon. That night is when the vortex is open and most effective. We only have five days." Fleur let go of Thomas' hand and walked away from the circle of stones towards the ridge to start her descent.

He noted how she walked, like royalty. He hadn't seen her so dignified as at that moment, though it seemed natural. He surmised this had been her usual state, before she lost her confidence. The transformation amazed him.

He understood what a vortex might mean in this context, as a center of energy originating from the core of the earth. Thomas knew he needed to understand who Brendan was. Fleur had called him Brendan on several occasions, and Thomas wondered if that was an indication he was involved. He concluded Fleur couldn't know his full name was Brendan Thomas Hayden; it wasn't documented anywhere. The thought was unsettling, especially as he was starting to suspect Fleur possessed intuitive powers.

Fleur walked down the hill ahead of Thomas. She appreciated him giving her time to be alone with her thoughts. Unlike the other two times at the standing stones, Fleur was eager and energized, as though she had taken back her power. She remembered the conversation she had with T'Eilin in her dream after the night she had painted in the conservatory. This time, before she approached the circle of standing stones, she had dropped into her heart like her meditation practice. That must have been exactly the right thing to do, for she felt the pure connection with the energy of the standing stones. A great peace settled on her when she spoke out loud in the middle of the circle, she felt the clarity of purpose within herself. Fleur had experienced a loving presence. She had also been given direction to find answers in her quest to help T'Eilin and lift the curse from her family line.

Fleur stopped to allow Thomas to catch up. She realized his concern and put him at ease. "Don't worry, I'm fine."

Thomas nodded, and asked the logical question, "Can you tell me what happened?"

Fleur stepped closer to Thomas, restraining the urge to rest her head on his broad shoulders. "I'm not sure what it looked like from the outside, but it was quite peaceful, like a warm hug from someone who loves me truly. I knew where to find the rune inscription. Now that I think about it, I had painted the exact location, hadn't I?"

Thomas nodded and smiled. Fleur expected that he had made the connection back to the painting. "Yes, I know," mused Fleur. "That painting has something to do with all of this as well."

Thomas commented, "I think you're right about the painting. If the woman in your painting is T'Eilin from your dreams, can you tell me who the man in the painting is?"

Realization flashed in Fleur's mind. She gasped, and stared at Thomas. "Brendan is T'Eilin's beloved. Do you think that you are somehow connected with Brendan from the past?"

"It's possible," said Thomas. "Brendan is my first name. I use the name B. Thomas Hayden for professional publications. It was quite a shock to hear you calling me Brendan last time we were at the stones."

"I didn't know your name was Brendan," she said. "It would explain a number of things, including why I painted your likeness alongside T'Eilin's."

Fleur frowned. "Do you think that you should come with me to Dublin?" She was shy asking Thomas.

"I would love nothing better," said Thomas. "We could be in Dublin by evening if we catch the first ferry in the morning.

"I appreciate your help, Thomas," said Fleur. "I suspect you prefer to have more time to plan things out, like I do. But things are moving fast, with only five days to resolve things. I have a feeling it's important that I see the image in the Book of Kells in person."

The glow of lights from the Factor's House in the distance spurred Fleur on. She was exhausted from the day's adventure, and looked forward to a quiet evening in front of the fireplace with a glass of red wine. She needed a reprieve from all the heightened otherworldly activity.

She and Thomas entered the front door as the last rays of the sunset winked over the trees. They were taking off their hiking boots in the entrance hall when a flurry of activity came from the library door. Matty rushed into the hall, excited to see them.

"There you are," she said. "You've got to come into the library. You wouldn't believe who we saw coming off the ferry when we were in town."

Matty stepped aside. Standing in the middle of the room was a large-boned woman with a felt hat sitting at a cocky angle on her head. "Well there, dearie," said the woman. "Aren't you going to give me a hug then?"

Fleur flew at the woman and snuggled into her ample arms. "Grana," she said. "It's really you! What are you doing here? How did you get here?"

"Dearie, one question at a time," smiled her Grana. "And we'll get to how happy I am to be here, to see that you are well now, to see dear Matty, and of course to meet my very own dear sister! But first, please introduce this young man." Fleur caught sight of Auntie G. beaming behind her Grana. How wonderful for the sisters to meet.

Fleur turned to smile at Thomas. Before she could introduce him, he stepped forward. "I'm Thomas Hayden," he said. "It's a pleasure to meet Fleur's grandmother."

"Well then, Thomas Hayden," said her grandmother. "What have you been doing with my granddaughter? I see you have resolved that issue about her inheritance." Fleur noted the twinkle in her Grana's eye, and knew her intuition told her this acquaintance with Thomas was meaningful. Also, Grana made sure they understood she knew that this Thomas Hayden was the same person who was responsible for the letter contesting Fleur's inheritance of the Factor's House.

"Fleur met Thomas at the university," explained Matty. "He's one of those posh lecturing types, you know, leather at the elbow. His specialty is history and buildings. He and his brother John, well they own this whole estate."

Though Matty was bold about most things, she was intimidated by Fleur's grandmother when it came to her affairs of the heart. More than once over the years, Fleur's Grana had given her advice about boys that Matty ignored, much to her detriment. Of course, Grana picked up the hint straight away, and cocked an eye in Auntie G.'s direction.

To Matty's relief, Auntie G. distracted her sister. "Eileen, dear," she said in her best Scottish lilt. "Let's get you upstairs and settle you in. We'll have a spot of tea with everyone in a few minutes."

When the two older ladies had gone upstairs, Matty asked, "Who do you think is going to be in charge between those two?"

Fleur chuckled. Auntie G. and Grana were indeed two formidable ladies, and it would be interesting to see them in action.

Matty laughed. "It's too bad I won't be here to see it," she said. "My flight is booked, and I'm leaving in a couple of days."

Fleur was still worried that Matty was rushing into this relationship with John. She turned to Thomas and said, "What do you think? Are they moving too fast?"

Thomas reassured Fleur, "I know my brother. Though John seems like a rough and tumble guy, he only takes action after a great deal of consideration; he especially never takes matters of the heart lightly. Trust me, you don't have to worry about his sincerity where Matty is concerned."

Matty smirked. "Ahem, I'm right here. And see, you don't need to worry," she said. "We are mad about each other, we belong together. John is coming to pick me up any second, so I'd better get dressed."

Fleur smiled at Matty's enthusiasm. "I'm happy for you. I'm going to have to say goodbye to you now, because tomorrow Thomas and I are going to Dublin for a few days. We leave very early in the morning."

Matty raised her eyebrows. "Good for you," she said. "Finally, you figured out your feelings about Thomas, eh?" With that, Matty gave a flustered Fleur a great big hug and ran up the stairs calling out, "I'll be back in less than a month. Keep the house all warmed up for me, if you know what I mean."

Thomas turned to Fleur after Matty clattered up the stairs. "Are you sure that with your Grana just arrived, you still want to go to Dublin?" he said. "Especially with me? I get the impression your grandmother is already suspicious of my motives."

Fleur wasn't concerned. For once in her life, she was doing what pleased her. "We need to go to Dublin," she said. "Time is running out before the crescent moon. Not only that, I want to go to Dublin with you. It's your city and I'd love to see it through your eyes."

Fleur saw Thomas light up, pleased she admitted she wanted to be with him in Dublin. "Besides, it will give Grana an opportunity to get to know her sister alone," she said. "I'm sure they will keep each other occupied with the many stories to share about their lives."

Thomas and Fleur discussed plans for the next day, then as Thomas was leaving, Grana and Auntie G. came down the stairs. "Good night, Thomas," said Auntie G. "We'll be seeing you in the morning, I expect?"

Auntie G. took note of the contented smile Thomas gave Fleur as he was leaving. When the door closed behind him, she wrapped her arms around Fleur in a hug, "It's so very good to see you're enjoying his company. He's a good lad."

Fleur agreed with Auntie G. "Oh yes," she said. "I'm learning just how good."

Eileen looked at her granddaughter with immense love in her eyes, "Dearie, I want you to be happy, and I can see that you are. In fact, you are more like yourself than I have seen you in a long time."

Those words were true; she had never felt happier than now, holding her Grana and her Auntie G. arm-in-arm as they made their way towards the kitchen. It was the best feeling in the world.

Grana and Auntie G. fussed over Fleur, preparing an elaborate tea of sandwiches and scones. She couldn't help but stare in wonder at how similar their mannerisms were.

"Isn't this marvelous," she said. "Did you ever think we would be so lucky to find family here in Mull, Grana?"

Her Grana smiled, eyes glistening with tears. "Nay, I didn't," she said. "I'm glad to have come to Mull to spend time with my very own sister. We'll have so many stories to tell each other."

This was the opportunity to let Grana and Auntie G. know that she was leaving for Dublin in the morning. "I'm so glad you're here, Grana," she said.

"But I'm going to Dublin tomorrow. I'll only be a few days. It'll give you and Auntie G. time together."

Her Grana had a twinkle in her eye when she said, "You do what you need to do, dearie. Does this have something to do with the woman in your dreams?"

"Yes, in fact it does," said Fleur. "Things have happened so fast in the past few days. "

Fleur considered it best to start with her painting. "A few nights ago, something magical happened," she said. "I was in the conservatory asking my great-great-grandmother Fiona for inspiration to figure out what work I'm supposed to do. Something came over me, like a spell, and I painted like I've never done before. I was lost in the creative energy that flowed over me. When I finished, I didn't even look at the painting, because I knew it was exactly as was meant to be."

Her Grana held her gaze. "It sounds as though you found pure alignment with your Inner Being. What happened next?"

"A few days ago, Thomas showed me an image of a woman in the Book of Kells, something he had come across in his research," said Fleur. "Remarkably, this woman looks like the woman from my dreams, and also from the visions I've had at the standing stones." Fleur paused to let that information sink in. Her Grana and Auntie G. nodded, as if what she told them was normal. Of course they would, as both women had strong powers of intuition, and they understood magical things that would be mysterious or foreboding to others.

"It's all unfolding nicely, isn't it now," said her Grana. "Let me ask you, the woman in the Book of Kells, does she also look like you?"

Fleur gasped. "In fact, she does," she said. "Not only that, but when I showed Thomas what I had painted, I was surprised to see a scene of the same woman, a man standing with her who looked like Thomas, and an older woman figure protecting them in front of the standing stones."

"Do you have any idea what role Thomas plays in all of this?" asked her Auntie G. "We talked about the stones revealing themselves only to certain people for a specific reason."

"My instinct tells me he is involved, but I don't know how yet," said Fleur. "Thomas found a loose page in Fiona Kintrell's diary, one I hadn't seen before. The page had drawings of runes, and those exact runes have been showing up in other places. I unconsciously placed them in my painting, and then we found the same runes on one of the standing stones. We think the runes must be a key, some direction on how to unlock the mystery."

Her Grana nodded her head and said, "That's why you're going to Dublin. The stones are guiding you to seek the key from the Book of Kells. I think you'll find more than how to end an ancient family curse. I believe you'll find answers to what you've been looking for all of your life. Yes, indeed I do."

CHAPTER SEVENTEEN

Thomas enjoyed the fresh air on the deck of the ferry, and was glad to see Fleur content as well. He laid his hand on hers and smiled when she clasped it. That small gesture gave Thomas the incentive to draw Fleur's body close to his, wrapping his arms around her back to keep her warm. He sighed when she rested her head on his shoulder. They stood entwined, watching the boat plow through the water, appreciating the comfort of each other's bodies, and enjoying the companionable silence.

Thomas felt Fleur's anticipation as they left the ferry and flew to Dublin on the commuter flight.

"The transition always amazes me," he said. "The island is so tranquil, like you stepped back in time. Then, you are thrust into civilization and all of this." Thomas waved a hand at the bustle of passengers lining up to board the plane.

Fleur grinned. "You're right about the island," she said. "It's lovely, but I must admit that I'm looking forward to being back in civilization."

Thomas kept still when he sensed she wanted to say more. "Thomas, you're being so kind to me," said Fleur. "I want you to know how much I appreciate everything you've done. Not just taking care of the travel plans, but wanting to help me in Dublin."

Thomas was happy to make things easier for Fleur. The desire to be with her was growing by the day. Though he knew he was not responsible, Thomas sensed he played a part in resolving the mystery of the visions at the standing stones. But the fact that he had feelings for Fleur was a more powerful incentive to help her.

"My pleasure," he said. "It would appear from all of the clues that I'm involved in this mystery. Don't forget that I selfishly want your perspective about the gender of the artist who painted the image I showed you."

Thomas heard Fleur stifle a chuckle, and turned to raise an eyebrow at her, causing her to blush. Thomas liked that Fleur could flush so sweetly. He was tempted to ask what she was thinking about, but left her alone. He suspected she was thinking about him. At least he hoped she was.

Fleur couldn't stop her face reddening when she thought about how sexy Thomas was. Those smoldering eyes piercing the core of her, the dark, wavy hair she wanted to smooth away from his face, the trim body she enjoyed feeling when they embraced on the ferry. His lips, very kissable, not thin-lipped like many men, and not too full. She was glad he didn't ask her what she was thinking about.

She blushed again when they arrived in Dublin as it hit her that she would be alone with Thomas in his apartment. On the way to the elevator, Thomas told her the history of the building and the surrounding area.

"I'm quite lucky to have this apartment," he said. "Recently, lofts in these old historic buildings are becoming more popular. You'll see in a minute, it's lovely."

As they approached Thomas' front door, Fleur babbled about how wonderful it must be to live in a central location, and that he must get lots of house guests to accommodate. She wanted to find out about the bedroom situation.

"I'm around the block from the college," said Thomas. "It comes in handy when I desire to lounge in bed before a morning class." Thomas grinned, leaving Fleur no doubt that he guessed her thoughts, which caused her face to go red yet again.

Thomas opened the heavy door and stepped aside for Fleur to enter. She stopped short, astounded by the space.

"My goodness," she exclaimed. "I've never seen a loft as stunning as this." Fleur gazed around the two-story living room that invited natural light in through a series of large windows on both levels.

"Ah, I know what this is," mused Fleur. "This room is an incredible example of the finest of eighteenth-century Georgian era conservatories, inspired by Palladian architecture. Look at the incredible symmetry of the room. The symmetry of a Georgian Double Cube." Thomas laughed at Fleur's accurate mimicking of his enthusiasm when he saw the conservatory at the Factor's House.

"You're almost right," he said. "I've attempted to restore the original design of the loft. This isn't a conservatory, but a close interpretation of one. I love the openness, the feeling of space and light."

Fleur wandered around the room, touching the well-worn leather furniture. A large painting of a beautiful couple holding twin baby boys captured her attention.

"That portrait," she said. "Are those your parents?"

Thomas touched the painting. "This was painted a month before my parents were killed," he said. "I'm told they were nice people, involved in the community and volunteering for many charities. That's how Catherine adopted us, she worked with my parents on many fundraising ventures."

Her fingers grazed his hand. "I'm sorry," she said. "I know how you feel. It's hard to come to terms with the fact you don't know your own parents. But we were both lucky to have people in our lives who took care of us and loved us just the same."

Thomas didn't say a word. Fleur saw he was overcome with emotion, and encircled her arms around him.

"Thank you, Fleur," he said. "I never realized what a relief it is to have someone else understand how that feels, other than my twin brother."

Thomas broke the spell, getting down to the practical matters of dealing with luggage and room arrangements. "I'm remiss in my hospitality," he said. "Are you thirsty?" He continued when Fleur shook her head. "Let me show you to the guest room so you can freshen up for dinner. I think that we should go out for a quick bite to eat, and then settle in for an early evening. We have a lot to accomplish tomorrow."

Having forgotten her unease about their possible sleeping arrangements, Fleur was delighted to hear the news.

"Ah," she said. "You have a guest room. I mean, yes, happy to see your guest room. I'll freshen up before going out. Do you have somewhere in mind?"

Thomas smiled as he led Fleur up the stairs to the open foyer level above the central living area.

The room Thomas showed her was furnished with overstuffed bedding and an armchair. "Oh, the bed, you could go off to sleep with a happy smile on your face," said Fleur.

Thomas' wolfish grin had Fleur blushing for a fourth time that day.

"The pub at the corner serves great food," said Thomas. "Shall we get a quick bite of dinner? Is fifteen minutes enough time for you to freshen up?"

Thomas pushed open the heavy etched glass red pub door of O'Toole's and stepped aside for Fleur to enter. The din of laughter, music, and chatter washed over her like an energizing wave. Her eyes adjusted to the dim lighting to find a small bar area jammed with people, and another larger area up a couple of stairs beyond the bar with more tables.

In the corner by the door, a group of musicians played lively Irish tunes with fiddles, accordions, and a keyboard. Some people around the bar were singing along with the musicians, while others stamped their feet in time with the beat. Fleur grinned with pleasure that she was experiencing Thomas' culture with him.

Thomas found a couple of stools at the bar. "Now that you're in Ireland, are you going to try Guinness? It's a gift from the leprechauns, you know."

"No, I've never heard that, but I'll try a Guinness," said Fleur. "Be warned, I'm a chardonnay type of girl."

Fleur frowned at the thick dark beverage as they clinked their glasses. Thomas took a large swig, licked his lips, and raised his glass to heaven. "The good stuff, and always best in Dublin."

Fleur took a tentative sip and made such a face of disgust that Thomas nodded to the bartender and said a single word: "Canadian." The bartender nodded, poured a glass of chardonnay, and placed it in front of Fleur. She laughed at being the brunt of their joke.

"OK, Mister," she teased. "If you're such as good Irishman, let's hear you sing a tune."

To Fleur's utter surprise, Thomas casually got off his stool, sauntered over to the musicians, whispered to the fiddle player, and proceeded to play the fiddle handed to him. It took but a second for the rest of the group to join in, and a rousing rendition of the folksong *Wild Rover* soon filled the pub. Thomas was animated as he sawed the fiddle, stamped his feet, danced his body, and sang louder than the rest of the band. He stayed with the musicians to play another half dozen songs, with some songs sung in the Celtic language.

Fleur clapped her delight throughout the evening, seeing Thomas yet again with new appreciation. Far from being the conversative man she first thought him to be, this evening at the pub showed her a fun side she couldn't have imagined.

They returned to Thomas' apartment arm-in-arm, sides aching from laughing all evening, Fleur flopped down on the sofa feeling quite at home, even putting her bare feet up on the hassock. She accepted a glass of wine Thomas offered as a nightcap.

She sipped the fresh chardonnay, "Thank you for a wonderful evening, Thomas."

Fleur learned quite a lot about Thomas. "I couldn't believe it when you joined the band," she said. "Where did you learn to play the fiddle like that? And how many Irish songs do you know all of the words?"

Thomas put his thumbs under his arms in a comical gesture. "Well there, us Irish be knowing all them Irish songs," he teased. "We learn-ed them Irish toons from ore memahs when we be babbies."

Fleur laughed at Thomas' silly leprechaun brogue. She loved his soft, lyrical accent. Thomas talked a lot that evening, more than usual, she thought, like an excited schoolboy showing his favorite girl all of his special belongings.

Whether it was the wine or the influence of Thomas' deep voice, Fleur nestled next to Thomas on the sofa. She felt more at home in her own skin than she had in a very long time.

Fleur was spellbound as he told her about the historical properties he had restored. His passion for this work was clear, and she immersed herself in his enthusiasm. He told her what he and John were planning for the Dowart Estate, not only to restore the castle and estate, but to run it like an intimate hotel, providing visitors an experience of an era long gone. Fleur had heard about these plans from Matty, but hearing the details from Thomas made it more sensational.

Though she was happy for Thomas and John and their plans, Fleur tensed as Thomas talked. She wasn't concerned about the Factor's House and her inheritance. She believed Thomas when he said it was sorted. However, his clear knowing of what he wanted to do contrasted with her own uncertainty about her path forward, her passion for her art, and her family. Not only that, she was worried about falling in love again.

Thomas was aware when Fleur's mood changed; she wasn't herself, and he remarked, "I'm sorry. How insensitive of me to be talking about my plans for the estate when you are not clear about your inheritance. Don't worry, we'll take care of that first thing in the morning. When we made last-minute plans to come to Dublin, I set up an appointment with the solicitor to finalize the details of the deed transfer."

Fleur appreciated how Thomas was sensitive to her emotions. "It wasn't that at all. You had already told me not to be concerned about my claim to the Factor's House. I was thinking about how lost I've felt these past few months, not knowing what my path is. You are so clear about what you want to do and who you are, it highlighted my own uncertainty.

"Grana always taught me everything is my path. Whatever I'm doing, that's my path. I need to flow, and stop all of the thinking. All that pondering I've been doing has made me feel stuck."

Thomas' caring gaze encouraged Fleur. Something opened up inside, and she wanted to share her growing feelings for him.

"The time we've been together has been wonderful. I feel at home with you, Thomas. I trust you, and I trust what you tell me. At the same time, these feelings scare me. I had a terrible experience with my marriage. I don't want that to happen again."

Fleur could see light in Thomas' eyes. Without saying a word, he drew her closer, looked into her eyes, and kissed her. At first, his kisses were loving, sweet kisses, on her eyes, on her forehead, and on her lips. Fleur murmured in contentment, a small sound that was Thomas' undoing. He deepened his kiss, and Fleur responded.

The sound of an ambulance on the street below broke through the fog of their lust. Fleur pulled away from Thomas. She remembered the appointment at the solicitors, and she wanted to be sure that her growing feelings for Thomas didn't get in the way of being clear minded.

"I think we'd better call it a night," said Thomas. "We have a long day tomorrow." Fleur appreciated that Thomas didn't belabor her stopping their romantic activity. He seemed to understand, and because of that her affection for him grew even more. That night, snuggled in the downy guest bed, she enjoyed her first dreamless sleep in a long time.

Fleur faltered when she saw the name Pheill McDonnell & Sons on the bronze plaque outside a building not far from Trinity College. Thomas sensed the tug of her emotions, and took her hand to reassure her. She appreciated the gesture of support. So much had happened since she opened that letter from Pheill McDonnell & Sons disputing her inheritance. Now here she was, at their law offices in Dublin, about to resolve things. At least that was her hope.

Fleur needed to be sure that Auntie G. and Grana were both taken care of, which meant that the only home that Auntie G. had ever known needed to remain in their family. To do that, the next logical step was to secure her ownership of the Factor's House.

Fleur and Thomas did not wait long for James McDonnell to join them. James was a childhood friend of Thomas. Fleur felt immediately at ease meeting him as he was warm, friendly, and exuded a manner of efficiency and clarity.

James first explained the property transfer based on the will of the Laird. The property included the Factor's House as well as four acres around the house. There was an additional clause giving Fleur the freedom to traverse the lands outside the perimeter of the castle, including the hilltop. Fleur understood that Thomas included that clause because of her interest in the circle of standing stones.

After reviewing the property deeds and documents, James showed Fleur a letter Thomas and John both signed explicitly revoking the suit they had previously lodged against her. Fleur touched Thomas' hand in appreciation after she read the letter. She knew this was also not a necessary step in the process.

Finally, James handed a thick file folder to Fleur. "This file documents all the tenants who have inhabited the Factor's House since it was built," said James. "It includes the factors who maintained the Dowart Estate as well as their family. Basically, it is your family tree going back to the year 1720."

Fleur gazed at Thomas, tears spilling through her smile of gratitude. It was clear that Thomas and his brother took great pains to ensure her inheritance and interests were well protected. The additional step of having their solicitor trace the lineage of factors for the estate was an extraordinary kindness that left her speechless.

"Let me know if you need more time to read the documents," said Thomas. "You don't need to sign anything today. You can wait for your lawyers to review it."

Fleur touched Thomas' arm. "That won't be necessary," she said, her voice soft with appreciation. "It's clear that you and John have honored your grandfather's wishes in transferring ownership of the Factor's House to me." Fleur signed the documents and breathed a sigh of relief.

Outside, Fleur reveled in the pure sense of freedom, walking arm-in-arm with Thomas along the streets of Dublin.

"It's a bit early for lunch, but maybe we should raise a glass to celebrate?" Thomas asked. "I know a great little restaurant around the corner."

Fleur loved the restaurant Thomas picked. "Look at the name of the restaurant. The Dragonfly, how perfect!"

Thomas grinned as they sat down. "I thought it might be," he said. "Dragonflies are symbolic of new beginnings."

"You're right," said Fleur, feeling a blush starting from her chest. "But I have to tell you, The Dragonfly Café is the name of the little diner in Antigonish where I work part time. Or where I used to work. I'm not sure what I'm doing now. I have to decide about what's next." To lighten her unsure mood, Fleur told Thomas stories of the characters at The Dragonfly Café.

"Aren't small towns wonderful?" he said. "I'm sure you've experienced similar characters in your short stay on Mull."

"Matty is our social monitor," said Fleur with a smile. "She loves meeting people and finding the nitty gritty about a place through their stories. She has met quite a few people who are like folks from home. Like Mrs. Donnegagh, the Tobermory librarian, is just as quirky, knowledgeable, and loveable as Mrs. Murray at the Antigonish library."

Mentioning Matty brought up the topic of what Fleur would do next. Thomas asked, "With your clear ownership of the Factor's House, and Matty deciding to stay in Mull to help John with his business, do you think you would consider staying as well?"

"Are you asking me because you'd like me to stay here to be near you?"

When Thomas turned serious, Fleur regretted her flippant question. "I'm sorry," she said. "I had no right to put you on the spot."

Thomas shook his head. "Not at all," he said. "I've been wondering how I could say goodbye to you if you decided not to stay."

Fleur was pleased, but didn't have a chance to reply. Thomas jumped up and grabbed her hand, all at once in a hurry to get out of the restaurant.

"Sorry to rush," he said. "But the college library will be closed in a few hours, and we should go this afternoon to see the Book of Kells. Monday is the perfect day, not too many people are around to view it. I'd like you to have enough time to settle in with the tomes."

The Trinity College library took Fleur's breath away. Never had she seen such enormous vaulted ceilings. Two levels of stacked shelves of books lined the entire room.

Thomas took her hand. "Isn't this place spectacular," he whispered. "Come this way, the book that I want to show you is on the second level."

Thomas approached the display case in the center of a small side gallery. Fleur stood still, holding her breath as her eyes adjusted to the gloomier light. When her eyes could focus, she gasped, not prepared for the simple beauty of the illustration on the open book before her. It was exquisite, and she could see immediately that it was indeed painted by a woman. The brushstrokes and the way the paint was applied confirmed that opinion.

Fleur stared at the image of the woman who resembled her own image and that of T'Eilin.

"It's her," whispered Fleur. She swayed and muttered, "I feel strange. Please hold my hand. I've come to do the work, but I don't know what it is. Do you know what it is, Brendan?"

Thomas held her hand and spoke in a tone she would understand through her trance. "I'm here," he said. "Don't be afraid, I'll keep you safe. Just try to understand the message you need to hear."

Still holding Thomas' hand, Fleur closed her eyes and nodded her head, as though agreeing. Thomas watched her, prepared to break the trance if she became distressed.

Only a few minutes passed when Fleur opened her eyes wide and pointed at the page in the display case, "Look, it's a hand."

Thomas was so intent on watching Fleur, he had not looked down at the page. Runes had emerged on the page, next to the woman's upraised right hand. Looking at the details, he recognized the same runes as those on the diary page, though some were missing from this rendition. The image appeared to be missing every other rune except for the fifth one to the right, where two were missing.

"You're right, Fleur," said Thomas. "The pattern looks like a hand. Perhaps the key is to lay your hand on the runes. Maybe it activates something to happen on the night of the crescent moon."

Fleur looked at Thomas and smiled at his enthusiasm. "Do you think so?" she said. "Maybe it has everything to do with the night of the crescent moon?"

Thomas remembered Fleur raising her hand to touch the runes. He reflected on the details of that day. "Wait a minute, I was holding your right hand," he said. "You must have used your left hand to touch the stones."

Realization hit both of them at once. "That's it, that's the key," he said. "The key is your right hand."

CHAPTER EIGHTEEN

AN ISLAND OF THE HEBRIDES, AD 560

The crescent moon shone upon the circle of standing stones, silhouetting the lone figure of a woman who lay deep in grief in the middle of the stone circle. This night of the waning crescent moon, when the moon recedes from its fullness and is reduced towards a new moon, brings with it a sense of surrender and reflection. The woman in the circle was in the throes of abysmal surrender, for her world had fallen apart. All whom she loved were lost, or so she thought.

The woman, T'Eilin the intuitive of the Irie tribe, cried aloud in great anguish. "No – I will not let him take away my power." She felt great anguish thinking she was the cause of so much pain, and she threw herself on the ground weeping.

As T'Eilin lay in the middle of the standing stones, she heard her grandmother speaking: "Do not forget who you are. Open your heart, be in the place of love where all creation happens. The illusion of time and space stops when you are in the place of love. All illusion of separateness stops. Then you can connect with the energy that creates life. Then you can do the work to be free, and to free your descendants ahead of you, and your ancestors behind."

T'Eilin lifted her head to the heavens and vowed out loud, with the standing stones as witness. "I hear you grandmother. I will work in this life, and in the next life, and as many generations and lifetimes as it would take, to break this curse."

T'Eilin slipped into a deep trance. Her grandmother's voice whispered into the wind, "Find the one who is marked. She will help you."

Brendan knew where to find his beloved when he was able to do so. T'Eilin was out of harm's way on the hilltop far from the village in the protection of the circle of standing stones. He needed to leave her there alone while he dealt with the aftermath of the event that had sent T'Eilin fleeing for her life. It pained him to imagine the grief she must be experiencing believing that her tribe's people were all dead. He knew she would rather have died herself than allow her people suffer. Brendan had insisted that she flee to save her life, convincing her it was the only way to save her people.

The surprise attack by Tonnick and his mercenary warriors had been short-lived. The attack had been brutal, interrupting the completion ceremony between Brendan and T'Eilin when the people were distracted and at their most vulnerable. But Tonnick and his group proved to be no match for Alcorat's leadership and the superior discipline of the tribe's warriors. Within minutes, the invaders were subdued and the threat to the tribe's people removed. Tonnick and his band of warriors were killed.

After the battle, Brendan turned his attention to separating the wounded from the dead, and attending to injuries, dealing with the most severe first. He was relieved when he found Diiaan hiding in the healing hut, and the Healing Mother on the ground, shaken but otherwise unharmed. Farmer Hinnian had thrown himself on top of the Healing Mother to protect her, though he himself had died in the process.

By the time the morning sun flickered over the horizon, the wounded tribe's people had been treated. Brendan was not alone in his ministrations. Diiaan worked tirelessly all night beside him, as did the Healing Mother. Meanwhile, Alcorat and the warriors restored the village such that all trace of the mayhem of the evening before was erased.

Though Brendan was extremely weary, he headed to the hilltop to find T'Eilin. He needed to reassure her that all was well with the tribe. Though they suffered losses, most of the tribe's people were unharmed and doing well.

T'Eilin raised her head from the ground where she had fallen into a nightmare-filled sleep. She blinked at the sun coming up over the trees, then bent over clutching her belly at the force of the pain at remembering the carnage of the evening before. Distraught by the images that filled her mind, she did not know how she would continue to live. Her people were gone. What was she to do? The only thing that kept her going was the knowledge that she and Brendan had created a child. The unborn child within her was all that mattered now. She must be strong to keep their child safe. This child was the future.

As she began to weep once more, heaving with the pain of the betrayal to her people, her attention went to a sound coming from the trees behind her. Instantly alert to the possibility of danger, the survival instinct to save her unborn child snapped her out of her despair and put her immediately on the defensive. If this was Tonnick come to kill her, he would not find her on the ground weeping, she thought.

T'Eilin stood tall facing the trees, prepared for what might come. She used the last ounce of her waning energy to stand erect. She was prepared for confrontation, but she was not prepared to see the person she loved more than life coming toward her through the trees and into the center of the standing stones.

She collapsed against Brendan's chest, unable to stand upright for the sheer relief of seeing him. "Is it really you?" she exclaimed. "I thought you were killed. I thought you were lost to me."

Brendan crooned and soothed her brow as he sunk onto the ground to support her in his lap. They remained thus for several minutes, bodies intertwined in complete relief, before T'Eilin found voice to speak again.

"My love, I am so glad you are alive," she said touching his face, arms, and hands to ensure he was truly there with her. "What of the people? Did they also survive the attack?"

Brendan stroked her hair to shield her from the pain. "We lost many people to the invaders," he said. "But Alcorat and his warriors were quick to respond to the attack, and many were saved. The Healing Mother is among those spared from the invaders' wrath. Farmer Hinnian sacrificed himself to protect her, throwing his body on hers. I found her unharmed."

Though overjoyed to hear that her grandmother was alive and well, T'Eilin felt sorrow for Farmer Hinnian. "His brave act has balanced his aggression towards the Healing Mother those months ago at the Speaking Session. All is well and in harmony now."

Finding strength from the knowledge that her tribe's people were well and needed her attention, T'Eilin stood up and shook the dust from her clothes. "We must go," said T'Eilin. "There are injuries to tend, and the dead to bury."

"The injured are doing well," said Brendan. "We looked after them immediately, which is why I did not come to find you right away. It pained me to think of your suffering here, thinking the worst of the attack, but I knew you would understand what had to be done for the people first."

T'Eilin touched Brendan's face in appreciation, and took his hand. They walked off the hilltop, connected by their physical touch and by their resolve to help the tribe's people.

T'Eilin stared around at the village grounds, unable to reconcile the order she saw with the last images in her mind of the invaders' attack. The tribe's people were going about their normal tasks as though nothing untoward had occurred. Such was the rhythm of life for her tribe, an acceptance of what is and a continuation of what is to be.

T'Eilin looked at Brendan with loving eyes when they arrived at the healing hut. He nodded his head to indicate he would wait outside to allow T'Eilin time alone with her grandmother. She hurried inside, eager to embrace her grandmother. Naghaire turned around from her task at the exact moment T'Eilin entered the hut and rushed toward her granddaughter. They held each other, lingering in their joy of seeing each other alive and well.

Naghaire was the first to break from the embrace with T'Eilin to say, "My darling granddaughter, I am well pleased to see you. I feared that ill had befallen you. Did you feel my energy calling to you while you were at the standing stones?"

"Yes, grandmother, I felt your loving presence and heard your words," said T'Eilin. "Your words saved me from my despair. I was distraught at thinking the worst had happened and that all the tribe were lost. It was a time of deepest grief for me."

Naghaire smoothed T'Eilin's hair and pulled her hand to guide her to the back of the hut where they could sit in comfort and discuss what had happened.

"You have a question," said Naghaire. "Please tell me what it is so that I can try to help you find an answer."

T'Eilin was still overcome by the emotions of seeing Brendan and her grandmother after thinking the worst had happened to them. She knew there would be more feelings for her to navigate through in the coming days as she tended to the injured and discovered who among the tribe had been killed by the invaders. For now, she needed to recover her strength, and so she focused on the one question that filled her mind. It was the matter of the curse.

"Grandmother, in truth I have many questions," said T'Eilin. "Mostly about the words you to spoke to me while I was at the circle of stones. We can discuss those questions in the days ahead, after we have tended to the injuries of the tribe's people. For now, you are correct, I have one question that is most on my mind."

Naghaire nodded her head, "It is the matter of the curse that most concerns you. Is that right?"

"Yes grandmother," said T'Eilin. "With Tonnick dead, does that mean the curse is ended? What now happens to our line, is it saved as our tribe's people have been saved? Or it too late because the curse had already been set in motion?"

Naghaire stroked her chin. "It is hard to say just what has occurred," she said. "We may not know now; it may become clear at some other time. Or we may never know. The only thing we can do is carry on with our own work."

T'Eilin rubbed her temple. Her intuition told her to leave logic behind and go to the feeling place of the heart. From that place, she added her own wisdom to that of her grandmother's to say, "As I vowed at the standing stones, it will be my life's work to strive for alignment with open heart and to teach my child and her child and so on down the line. The teaching I must embrace is that love is the place where all illusions cease to be and where creation happens. I vow also to find the descendant marked to help us, because I know that her work will help our ancestry just as it will enable her to find peace and wellbeing."

In the months that followed, T'Eilin stayed true to her heart. She built a life of service to the tribe's people alongside Brendan. He continued his work to teach the people, and T'Eilin continued to minister to their physical and intuitive needs.

When two moons had passed since Tonnick's attack on the tribe, T'Eilin knew it was time to tell Brendan about his child growing inside of her. She thought carefully about where and when to tell him the news, aware that this event would change the path of their ancestry.

She chose to tell Brendan on the night of the waxing crescent moon, as that moon holds the energy of optimism for great change. The obvious location was the standing stones. The circle of stones was her connection with spirit for most of her life. Brendan readily agreed to go with her to the standing stones that evening, aware that it was important for her to perform a ceremony on the night of the crescent moon.

T'Eilin and Brendan crested the ridge of the hilltop just as the crescent moon came out from behind clouds hovering high above the horizon. The moon was clearly visible from the middle of the standing stones. T'Eilin greeted the spirit of the circle of stones, and then motioned for Brendan to join her to sit in the middle of the circle of stones.

T'Eilin took both of Brendan's hands in her hands, and looked deeply into his eyes with unabashed love. She heard Brendan swallow and smiled at his recognition of her love for him. "Beloved," she whispered. "I wanted us to be in this sacred place when I told you the news. I am with your child. A daughter is to be born to us. She will continue to do our work, teaching her children and their children about our eternal love."

Brendan leaned forward, cradled T'Eilin's face, and rested his forehead against hers. No words were needed, for T'Eilin felt the utter joy in his heart.

Before they left the standing stones, T'Eilin asked Brendan for a moment alone. She walked to the eastern quadrant of the circle of stones and placed her hand on the furthermost stone lining up with the rising sun. She spoke words of intention aloud, "May the hand of my descendant find the energy of the hand I now place upon this stone. May the work be done as it should, by myself, by our ancestors, by our descendants. Through me and through the child I carry. May this be a key that unlocks the energy of love, and may it bring about the cessation of time and space such that we find our oneness. This I ask, and so it is."

T'Eilin bowed her head and left the standing stones secure in the knowledge she set something in motion that would prove to be important for her ancestry.

CHAPTER NINETEEN

ISLE OF MULL, SCOTLAND, 1987

Fleur had a chance to catch her breath before they traveled back to the Isle of Mull. She had appreciated Thomas' suggestion that they stay an extra couple of days in Dublin. Though she had wanted to get back as soon as possible, she admitted she could use some space to process everything. There was enough time before the night of the crescent moon for them to return. Besides, she was excited for Thomas to show her around his city.

She loved that the city was vibrant with music, and enjoyed walking with Thomas along the River Liffey through the center of Dublin, listening to the entertainers serenading the crowds. In the evening, she and Thomas enjoyed chatting at the outdoor cafes along the river.

They discussed at length what they witnessed at the college library. The sudden appearance of the runes on the page of the Book of Kells was nothing short of magic. Thomas had contacted an archeologist friend who studied runes to find out the runic meaning of the symbols. He had faxed a copy of the diary page of runes ahead to his friend, and they had an appointment to meet.

Fleur stood back as Thomas knocked on the door to his friend's office in the archeology department of Trinity College. A bespectacled, distracted man came to the door, and welcomed Thomas with a hug.

"There you are, old scoundrel," said the man. "Ah, you must be Fleur? Lovely. Come in."

Fleur had been concerned about what a stranger might think of the strange occurrences, but Thomas reassured her that Malcolm would not pry about the origins or the story behind the runes.

"That was an interesting page you sent me," said Malcolm after they had exchanged pleasantries. "I presume if these runes came from an archeological find of any significance, you'd share with me more than just an illustration of runes."

Thomas patted his friend on the back. "Absolutely," he said. "You would be the first person I'd contact. Can you decipher their meaning?"

Malcolm nodded his head and said, "These symbols are the Elder Futhark Germanic runic alphabet, used between the second and eighth centuries. The transliteration of runes is difficult without context of where they are from. You see, runes are not letters, or a code. Each rune has a sound and a meaning attached to it, and there is a lot of guesswork to come up with their transliteration."

Fleur had only heard of runes in a mystical context. "Are runes magical?" she asked.

"The Elder Futhark runes, though the simplest to learn, were rarely used to convey information," said Malcolm. "They were usually short inscriptions written in riddles and codes. To the early Germanic tribes, the act of writing something had seemed to be magic, so in that sense I suppose they were."

"And their meaning?" asked Thomas.

Malcolm handed a piece of paper to Thomas with the runes on the top and English words on the bottom. "My best guess is this is the meaning of these runes," he said. "Forgive the words flowing together. There is no punctuation in Elder Futhark."

Fleur leaned over Thomas' shoulder, and inhaled when she read the words. They made complete sense related to her situation, as if they were meant specifically for her. Which of course she now believed that they were.

The translation on the page that Malcom gave them was this:

ancestors live through you heal your pain and the pain of your ancestors heals

Thomas thanked Malcolm and made a tentative date to meet up when he was next in Dublin. Then, he and Fleur made their way to the car to continue their journey back to the Isle of Mull. If all went well, they would arrive at the Factor's House in time for tea.

By the time Fleur went into the kitchen for coffee the next day, Thomas was chatting with her Grana and Auntie G.

"Good morning, sleepy head," he said, grinning when he spotted Fleur coming through the door. "Slept well?"

Fleur admitted to feeling perkier, in large part because of the soothing dreams she had about her great-great-grandmother throughout the night. She felt energized and ready for action.

"Good morning, Grana and Auntie G. Sorry for not telling you about our trip to Dublin last night. I was shattered and needed to sleep. How was your visit while I was away?"

Grana answered first, amusing Fleur that she and Auntie G. completed each other's sentences. "Dearie, we had a wonderful time," she said. "We spent hours chatting ..."

Auntie G. jumped in, "...and telling all our stories. We had a marvelous time getting to know one another."

"Did Thomas tell you about Dublin?" asked Fleur.

"No, mo mhuirnín, that's your story to tell," said Thomas.

Fleur blushed at the endearment Thomas used for a second time, and made a note to find out what it meant. She explained to her relatives everything that happened at the standing stones prior to their departure to Dublin, and what happened at Trinity College when they went to look at the Book of Kells. They didn't appear to be astounded about the runes emerging on the illustration. Grana and Auntie G. both took all she relayed in stride, as though the magical things she experienced were everyday occurrences.

Her Grana became particularly attentive to the transliteration of the runes provided by Malcolm. "The message from the runes seems to be in sync with my grandmother's words to me, and what Dante's also said to you," she said. "There's no doubt you are supposed to heal not only yourself, but your ancestors."

Fleur asked if they knew what a vortex might mean in relation to the circle of standing stones. She wondered if they knew what might be revealed on the night of the crescent moon.

"I don't know specifically in this situation," Auntie G. said. "However, I believe that every thought that has ever been thought still exists through the ether of time, even to this day. There is a web of thought that can impact us, influencing our own thoughts and behavior if we allow it."

Her Grana added, "A vortex is a center of energy in the earth. Perhaps a vortex at the standing stones is opening for you to find answers from your ancestors. Maybe you'll find out the meaning of this ancient family curse. With all that you've experienced already there, you know better than anyone the power of the place."

"Don't fret, dearie," said Grana, sensing Fleur's apprehension. "We are never given more than we can handle. Besides, I'll be there to make sure you are safe and well."

Fleur said to her grandmother in surprise, "You'll be there when I open myself up to the vortex? Are you sure you are able to walk all the way up to the hilltop?"

Fleur heard her Grana sniff. "Dearie, I don't intend to hike up the hill, though I'm sure I could. Even with this bum leg. No – your Auntie G. and I talked about this, and I'm going with you – using the old ways. While you were away in Dublin, my sister awakened the great knowledge in me that I had almost forgotten I had, so rest assured, I will be there to support you."

Fleur and Thomas had a few moments to speak alone. They arranged to leave later in the afternoon in order to arrive at the standing stones well before dusk, as the crescent moon appeared in the eastern sky. Fleur would spend the rest of the morning in meditation to clear any resistant energy or thoughts she might be holding. She instinctively knew that her mind needed to be peaceful before she approached the circle of stones.

Fleur was bereft when Thomas left her alone for a few hours. She wondered how she had come to rely on his strength in such a short period of time. She went to the conservatory to gird herself for this evening's activity. The minute she crossed the threshold into the room, a joyfulness that expelled all worry wrapped around her. She sat in front of the painting she had created and filled her mind with loving thoughts.

Somewhere here is the solution to this mystery. It is a gift for me. It brought me to painting again. Thank you, great-great-grandmother, for your inspiration. Was it only a few days ago that I had painted this canvas? So much had happened since then.

In this room, she indulged in a daydream. She thought about the couple portrayed in her painting and how they might have lived together. Fleur didn't fret about who the couple was, whether it was Thomas and herself, or T'Eilin and Brendan. She realized that the painting was a symbol of love and hope, perhaps no more than that.

Fleur let her mind drift to thoughts about her own future. She imagined what it would be like to stay on Mull at the Factor's House with her Auntie G., and maybe with her Grana. Fleur imagined opening up this magnificent conservatory for other artists to enjoy. In that moment, Fleur imagined the Factor's House as a retreat center where artists could come to reignite their talents, much in the same way she herself had rediscovered her artistic voice again.

When it was time to meet Thomas to go to the standing stones, she felt refreshed, ready, and eager.

Thomas saw a tear in Fleur's eye as she said goodbye to Grana and Auntie G. He put his arm around her shoulder to give her encouragement, and whispered in her ear, "Mo mhuirnín, my beloved, all will be well."

They arrived at the top of the hill well before dusk, just as the faint outline of the crescent moon became visible like a sliver of hope. This night of the waxing crescent moon, when the moon moves toward fullness, holds the energy of optimism for the future. So much was unknown, yet Fleur showed great courage to face these mysterious events. He expected his role would be to stand by, trusting he'd know what to do if she needed his help.

Thomas took comfort in the determination and courage that he saw on Fleur's face. She walked without hesitation into the middle of the circle of stones and announced her presence, "Do you see me, Source Energy? I am Fleur, and I am here to ask for clarity and understanding. I am here to clear the ancient curse from my ancestry."

Thomas watched from the edge of the circle, knowing Fleur needed to feel autonomy as she greeted the presence within the circle of stones. Fleur nodded her head as though in agreement, and then she walked to the stone with the rune engravings. Thomas held his breath. Fleur placed her right hand on the runes. She was in control, not like the first time he had met her at the stones.

The space between Fleur's fingers glowed in the dusk as she rested her right hand on the stone. Lights pulsated from behind her hand. Fleur did not flinch. Thomas heard a buzzing sound like thousands of voices in the distance. The lights around Fleur's hand appeared to float towards her head and meld into the crescent moon birthmark on her neck, similar to when Thomas found her unconscious. Unlike that time, the merging lights did not cause Fleur discomfort. She turned, walked back to the center of the circle of stones, sat on the ground humming to herself, and became still, as though she had fallen into a trance. Thomas could only wonder at the visions she might be having. He had to trust that his presence would help keep her safe.

Fleur was aware of Thomas' concern, but could do nothing to assure him. She needed to focus on allowing the powerful magic to happen. Previously, she had been less sure of herself; now, she sensed her power and she knew how to use it. She had overcome her fears – of opening her heart, of painting, and of loving again.

As Fleur settled herself deeper into her trance, four women of differing ages appeared to her in a vision. She recognized two of the women, T'Eilin and her Grana. It was a great comfort to see her Grana. Bowing her head towards each of the four women in turn, Fleur waited for one of them to speak first.

T'Eilin was the first to speak. "I see you, Fleur, the last of my line," she said. "I am T'Eilin, and I have summoned you. I am your ancestor, the intuitive for the Irie tribe. I left a legacy of suffering and sorrow, and have summoned you to save our ancestry from an ancient curse."

Fleur stared in amazement upon seeing T'Eilin so close to her. T'Eilin was not only physically like Fleur, but even her mannerisms were the same, the way she held her posture, the angle of her head, how she moved her long blonde hair away from her neck to receive airflow. Fleur saw that T'Eilin even had the crescent moon birthmark on her neck in the same spot.

"I am honored to have been summoned," she said. "What am I to do? What is the work?"

T'Eilin took a step closer to Fleur as she spoke, "You are to align with your true self, your Inner Being. The work is to close the gap between you as human, focused physically here on this earth plane, and you as a higher being, eternal in nature and energetically focused."

Fleur furrowed her brow, not understanding. "Please be patient with me and explain further."

T'Eilin smiled and reached out a hand as though to touch Fleur. "I denied my very nature when I denied love," she said. "My resistance and split energy caused a rift in our ancestry. I gave my power away to a man whose behavior I took responsibility for when it was not my fault. This pattern has rippled through time. Every generation paid the price. A line of women not knowing true love, either a man's love or a mother's love. Daughters of my daughter, and their daughters raised by their grandmothers, wondering why they did not know a mother's love. Daughters of my daughter, and their daughters giving their power away when love seemed to scorn them. You are the last of the line to have had the same experience in both areas. You know the pain of it, and it rests with you and your ability to heal it now for all generations."

Fleur was amazed to hear that the pain she experienced had been shared by many before her. She asked, "What am I to do?"

"You are the conduit to stop the generational pattern and habit of behavior that started with me," said T'Eilin. "In my state of pure positive energy now, I know life is a joyous gift. We get to play, to choose either to live savoring all things as one thing, that which we perceive to be bad and that which we perceive to be good. Or we live in misery, fighting all the moments of struggle so that the universal source of all must give us problems to stimulate our growth and expansion. I stand inside the vortex, knowing of my misstep."

T'Eilin bowed her head as though in sorrow, then raised it high to say, "Fleur, I summoned you here to do the work. You have followed the clues I left over the ages, the dreams, the illustration that my beloved Brendan showed how to make on parchment, the runes. I have gathered representatives of generations of our line to clean the non-truth of this generational pattern of guilt, sacrifice, and responsibility that has rippled through time. This I say, and so it is. I love you, I am sorry, please forgive me, thank you." T'Eilin bowed towards Fleur and stepped away.

"Thank you, T'Eilin," she said. "You honor me with your presence and your words. I shall endeavor to live a life that will benefit all by staying true to my nature, taking back my power, and being open to the magic of life."

As Fleur wondered what would happen next, the older woman standing next to T'Eilin stepped forward and spoke. "I see you, Fleur," she said. "I am Naghaire, grandmother to T'Eilin and Healing Mother of the Irie tribe. In my physical life, I was given the knowledge that the wellbeing of our line of women had been disrupted before T'Eilin's time."

Naghaire took a breath and looked at T'Eilin with great tenderness. "It was not T'Eilin's fault, but she kept alive the habitual pattern of feeling responsible for those around her. She gave up her dreams to sacrifice for others. In my ignorance, I put the ancient legend of a family curse in her mind. So, when a man stood before her who spoke aloud curse-like words, T'Eilin gave him her power by believing this non-truth. She had great ability as an intuitive, but could not see this. It is a great power to stand firm in love, and to see the opportunities for love. Fleur, I encourage you to take back your power, know who you are, and live a full life awakened to all of your potential."

Naghaire ended with the same words as T'Eilin, "This I say, and so it is. I love you, I am sorry, please forgive me, thank you."

Fleur looked toward Naghaire, nodded her head, and said, "Thank you Naghaire. I am honored with your presence and your words. I have faith that your words will bring clarity."

Fleur guessed that the woman standing next to her Grana must be her great-great-grandmother, Fiona Kintrell. "I see you, Fleur" said the woman. "I am Fiona Kintrell, your great-great-grandmother. You read the diary containing my deepest thoughts. You know how much I enjoyed the opportunities and talents I was given. I was called to do the work through my painting, and I did so wholeheartedly, guided by the collective consciousness I called Lliam, whom I met at these very same standing stones."

Fleur wanted to ask so many questions, but held her peace. "I left my country and family to protect Eileen, your grandmother," said Fiona. "I was aligned with that decision at the time, but as the years went on, I felt trapped, like I had given up the only life I knew to protect my beautiful granddaughter. My misstep was that Eileen didn't need protection in the first place. She didn't need me to sacrifice for her. I became hardened, and shut the door on the past. As a consequence, your grandmother did not know her roots, and neither did you. I gave away my power. In alignment I was strong, but when non-truths entered my thoughts, I lost my power." Fiona concluded with the words "This I say, and so it is. I love you, I'm sorry, please forgive me, thank you."

Next, Fleur's own grandmother stepped forward to speak, smiling at her lovely granddaughter. "I see you, my beautiful granddaughter," she said. "I am Eileen Kintrell Lewis. I had the privilege to raise you from infancy, and you have been the love of my life. When I intuited years ago that I had a sister in Scotland, I did not reach out to her. In this way, I failed you. I know that you felt lost and needed to know where you came from to know who you are. But you have always known who you are. Now you will acknowledge this truth and go forward with courage. This I say, and so it is. I love you, I'm sorry, please forgive me, thank you."

It was a great effort for Fleur to hold her emotions in check as her Grana spoke. She wanted to rush into her Grana's arms. Naghaire stepped to the front and said, "Here in this vortex where the energy of the standing stones connects us, we, your ancestors, have taken responsibility in our own way for our actions. The cleansing is done. The healing words of forgiveness have been spoken, and have released the pain that bound us to the past. Divine thoughts, words, deeds, and actions will flow to positively impact your life. You are freed from the past."

Her Grana spoke after Naghaire. "Remember every step you take is a step on your path," she said. "Whether you are aligned or not, it is a moment-to-moment process. All is the path. The work of alignment is you coming back to who you are, your very nature, and that is love and joy to your very core. When you live from your true nature, you will influence others. For one person who is awakened to this truth can carry thousands who are asleep."

As the vision of the four women faded, Fleur's heart brimmed with the love that these women from many generations showered on her. She knew that although she might not be able to see them going forward, the ancestors would always be with her. Her words and actions would always reflect her ancestors. She felt such a sense of connection to family like never before, and she was eager to get on with her life's purpose.

CHAPTER TWENTY

Fleur awoke early in the morning, before even Auntie G. or her Grana roused from sleep. She was refreshed from her slumber and the pleasant dream she experienced about T'Eilin and Brendan. The dream gave her answers to some questions she had about what had happened to them, but there were still pieces of the puzzle unanswered.

She had been too exhausted the evening before to do anything but fall into bed when she and Thomas returned to the Factor's House. Even seeing her Grana at the door, and knowing that she likely had answers to her questions, did not stop her from going to her bedroom.

The power exerted to produce the vision must have been potent indeed, for when it was over Thomas noted that only a few minutes had passed between when Fleur had sat in the middle of the stone circle and when she got up to leave the circle. To Fleur, it was as though an entire evening had passed. Fleur planned to talk with him at length about what transpired when she saw him later. After all, he was now a part of it, not only in helping her to solve the mystery, but also from his remarkable resemblance to Brendan. That piece of the puzzle still needed to be sorted.

She resolved to discuss all aspects of last night's vision at the standing stones with her Grana later this morning. There were many things about the vision that she did not understand, and perhaps her Grana could help her.

Meanwhile, the idea came to Fleur to see if she could merge with T'Eilin's energy by being near the painting; perhaps she could discover the answers to some of her lingering questions.

Fleur clicked on the conservatory lights and blinked at the brightness. She felt like an intruder tiptoeing into the room so early in the morning. Standing before her painting of T'Eilin, Brendan, and T'Eilin's grandmother, Fleur took a deep breath, dropped into her heart, and asked to connect with

T'Eilin's energy. She had come to know the power of this meditative stance and was confident in her abilities to access non-physical energy. She asked T'Eilin to provide the answers she was seeking.

Fleur stood mesmerized in front of the canvas as visions appeared in her mind. In the first vision, Brendan was teaching T'Eilin to read and write, and to draw illustrations on parchment. Before long, she illustrated his text, and completed a drawing of the blonde woman in the Book of Kells based on her own features. She copied the clothing the woman of that period wore from other illustrations in the parchment. When T'Eilin finished her work, Brendan sent the packet of parchment back to the monastery.

The next vision was located at the standing stones. T'Eilin was lying on the ground weeping about the attack by Tonnick and his warriors. Her despair turned to intense love when Brendan appeared before her. She was astounded that he was alive, and that all was well with her tribe. They walked hand in hand toward the village to begin anew.

The final vision, again at the standing stones, was of T'Eilin telling Brendan about the child she was carrying; a daughter to carry on the work of their love. Before they left, T'Eilin walked to the eastern side of the circle, lay her right hand on the stone, and muttered an intention. A set of runes appeared indented in the stone around her hand. T'Eilin smiled, satisfied that these would provide the key for her descendant.

As T'Eilin turned away from the stone, she paused and looked directly at Fleur, giving her instructions: "You are me come to live the life meant to be."

Fleur blinked her eyes as the visions faded. She was in awe of the words T'Eilin spoke, for they answered many questions. She would remember those words and resolved to discuss their meaning with her Grana.

After her experience at the conservatory early in the morning, Fleur went outside for fresh air. She enjoyed the approach to the front of the house, surrounded as it was by lush, fragrant greenery and colorful flowers. Glancing to her left, she was glad to see her Grana outside in the garden enjoying a cup of tea.

Grana looked up from her book. "There you are, dearie," she said. "I trust you've had a chance to sort yourself out. It's a lovely morning, all fresh and new."

"That's exactly how I feel this morning, fresh and new," said Fleur. "Is it a good time for us to talk about last night, about the vision I experienced?"

"Sit down, dearie, and let me pour you a cup of tea," said Grana as she filled the extra cup lying on the tray. "I expect the first thing that you'd like to know is if I experienced the vision also, and how could that happen?"

Fleur nodded her head. "That puzzles me. At the time it seemed natural that you would be a part of my vision, and it gave me great comfort that you were with me. But this morning, I'm confused."

"I know you must be believing the vision was similar to a dream, for it's easier to understand," said Grana. "In fact, what you experienced was a lifting of the veil between things seen and unseen. That tells me that you have a clear power of clairvoyance, perhaps exposed as a result of being summoned by T'Eilin in the dreams. It's a power that allows you to see things that no one else sees. From what I gathered last night, you are able to control this power, unlike the first time it happened to you."

Fleur sipped the hot tea, considering her Grana's words. "If I have the power of clairvoyance, how is it that you took part in my vision?"

"Understanding how clairvoyant powers develop may help," said Grana, leaning across to pour herself another cupful. "If I remember, the dreams about T'Eilin coincided with you rediscovering your meditation practice. As you know, meditation quiets the mind enough for you to receive divine communication. I believe your successful practice allowed you to open the veil; well, you can think of it as opening your heart. When you came to Scotland, especially near the source of the vortex energy of the circle of standing stones, your dreams stopped and the visions started. Is that right?"

Fleur glimpsed where her Grana was going with this line of thought. "Yes, you're right. Perhaps you were able to join me through a meditative process," she said.

"It came to me when Auntie G. and I were discussing the family abilities," said Grana. "There is such a strong connection, I was able to experience what you did, though I wasn't physically with you."

"Do you mind if I recap my understanding of last night's activity?" she asked. "It would help me if I can verbalize it."

Her Grana nodded, and encouraged Fleur to speak her thoughts out loud. "I believe healing work occurred last night. All the women concluded with the same mantra, believing that they did not do what they were supposed to do in their lifetimes.

"They spoke words of universal forgiveness," Fleur continued. "From my perspective, what they did last night was powerful healing. My instinct tells me the ancestral curse is cleared. But I think what was identified as a 'curse' was generational patterns of behavior based on non-truths. I wonder what will happen now?"

Grana smiled, for she knew her granddaughter to be anxious to know the answers immediately. One of the things that Fleur needed to learn was patience when it came to matters of spirit.

"No surprise that I dreamed about T'Eilin and Brendan last night," Fleur said. "Then this morning I wondered if I could find answers by standing in front of my painting and intending to communicate with T'Eilin. I was successful and experienced a vision like the sequel to the invasion."

"What happened at that point?" asked Grana.

"The first time I experienced the invasion, the vision ended with T'Eilin crying, feeling responsible for cursing her line of descendants. But this time, as she was weeping at the stones, Brendan appeared in front of her. He embraced her and told her that all was well, the invaders had been beaten back, and that Tonnick was no longer a threat to them."

"What was the conclusion?"

Fleur was excited about the next part, for it spoke of hope for the future. "The vision ended with T'Eilin and Brendan walking hand in hand back to the village to continue with their lives, to raise their daughter yet to be born, and to bring the light of knowledge to the tribe's people, as Brendan had started to do."

Grana figured that the dream was an indication that the healing at the standing stones had been completed. "I would say that tells you all is well with our family line."

"I agree," said Fleur. "There was one more thing." She paused to remember the words she heard. "Before the vision faded, T'Eilin turned around and looked back at me. She spoke these words to me, 'You are me, come again to live the life meant to be. Thomas is Brendan, come again as the eternal soul mate. Love each other well, love the child you will bear with him. A daughter also with the power to see what no one else sees. Most importantly, keep in sight the mark of the crescent moon. For that symbol from your birth marks you and your descendants with the sign of your eternal love.' "

"I would say, dearie, that answers all your questions," said Grana. "Now it's up to you how you live your life going forward."

One week after the experience at the standing stones, Fleur sighed in contentment, snuggled in the crook of Thomas' arm as they sat on the couch in front of a warming fire. Fleur was delighted that she and Thomas were focused on the future, and not the past. She had suspected that there was a connection between T'Eilin and Brendan's story with her and Thomas' story. Now that she knew for sure there was, she could leave speculation behind.

"Have you decided what to do about the Factor's House?" asked Thomas. "Though I'm not sure that you need to do anything."

Fleur smiled at his words; they echoed what she'd been sensing lately, that action wasn't necessary. It was best to allow things to flow. Not a mindless floating, but a conscious effort to first tend to the energy of joy and happiness. Everything else would be taken care of when she followed her intuitive nudges to inspired action.

"You know what I think," mused Fleur. "I think that you're right, I don't need to do anything." She let that pronouncement hang in the air for a few minutes.

Fleur turned to gaze into Thomas' eyes. "But I've made a decision about the future." She could feel his heart thump in anticipation of what she was about to disclose. "The Factor's House is my home, and I'm going to live here."

Thomas sighed, a contented sound that delighted Fleur. She pushed herself back from his arms to see him better. "I'm going to create a retreat for artists. The conservatory and the landscape in this area are perfect for painting, and the island is a haven for exploration, both in the physical sense and the non-physical sense." Fleur chuckled at the thought.

Thomas, however, cringed. "I'm not sure I have the nerve to go through anything like that again. But for you, I'd do it every night of the week."

Fleur laughed. "One look at another ancestor and you'd be out of here, historical value or not."

"Anyway, back to my plan about an artist's retreat. Of course, Auntie G. would need to agree with that idea first," said Fleur, then paused to consider. "I feel sure that Grana would love to live at the Factor's House, at least for a while to get to know her half-sister. We'd have a lot of fun putting down new roots. After all, this is where we came from."

Fleur's mind raced, thinking about all of the great exploits she and her small family would have at the Factor's House. It would be a new beginning for all of them.

Fleur marvelled when she remembered her friend's decision. "Matty is supposed to return to help John build the travel business. She can help me too. Oh, and who knows, Terrence might decide he needs to live closer to Mark."

Thomas grinned at Fleur's enthusiasm, and said, "Is there any other reason that you might want to stay on Mull?"

Fleur flickered her eyes. "Hmmm... let me think."

Thomas tickled her sides until she admitted that there might be one other reason. "I give up." She wiggled away from his tickling fingers to admit, "There might be someone special I'd like to get to know much better."

The decision to stay on Mull held great promise. Fleur didn't know where it would lead, but it felt right. She wanted to remain near the standing stones for the guidance they provided.

Importantly, there was Thomas. She had feelings for Thomas, and she knew he had feelings for her. If things developed further with Thomas, especially in the light of T'Eilin's words, it would be wonderful but not necessary to her happiness. She felt strong in her own self, as though she had found her home in the land of her ancestors. She had found love all around her, and best of all, she had found herself. She came to understand that true love meant not giving her power away, but rather taking control of it from her heart.

As Fleur sat on the couch nestled beside Thomas, she had a sudden intuition that there was a presence in the room with them. A thought was transmitted directly to her mind; from where it came, she could only guess. Maybe T'Eilin, or Naghaire, or Fiona, it didn't matter. She felt sure that the thought came to her from one of her ancestors, and that notion felt comforting indeed. Love your life, you never get it wrong, and you never get it done. Life flows eternally, unfolding like a beautiful work of art created with love by your own hand.

THE END

A NOTE TO READER

This is a work of fiction inspired by my spiritual journey and lessons gleaned from thought leaders and teachers over the years. My intention to share these teachings in an entertaining manner resulted in my writing *Mark of a Crescent Moon*, a story about strong women and family lines influenced from ancient times and set free in modern times. Those ready to hear the lessons will. Those not ready to hear will enjoy an engaging story. I hope that all will benefit.

With heartfelt appreciation I ask you, Dear Reader, to take a few minutes to place your comments either on Amazon or on Goodreads so that we might all benefit from your feedback. Also, find me on Instagram (@clarafay. author) and Facebook (@clarafayauthor) and let's have a conversation.

A NOTE OF THANKS

An author's journey begins with a dream, blossoms with the support of so many people, and ends with heartfelt gratitude. Though I have enjoyed the art of writing all my life and had created a career around it in the corporate world, this is my first foray into crafting a novel. It has been an interesting and joyous experience.

Thank you, Melissa Jeglinski, for patiently teaching me the basics of novel structure.

Thank you, Annalisa Parent, for coaching me on how to polish my manuscript as well as my author's mindset.

Thank you, Alexa Bigwarfe, for your informative Women in Publishing Summits and webinars.

Thank you, my children, Marie and Alex Fay, Laura and Adam Kirk, Kate and Michael Fay, and my grandchildren, Maia-Jane Fay, Linc Fay, Luke Fay, and Serena Kirk, for the love and joy you bring into my life. You have inspired the realization that living one's authentic life well benefits our descendants.

Thank you, my dearest friends, Beth Latwaitis, Maureen Murray, and Sherry Chadwick, for your interest and excitement.

Special thanks to Sharon Bridget Doyle, whose guidance taught me the value of alignment in my spiritual journey.

And thank you, Ian Cummings, my partner, for sharing a great life with me. And for showing me the wonders of your homeland with its moors, mountains, and ancient sites, and especially your interest in megalithic standing stones, all of which inspired this story.

ABOUT THE AUTHOR

Clara Fay lives on the beautiful island of Bermuda, where she built a lifelong career as a communication professional for a prominent global company. She loves to explore the islands of the Scottish Inner and Outer Hebrides, so completely different from her semi-tropical island home. She leverages her communications expertise, and her keen interest in spiritual awareness, to capture the mystical atmosphere, and unique antiquity, of these Scottish islands in her debut novel, *Mark of a Crescent Moon*.

.